THE REQUEST

THE REQUEST

By

KENT WALKER

Printed in the United States of America

First Printing, 2020

ISBN-13: 978-1-949003-66-6 print edition
ISBN-13: 978-1-949003-67-3 ebook edition

Waterside Productions
2055 Oxford Ave
Cardiff, CA 92007
www.waterside.com

TABLE OF CONTENTS

Chapter 1

Signals

He had no idea his life was going to completely and tragically change in less than an hour as he was awakened with a startle.

"Carl, you up? You're going to miss the bus!" the voice screamed through the door.

"Oh crap!" Carl squinted through hazy eyes at his alarm clock wondering why it did not go off. "I'm up, I'm up!"

"Get ready, your dad and I will drop you off at school on the way to the bank. But hurry, it's late," his mother ordered.

It was the last week of junior high and Carl had mixed emotions about the change. He looked forward to starting something new. But he dreaded having to be low man on the totem pole again. It also had been an unsettling few months because for the first time in his life he heard his parents arguing. The thin walls of their modest house made it impossible not to hear every word, and the fights were always about one thing. Money.

His dad had been a retail manager at a hardware store for as long as he could remember until he decided to go out on his own with a new franchise, ignoring the big box store trend of the 1980's. It was not going well. His dad was away a lot more and his mom had less money to keep the household afloat.

Carl knew from overhearing their heated discussions they were going to try to get one last bank loan, again. The stress in the house was increasing. Carl was hoping that things would go well at the bank. Otherwise it might be a long summer.

After he jumped out of bed and rushed to get dressed they loaded into the modest family car and headed off. They were pulling out of the driveway when his mother turned and said, "I got a call from the high school and they said you hadn't selected an elective. They said we'd have to let them know today or they will assign one for you. Have you given it any thought?"

"Most of my friends are trying to get the computer class."

"Computers! That's just a fad. Why don't you get a class that can be productive? How about woodshop?"

"No way! I don't want to build stupid birdhouses," Carl said with exasperation. "I want to get into the computer class."

"Fine, I'll call today."

Carl sat in silence the rest of the drive to school and listened to his parents discuss the loan application. He could tell they were agitated and his father was driving a lot faster than usual. The tension eased slightly as they pulled into the parking lot.

"Sorry if I made you late. The alarm didn't go off."

"No problem Buddy, we can make up the time. Traffic looks light," his dad said with a forced smile. "Maybe we can do something fun this weekend. We haven't been fishing for awhile."

"That would be great." Carl knew it was not going to happen. His dad did not have any spare time for fishing or anything else for that matter.

He grabbed his backpack as he climbed out of the back seat. He could hear his mom over the smack of the car door closing, "Love you, Honey. We'll see you tonight." The car sped off.

As he ran up the steps he saw his friends sitting near the top. "Hey look, it's the good citizen!" his best friend, Joe, cried out as Carl approached.

A couple of days before, it was announced that Carl was going to be recognized for receiving the highest amount of good citizenship awards over the last three years. For his parents, it was a source of pride. For his peers, however, it was kindling of relentless pokes and jabs.

As he sat with his buddies he heard them talk about plans for their upcoming summer vacations. They almost all included family get-togethers. That was one thing that Carl could not relate to.

He was born to his parents late in life. His mom often called him their "little miracle" because they were told they would not be able to have children. The doctors were almost right, he was an only child.

His father was an orphan and the only living relative on his mother's side of the family was her older sister, Aunt Sally. So there were no cousins or grandparents and his family get-togethers usually consisted of him and his parents. His aunt was not estranged, but almost. Once a year or so she would stop by to visit or they would go to her house for Sunday brunch.

Aunt Sally had married well and divorced even better. She was in her mid-forties and was in a position financially where she would never have to work a day in her life and still be very comfortable. Carl overheard in one of his parents' fights how disappointed they were she would not help them get through the current rough spot with a loan. Sally did not like to share. Carl also got the feeling she did not like kids. She was aloof and put off while putting on a mask of caring.

Sally lived ten minutes away and there were always plans for everyone to see each other. But more times than not, Aunt Sally would call at the last minute with some lame excuse of why she would not be able to make it.

After the bell rang, Carl and his friends headed to their classes. His first period was study hall and he shared it with Joe. With only a few days left in the school year and most of the exams completed, the staff gave the students some leeway. The room was filled with sounds of students trading notes and talking about their plans for summer when in the distance they heard a siren. Everyone looked up as it was getting louder. Joe stood and yelled, "Hey look, they're coming to get Mr. goooood citizen!" The room erupted in laughter as Carl sank in his seat and the siren faded. "You really can be a jerk sometimes," Carl said after everyone calmed down.

The rest of the day was routine with the exception of signing yearbooks. After lunch, there was a school-wide assembly and Carl received his outstanding citizen plaque. The crowd cheered and clapped loudly and he could not keep himself from blushing from all the attention as he walked in front of the crowd to be congratulated by the principal and handed the plaque. His blush grew more intense as he saw Joe and realized he would be in for a lot more ridicule.

His last class of the day and last exam of the year was algebra. He excelled at math and finished his test long before the other students. He never received anything short of an "A." He struggled in other subjects, but when it came to numbers he was a wizard. He had time on his hands as the rest of the students were crunching numbers trying to get a passing grade when the door opened and the school secretary came into the room and whispered to the teacher. He looked at Carl and used his index finger to signal him to come to his desk. "What's up?" Carl asked.

"You need to go to the principal's office."

He felt like he was hit by a brick. He received the citizenship award not more than two hours ago and now he was being sent to see "The Yoda." Yoda was the nickname, or at least what the students called the principal behind his back, because other than not being green and a lot bigger, he looked a lot like the character from Star Wars.

He had no idea what this could be about as he entered the administration offices and was led to Yoda's office. When he walked in he noticed two other people. One was a kindly looking woman with a sad expression on her face. The other was a cop. Now Carl was freaking out. There was no way he could have done something bad enough to get the police involved.

Yoda stood, walked around his desk and put his hands gently on Carl's shoulders. "Carl, I'm sorry to have to tell you this, but there's been a terrible accident."

The adults did their best to gently tell Carl what happened, not in the way the details were told by the witnesses for the police report.

The car was southbound as it approached the intersection driving faster than it should. The driver was faced with an unexpected choice. The stoplight had turned yellow in that moment when a driver thinks, "I can make it" or "I should stop." Even though a car to his right and just ahead of him started to slow, he sped up. Unfortunately a large, fully loaded delivery truck was eastbound as it approached the intersection. The truck driver was behind schedule and driving too fast, himself. He could not see the traffic coming from his left, but he could see that one car was slowing and thought the crossing traffic's light had turned red. He kept his foot on the gas pedal and made no attempt to slow down. It was too late as the truck driver saw the car enter the intersection.

"Horrific," was the word used by the witnesses. The mid-size sedan was no match for the five tons of truck and cargo as it slammed into the driver's side of the car. There was no fire, but the aftermath looked like there had been an explosion. Glass and debris were scattered and one of the side view mirrors of the truck was found half a block away. No one could agree who was at fault and in the end it was chalked up to one of those one-in-a million freak accidents.

At one instant Carl's parents were alive. Rushing to the bank and worrying about the mortgage, wondering if they would be able to stay in business and praying the bank would say yes. In the next, they were gone. They did not have time to have concerns about the fate of their son.

In Yoda's office Carl had not realized he stumbled and used the desk to stop his fall. As he leaned on it he noticed a humming in his ears that was almost deafening. His body felt like it had been engulfed in a tank of thick glue where even blinking his eyes took effort.

The only real loss he endured before was when his dog was hit by a car years ago. He was devastated, but things got better when his parents surprised him with a puppy a few weeks later. They called him "Mutt." Everyone who saw the animal immediately understood the appropriateness of the name. It might have been the ugliest dog in town, and Carl loved him. It seemed strange for him to even be thinking about Mutt, but he could not help it. He knew his pet was stretched out on top of the couch staring out the window waiting for his masters to come home.

"Carl, are you okay?" He could hear the noise but not the voice or what it said. He had to do something. He had to do something *right now*! But what? Run? Cry? Scream?

"I need to go the bathroom," Carl half said and half screamed.

Yoda lead him to the employees' restroom. "Take all the time you need, Carl. We'll be right here."

Carl was in a haze when he entered a stall and vomited violently. The heaves were relentless. But, there were no tears. "Why?" he wondered.

He regained a little control and stood up. He was exhausted from the physical effort of empting the contents of his body. But the pain was still there. He walked to the sink and washed his face. He looked in the mirror and for the first time saw a couple of fine hairs sticking out of his chin. "I wonder who's going to teach me to shave now..." he thought.

He stayed in the restroom for a while at a complete loss. Then all of a sudden, almost like a switch had been flipped, he stood up straight, walked out of the bathroom and straight to Yoda's desk.

"What's going to happen to me now?"

"Well, we're not entirely sure. We called the number on the emergency contact card we have on file and left several messages. But so far no luck there," said Yoda. Carl knew the only number on the card would be Aunt Sally's. "Maybe one of your friend's family can take you in for a couple of days while we figure out how to help you."

"I want to go home!"

"That isn't a very good idea, Carl," said the woman. "We know how hard this must be, and we are only here to help you. I'm sure we can figure something out that would be best for you."

"Going home is what's best for me. I've been there alone a ton of times. I don't see what the big deal is."

"If we can't find a friend or a relative who you can stay with, we have a great place with lots of kids your age. You would fit right in," the woman said. "There will also be people that you can talk to."

"No way," Carl said and now the tears started to flow. "I want to go home."

The conversation went on. Then Carl had enough. "I'm sorry, but I have to go to the bathroom again, and I know the way so you don't have to show me," he said as he stood up and walked out the office door.

As he entered the outside office area he looked over his shoulder and saw the adults were not following him. He started to walk faster toward the door and into the hallway. When he got further from the administration offices he started to run, and the good citizen did not stop running until he got to his house.

Chapter 2

Decisions

Twenty-seven years later Carl sat at his desk in his woodshop fighting back tears and memories but was loosing the battle. It had been over twelve hours since he received the request for the project he had to start, but his hands still trembled.

He forced himself to focus on the decisions he had to make. First, what kind of wood to use. It needed to be durable but he also wanted it to be beautiful. He decided on Santos Mahogany. A hardwood with blends of honey colors and creamy coffee highlights that reminded him of the diversity of life; complex, flowing and beautiful.

Usually he would take into account how the wood worked with him. Some were easier to cut and others more forgiving of slight mistakes. They all had their own perks and personalities, but this time that did not matter.

At forty one, Carl had established himself as a master craftsman who was well respected by everyone who knew him or had seen his work. As the craftsman, he was considered to be unequalled. Jobs other wood workers thought to be impossible were the projects he completed consistently over the years. Whether it was custom cabinetry in a multimillion-dollar home remodel or restoring family heirlooms or anything at all that dealt with wood, he was not just a master, he was *the* master.

As the man, his life was as admirable as his woodwork. Salt of the earth, kind, loyal, honest, fun-loving and every positive attribute a man could receive was used to describe Carl. He was known to be a good, loving husband and father of two sons and a daughter.

As Carl stood in the middle of his shop surrounded by the tools of his craft, he took pause. The walls and counters were filled with every tool imaginable to manipulate and coax the raw material of wood into a finished piece. Some were state-of-the art that included micro chips and technology that was only a pipedream a few years before and costing as much as a used car. Others, the ones he loved, were old. To the casual observer they appeared to be an accumulation of junk from a bygone era.

Coffee in hand, he sat at his desk where he sketched the plans of his projects and kept his records. Next to his new smart phone lay a broken hammer, its head cracked and handle split. He had forgotten to throw it away.

He stared at the two, old broken hammer and new smart phone, representing two completely different worlds and times. He leaned over and picked up the now useless tool, examined it and thought, "That should've been me. Broken."

He walked toward the door of his shop and looked at the workspace. The tools were arranged in exact order as were the other materials. Lights off, door shut and locked, time to transform from Carl the craftsman to Carl the husband and father.

Carl believed he was blessed that he could have his workshop on the same property as his home. The parcel was large, and he deliberately built the house and workshop on opposite ends of the property. This meant every morning and evening when he worked he had a ten minute walk on a gravel path that crunched beneath his work boot's every step. He found the sound to be soothing, almost hypnotic.

At the beginning of his workdays he would have a transformation. Some might call it "getting into the zone" or "getting the artistic juices flowing." To Carl, though, it was not quite a "Zen" thing. He was just getting ready to do what he did. There were rare occasions when he did not feel it. On those days he would not unlock the door to the shop. Instead he would head to the house and fill the day with anything but woodwork.

Carl was no kind of loner. You might catch him at the local tavern bellied up to the bar with his buddies. He could go on for hours with a beer in hand while arguing why his favorite team was better than theirs. He and his wife went out often and there were always invitations from friends for weekend barbecues. His favorite times were when he watched his children's plays or sporting events. But once inside the workshop he was in a different dimension. It was not that people were not welcome. No "do not disturb" signs or suggestions. It was just understood that once he passed the threshold he was in a place that no one could reach. The only contact to the outside world was a phone line to his fax machine. He muted the ringer the day he bought it and always turned his smart phone off when he went into his shop.

On his strolls home at the end of the day his transformation back to the real world ended at his front door. He always walked straight to the house, no stops, no lagging. This time he paused to sit on an old tree stump and looked up at the stars. He needed more time to transform. After a few minutes he continued, and as he walked around a bend of trees he saw it.

The sight of the home made him glow from within, as it always did. A single-story ranch style that held all the charm of a mountain villa and warmth of the love he built it with. He contracted out the electrical and plumbing work, but everything else he built with his own hands and with help and encouragement from his wife.

As he took the steps up to the porch, looking forward to the nightly ritual of hugging and kissing his wife and catching up with his children, he stopped. He could only think and feel one thing.

"Thank God for Aunt Sally."

Tonight was a good night. All three kids were home and Carl and his wife enjoyed a dinner with their teenagers. After the last dish was put away and counters wiped off, the kids went to their rooms to study. His wife said she was going to read in bed for a while. Carl said to her, "I'll be there in a bit," and kissed her goodnight.

He walked into the den and to the corner bar. He was not a big drinker, but a few times a week he would allow himself the indulgence of a shot or two of his favorite Bourbon. He developed a ritual over the years. First he wiped the glass clean with a bar rag. Then slowly pour two fingers of the liquid into the tumbler. Then, the most important part, he counted out three large ice cubes and gently lowered them into the glass. One cube did not make it cold enough. Two cubes did not sound right. Carl loved the sound three ice cubes made as he swirled the drink between sips.

He sat on the over-stuffed couch and soaked in his surroundings. He smiled as he thought about the times his or his children's friends came into the expansive space for the first time. Some thought it made them feel they were in the Captain's Quarters of a tall sailing ship from years ago. Others said it was like a luxury car on an old-time train. No matter what the comparison, all agreed they had been transported to a different place and time.

It was rare Carl would indulge in more than one drink. But, tonight was going to be one of the exceptions. He poured four fingers of the alcohol into the glass and added three new ice cubes before he sat back on the couch. He slowly lifted his feet and rested them on the coffee table and looked at the tumbler and decided not to sip. He quickly swallowed it all at once, wincing from the sudden burn in his throat. He crossed his hands on his lap, still holding the glass. Carl rested his head back, closed his eyes and let himself drift back to that day that happened twenty-seven years before.

CHAPTER 3
TRANSITIONS

The run from the junior high school to his house exhausted him. Completely out of breath and drenched in sweat, Carl collapsed in a chair on his front porch. He saw Mutt looking at him through the window wagging his tail and being fidgety. Carl leaned over, rested his head in his hands and whispered, "Just a sec, boy. Let me catch my breath."

It took him awhile to recover, at least physically. His mind was still racing, trying to come to terms with what happened. He got up and walked to the front door and turned the handle. Locked. "Damn it!" he screamed realizing he left his backpack in Yoda's office when he made his escape and his house key was in it. He walked around the house to try the back door. It was locked, too. With his dad being, or had been, in the hardware industry, all of the locks on the doors and windows were top notch leaving no chance for them to be jimmied open. He sat on the porch chair completely defeated and thought, "I wonder if breaking into my own house is against the law. Is this even my house, anymore?"

He walked to the yard, picked up a rock and went back to kitchen door. It had a small window in it. His plan was to break it out, reach in and unlock the door from the inside. He stood back a few feet and took aim and hurled the rock at the window. It missed. Instead of hitting the window it hit the door, leaving an ugly gash.

Frustration took over as he spastically picked up the rock and smashed it into the window. It worked this time. The glass shattered. It also left a large cut on his arm, but he did not feel the pain.

He reached through the broken window and unlocked the door. Mutt immediately ran up, reared on his hunches and started licking him. It was the first time Carl felt better since almost falling over in Yoda's office. He petted the dog, let him out and crept into the kitchen. The house was quiet, too quiet and he became unsettled again. As he passed the breakfast nook he saw two cups of half drunken coffee, one with lipstick smears on it. He touched one and it was stone cold, just like he felt.

He had never before been uncomfortable in his own house, but now felt like he was walking into a dark cave. He checked every part, all the while hoping there had been a terrible mistake and his parents were okay. He wanted to find them taking a nap or watching television, but he knew. No one else was in it. He ran through the rooms and saved his parents' one for last. He could not remember the last time he had been in there and felt like he was intruding. Every time before it was neat and clean. This time the bed was not made and he could see his dad's pajamas and his mom's nightgown piled in a heap. Entering the master bathroom he saw clutter on the counters. The toothbrushes, razors and makeup had been placed on the counter haphazardly.

The silence was driving him out of his mind. Carl grabbed the remote from the night table and turned on the television, hoping it would take away the loneliness. It was tuned to a local channel and an early edition of the news was beginning to air. The top story was the tragic accident that morning. The images of the twisted wreck were clear, and although it was hard to tell from the damage, Carl could still see it looked like his family's car. When he listened to the reporter describing the wreck and where and when it occurred, Carl felt like the floor had fallen out from under him. "Oh, my God," he slowly said to himself as he realized the sirens he heard at study hall were in response to his parents' death.

The shock and desire to disbelieve the situation replaced the surge of energy his adrenalin levels created. And then the crash. In just a few moments he went from going a million miles an hour to a full stop, like he had run into a brick wall.

The exhaustion overwhelmed him and his legs grew weak as he sat on his parents' bed. He reached over, grabbed his dad's pillow, then his mom's, and held them to his chest, squeezing as hard as he could. He held them to his face and inhaled to breathe in their scent as he started to sob uncontrollably. He fell over onto his side, clutched the pillows tight again and cried himself to sleep.

Two hours away, Sally was enjoying her impromptu holiday. When she woke up that morning, she decided to go to the city, have dinner with her girlfriend and, of course to shop.

She picked up the phone as she got out of her lavish four-poster bed to call her assistant, Ruth, who took care of the mundane day-to-day details Sally thought were beneath her. After several rings a sleepy voice answered. "Hello."

"Ruthy, I need you to call the Hilton and make reservations for tonight. Then, call Dominick's and make dinner reservations for two at six this evening. Get me that table I like."

Ruth hated being called Ruthy, and her boss knew it. But, the pay was good. So she put up with it along with other countless annoyances Sally dished out daily. She turned on the light and looked at her clock to see it was just before five-thirty A.M. She always had to keep a pen and pad with her because she knew she could get a call at anytime, day or night, and if she was not prepared or did not follow Sally's instructions to the letter there would be hell to pay. "I'll call the hotel right away, but the restaurant doesn't open for another six hours. I'll call then."

"Ruthy, Ruthy, Ruthy, we live in a day of answering machines. Call Dominick's right now and leave a message. I don't want to lose that table just because you delayed."

"Good idea," Ruth said, trying to appease her boss.

Over the next few hours, Sally got ready and loaded her over-night bag into her car right after calling her friend in the city to tell her about the dinner plans. She got in and pointed the big Mercedes-Benz out of her enormous driveway to start the two-hour drive.

Sally was a living contradiction in the way she saw herself compared to the way others saw her. In her mind she was glamorous, others would say gaudy. She always told her friends how gracious she was; no one had the heart or courage to tell her that calling yourself gracious was about as ungracious as ungracious could get. To say Sally had a problem controlling her temper would be an understatement. She was quick to fly off the handle, often for little or no reason. Sally could be generous at times. When it served her purpose or she had an ulterior motive.

She grew up in an average home with a loving family. She had plenty of friends and loved animals. While in her freshman year in high school, Sally got a part-time job at the local veterinarian's practice and found her calling. She always had pets, but when she started to care for other people's, she was hooked. She wanted to become a veterinarian. She knew her family's financial resources were limited and her only chance of making her dream a reality was to get a scholarship. So she dove into her schoolwork which resulted into an impressive GPA. Her plan worked. In her senior year she received a full scholarship to one of the best colleges in the country. Her family was proud and she could not have been happier.

The roots of Sally's slow transformation from the fun loving and well liked girl to diva-bitch could be traced to the summer after high school. The college had an orientation all freshmen were required to attend without their parents. It was on this trip she met her future husband.

On the last night of the orientation she went out with her new friends for dinner. While waiting to be seated she had a conversation with a very handsome and charming man. He was five years her senior and Sally was swept off her feet.

To the outrage of her parents, Sally did not come home the next day. She stayed for an extra week. Her future husband came from a very wealthy family and had all the money he needed to wine and dine the impressionable young Sally. After she returned home there was not more than a few days that passed before they would see each other again. He would either fly out to visit her, or fly her to his home.

Within two months wedding plans were being made. She had never been so happy even though she felt like she was living in a whirlwind. The first hint of trouble was when he suggested she wait a year or two to start college. He explained he wanted to give all of his attention to her, but the reality was he wanted all of hers. "You don't need the scholarship; we have more than enough money to put you through school, when you're ready..." If he had said, "When I'm ready," it would have been honest.

After a couple of years of marriage, Sally had her first doubts about the choices she made. He was still kind and loving, but also more controlling. He expected her to be the perfect society wife and to be at his beck and call at all times. It was okay if he went out with friends for drinks or a round of golf, but insisted whenever Sally left their home it was with him. He also made a rule never allowing pets. He claimed he had allergies to animals, but she never heard him sneeze, not once.

It was also his rule they would not have children. At least not right away. Again, he did not want any competition for Sally's attention. His controlling behavior intensified as time went on.

With each passing year a little bit of her confidence slipped away to be replaced with bitterness and resentment. But she always kept on a happy face and acted like she was the most content young woman in the world. Her husband demanded it. Her family became distant as the daughter and sister they had once known slowly evaporated.

On their tenth anniversary all traces of the kind, optimistic Sally had completely faded and was replaced with a cold-hearted and angry one. Although he never abused her physically, he might as well have. Bruises fade and broken bones heal. The damage he inflicted became firmly entrenched into her soul. Sally's only relief from the suffering was when she was abusive to the house staff. The maids could never clean well enough and the cook never got it just right.

It was on a day just shy of their fifteenth anniversary something snapped in Sally. Now she was able to turn her bitterness on him, but in a very cunning manner.

He had been away from home more, and after a little investigating Sally learned of his affair with a younger woman. Instead of being hurt, she saw it as a way out. He made it clear that if she left, she would not receive a dime. She had other plans. It seemed her husband's wealth was not always gained by proper means and his tax returns were worthy of an award for good fiction, and she was privy to all of the information and records. It made her attorney's job much easier.

She was prepared on the night she walked into his office, threw a large stack of files on his desk and dictated the terms. She explained she did not care about his affair, but knew the humiliation he would endure if word got out. She also explained the large pile of papers in front of him were copies made from the records at her lawyer's office. "It's very simple Dear, you can write the check to me from your office or to the IRS from your jail cell."

He quickly became compliant and within a week Sally was a very wealthy woman in her own right. And also a very single one, but the change in living conditions did not alter the woman on the inside.

As Sally handed her keys to the valet she barked, "Watch the paint and make sure my bag makes it to my room by noon." The young man in the silly doorman's uniform felt like he had been slapped.

She went directly to her favorite boutique a few blocks away. As she walked down the crowded sidewalk she pretended not to notice the many people who looked at her. In her mind it was because they thought her to be attractive. She bore a striking resemblance to Jacqueline Kennedy Onassis. But the beauty did not translate to

Sally. They say that true beauty comes from within. Well, so does true ugly and all the makeup in the world could not cover hers.

One of the clerks saw Sally approaching the boutique, empty of customers. She turned and yelled to her co-workers, "The bitch is back!" They quickly practiced their fake smiles and got into their "kiss ass" characters. They knew there would not be any tips, but the commissions were worth the effort. They also knew that their faces were going to be very sore in a couple of hours. Maintaining fake smiles took a lot of physical effort.

The day of shopping went as planned and at six that evening she was in the lobby of Dominick's with her friend, waiting to be seated. They were catching up and planning their shared vacation to Paris in the fall when the waiter told them their table was ready. Luckily for Ruth, it was the table that Sally demanded. Sally enjoyed the evening and was completely oblivious to how much her life had changed that morning at an intersection close to the school.

Carl was in too deep of a sleep to notice the two adults hovering above him. It took a few gentle nudges to wake him and as he finally opened his eyes he could see the policeman and the lady that were in Yoda's office earlier. "We need you to get up, son," said the cop.

"Why?"

"Come on, just get up and we can go to the kitchen and talk. We also need to clean up that cut on your arm."

Now fully awake, Carl felt rebellious, "Don't you need a warrant or something to be in my house."

"Not when we have probable cause of a crime being committed, and with the broken glass in the back door we had every reason to believe there was. Now come on, let's go into the kitchen, clean up that cut and figure out how we can best help you." The cop was trying to sound kind and gentle, but Carl could tell he was not used to having his authority questioned.

Reluctantly Carl did as he was told. In the kitchen the woman asked where the first aid kit was. "I don't know. My mom takes care of that," then he caught himself, "At least she used to."

After searching she found the medical supplies and treated his wound. "You're lucky; if this had gone any deeper you would have needed stitches."

"Yea, I'm feeling pretty lucky, alright."

The woman explained she talked to the parents of one of Carl's friends. They were willing to let him stay at their home for a few days until everything was worked out. She also told him that since the school year was over in a couple of days and he met all the requirements he could pass on going to class, if he wanted.

"Why can't I just stay here? I'm old enough and I can take care of myself."

After going back and forth, Carl could see they were not going to budge and gave up. There was a pile of clean clothes on the washing machine his mother folded the day before. He picked out things he would need the next day and the lady asked, "Do you have any idea how we can contact your aunt. She seems to be your only relative."

"No and she is."

The feeling of utter loss of control seemed fitting to Carl as he was shown the back door of the police cruiser. He might as well be under arrest.

"Wait, wait! What about my dog! I need to stay here and take care of Mutt!" he said, thinking that he might still have a way to convince them to let him stay.

"We're going to put him up at a local kennel. Don't worry, he'll be well taken care of and waiting for you once we know where you're going to be placed," the woman said.

The word hit him like he had been punched in the gut. Placed. "What the hell does that mean?" he thought as he sank into the back seat of the police car in surrender.

The car was silent on the short drive to his friend's house and the rest of the evening went as anyone might have predicted, almost.

There were condolences, hugs and trying to help him feel better by telling him how welcome he was. Joe's mother made up the guest room and showed Carl where everything was. Carl thought this was strange; he spent the night at his friend's house countless times and already knew where everything was.

After the policeman and woman left it was close to bedtime and it became awkward. Joe told him he could sleep in his room. Carl could tell his friend was uncomfortable. "That's okay, I'll crash in the room your mom made up for me."

Everyone said their goodnights and Carl went into the guest room, locked the door, turned out the lights, sat on the bed and waited. It took over an hour for the house to quiet down. Carl crept toward the faint light that came through the window. He slowly opened it and crawled out into the cold night air and for the second time in the last ten hours, and maybe his life, Carl had chosen to break the rules.

It took him ten minutes to walk to his house and he breathed a sigh of relief when he saw that no one fixed the back door window. He reached in, more carefully than last time, and unlocked the door. It was the first time since his parents brought Mutt home he was not there to greet him.

It felt safe turning on the lights in his room. It was in the back of the house with little chance being seen from the street.

Carl was calmer now. He sat on his bed and picked up his alarm clock. It was the type that had sliding control switches for setting the time and turning on the alarm on it's top. Then Carl saw it. The switch that controlled the alarm was not slid all the way. It was less than an eight of an inch off the "on" mark, still enough not to turn on the alarm, but also just enough to make him think that he did.

His eyes filled with tears as he hurled the clock into the wall, breaking it into pieces. He wanted to make sure it would never work again.

He turned off the lights, crawled under the covers still wearing his street clothes and for the second time of the day, and maybe his life, cried himself to sleep.

⚜   ⚜   ⚜

"Carl, Honey, are you coming to bed?" His wife's voice jolted him out of his trance. "Be there in a minute," he called back as he looked down at his glass. The ice had melted.

He put the glass away, and wondered if there really was a heaven. "I sure hope so," he thought.

He went into the master bedroom, brushed his teeth, and changed for the night's sleep. After leaning over and kissing his wife he laid his head on the pillow. Maybe it was the extra Bourbon or allowing himself to purge some of the old memories, but he had the deepest sleep of his life.

CHAPTER 4
MESSAGES

Carl did not follow his normal routine when we got up the next morning. Usually he and his wife would get up early, rustle up the kids and make breakfast. He would then get cleaned up and have coffee with her before he went to his woodshop.

It was different this morning. He was swinging his feet off the bed the moment he opened his eyes and before they hit the floor he felt a need to get to the shop right away. He quickly brushed his teeth, decided to skip the shower and got dressed. "I'm going to start earlier today," he told his wife.

"That's fine; I'll get the kids off. Have a good day, Honey," she said perplexed as he left the room and noting this was the first time he did not give her a kiss before he left.

Carl did not need time to make the transition from husband and father to master craftsman. It happened before he woke up and as the gravel path crunched beneath his footsteps he was almost running.

When he reached into his pocket as he approached the door to the woodshop he realized he was experiencing another first. He laughed at himself realizing in his rush he forgotten his keys. He stared at the big, heavy padlock and was reminded of a time from many years before.

✤ ✤ ✤

Carl thought he awakened from a bad dream like hundreds of times before. He would be in the middle of an impossible situation, only to wake up and realize that it was not reality and have feelings of relief wash over him. Not this time. He was immediately aware that Mutt was not nestled at his feet and as he looked at the pieces of the clock on the floor knew right away he was living a nightmare. He also knew there was going to be no relief from the fear anytime soon.

As Carl sat up he did not know what time it was, but could tell it was early from the sunlight.

He dragged himself to the bathroom to take a shower. As he stepped into the steamy hot stream of water he could feel his body release the tension. It should have given him relief, but it did not. The more he allowed himself to think clearly, the more he understood the gravity of his situation. Although there was the pressure of time, he stayed in longer than normal hoping to wash away the grit from the inside, too. He stepped out and grabbed a towel. The mirror steamed up and Carl rubbed a small spot off the glass. He took a hard look and said to his foggy reflection, "I'm screwed."

Carl had not eaten since the lunch break at school the day before and his stomach ached. He went into the kitchen and remembered this was the day of the week his mom did the grocery shopping. He recalled his mom telling him it was the day the sales started and the "day old" discount section had the best selection.

He found old bread and a nearly empty jar of peanut butter. As he made a sandwich and poured the last of the milk, he realized he had to come up with a plan. He looked at the clock on the wall and knew he had little time before it was discovered he snuck out of his friend's house, so he had to act fast. "But what?" he thought as he devoured his makeshift breakfast.

He felt better as a strategy took form. He searched his parents' room for money, finding about thirty bucks. Not a lot, but enough for what he wanted to do. He learned his lesson last night and knew they would come looking for him as soon as they found out he bolted. So now, where to hide? The lady told him he would be excused if he did not want to go to school. So they couldn't be upset if he didn't show up. Right?

He walked out the kitchen door and saw Mutt's food dish was empty. Out of habit he started to fill it until he caught himself, Mutt was not there.

He walked to the mall. He wanted to look like any other kid who was walking down the sidewalk, not one that was in hiding or on the run.

At the box-office of the multi-screen theater complex he saw he had a few hours to kill before the first movie started. "I can do this."

To him it was simple. He could not be seen, so what better than to hide in a place where you can not be. He would buy a ticket for the first show, go in and sneak into other theaters all day as the movies ended. He did not care what movies were showing. He needed time to think, not to worry about being caught and as far as he was concerned, this was perfect.

He laid low in the food court, trying not to bring any attention to himself. He did not realize he was being paranoid; who would give a second look to a kid in the food court? When the time came he walked to the box office and thought everything was going to fall apart before it had a chance to get started when the attendant asked him, "Aren't you supposed to be in school?"

"I'm from out of town visiting family. My school let out last week and I'm killing time until my cousins get home," Carl said, trying to sound confident. It worked. The attendant handed him his ticket and Carl disappeared into the complex, becoming the ghost of the theaters until well into the night.

Sally woke up early and ordered room service. When the knock came a half hour later, she opened it. "Took long enough."

She decided to go home early so she could arrange her purchases. "I may have to have that carpenter enlarge the closet, again," she thought as she got dressed.

She called Ruth and told her what time to meet her at the house, then had the hotel staff load her bags into her car. Even though the trunk was massive, they still had to put a few of the full shopping bags in the back seat.

As she walked away from the front desk after checking out, the clerk let out a long breath. He held it in as Sally went over the bill, remembering times before when she would have temper tantrums over some minor charge. It went well this time, no tantrums, but she still was unpleasant.

Her car was brought to her and she navigated the crowded city streets beginning her trip home. The night before her friend asked her the same question she been asking for years, "You love the city so much and come so often, why not just move here?"

Sally had her stock answer, "I love my house and have family close by. It wouldn't be right. They would be disappointed." She neglected to tell her friend she saw her "family" maybe once a year. If Sally been honest she would have told her friend her decision not to move to the city was for only one reason, status.

In her hometown it was easier to be the richest and highest up on the social ladder. The town was just big enough to have all the comforts and conveniences she wanted and small enough so her house would be one of the biggest and most envied. It was not the largest house in town, but it was close.

If Sally lived in the city, there would be too much competition in the social pecking order. Although she was very wealthy, in the city her balance sheet would have been mid-stream. Old money, new money, it did not matter there. The only thing that did was the number of digits, and the bigger the amount, the better. In her hometown she was the queen and that was just the way she liked it.

Sally saw Ruth standing in front of the house as she pulled up the driveway. She pushed the button to remotely close the iron gates behind her and pulled up next to her assistant. "Ruthy, call the maid and tell her to come right away. I need her to hang these new dresses up before they wrinkle," she said as she walked by her. No "hellos" or "good mornings," just straight to business.

Sally walked through the front, over-sized doors and straight to the large kitchen in back of the house and noticed something odd. Next to the phone was a rarely used answering machine. She never gave out her number, instead she would have her friends and associates contact Ruth who would then sort out the messages for Sally to call back. She thought the process made her look more important and could not think of one person, besides her assistant, that had the house number. That is why she found it odd to see the light on the machine blinking and the little window flashing the number twelve.

The machine was so rarely used that Sally needed Ruth's help to retrieve the messages, all of which were the same. The only difference was they sounded more urgent as they progressed. All requested Sally call the local junior high school as soon as possible.

Sally stared at the silent machine after the last message played, dumbfounded. "Isn't that the school your nephew goes to? Carl, right?" Ruth asked.

"Yeah, I think so. But I have no idea why they'd want me to call. If he got into trouble or hurt they would call his mom. She's home all of the time, as far as I know."

After a couple of moments she shrugged her shoulders, turned to Ruth and said, "I don't have time for this nonsense. Come on, Ruthy, help me bring in the shopping bags and when the maid gets here you can call to find out what's going on."

The maid arrived twenty minutes latter. After Sally gave her specific orders on how she wanted the new clothes placed in the huge master closet, she turned to Ruth, "Ruthy, go ahead and make that call. I'm going to be in my study and rest awhile."

Minutes later Ruth was nervously approaching her boss's office, portable telephone in hand. She knew Sally was not in the best of moods, as usual, and dreaded telling her what they said. "Sally, I'm sorry, but they say they can't give out any information to anyone but a family member. I tried, but they insist on talking to you, right now."

Sally looked up and was agitated. She stuck her hand up and motioned Ruth to give her the phone. Five minutes later she was sitting back in her chair starring blankly into space, completely pale. Her thick make-up could not hide the fact all the blood had drained from her face.

She was in a void all to herself. All of her senses shut off and she looked like she was comatose. It felt like hours, but it was only a few moments; she considered and examined every possible outcome of her new scenario. The countless choices she had to make now and in the future were given full and thoughtful consideration and every option was thoroughly examined. No matter how hard she tried to spin the facts or wish away the new situation, she always landed on the same conclusion.

Ruth leaned over her, surprised she was genuinely concern for her boss. "This is a first," she thought. Saying out loud as she put her hand on Sally's shoulder, "Sally, are you all right, do you need me to get help?"

Sally reached up; putting her hand on top of Ruth's and looked up at her, then back at the wall. In a very small and hollow voice she repeated what her last living relative on earth said a few hours before. "I'm screwed."

Sally recovered from her lapse and snapped back into her old, demanding self. There were things that had to be done, and done quickly. She sent Ruth to bring her a glass of iced tea, and a shot of brandy. She thought the tea would revive her as the booze settled her nerves. Her first call was to the school to inform them she saw no reason for her to have to go there. Instead she demanded whomever needed to talk to her come to her house. Then she called her attorney to start the process of finding out if there was a will and to make sure it was legal to go through her sister's records.

As Ruth carried in a tray holding Sally's drinks, she was immediately bombarded with orders. "Put that down and start taking notes, Ruthy."

Ruth's pen was flying across the pad frantically as she took notes on all the details Sally wanted handled, to include the funeral arrangements. Her last order was to pick up a newspaper right away. As she stood there waiting for more, Sally looked at her, "Well go on. Get started now!"

The person at the school told her Carl was missing, last being seen the night before. Sally caught herself thinking, "It would be so easy if he didn't turn up." But, hope for the best and plan for the worst was one of her mottos. She ushered the maid to the guest bedroom furthest from hers and told her to remove anything of value and clean it thoroughly. Then she handed her a handful of hundred dollar bills and instructed her to buy the largest television that would fit on top of the chest of drawers. She remembered hearing boys Carl's age liked video games and watching tapes on VCRs. So, she told the maid to pick up these items also and ask the store clerks for the most popular games and movies to purchase. The maid was shocked, "This is very nice of you."

"Nice? I don't want him to have any reason to leave this room!"

When Ruth returned with the local newspaper, Sally unfolded it. The picture of the wreckage and accompanying story was on the front page. She read the report twice and soaked in the image. She softly laid the paper on the table and whispered to herself, "My God."

Hours later the junior high principal and the social worker were at Sally's front door. Ruth let them in and led them to one of the living rooms. She informed them her boss would be there momentarily.

Sally spent time getting into character before making her entrance. She had to display she was in complete control. But she could not come across as hard and not caring. After rehearsing she felt like she had the perfect mix and entered the living room.

She introduced herself and was taken aback when the man stood up; Sally thought this might have been the strangest looking man she had ever seen. If he was any uglier he might not qualify as human. But, he also looked vaguely familiar, like she saw him or his picture before. She shook off the shock and got down to business.

The scene that played out was similar to the one from the night before when Carl was dropped off at Joe's house. Condolences passed out freely and how shocked everyone was. The main difference was Carl's well being was in the middle of the discussion. With him not being there, the adults were free to speak their minds and lay out their concerns. The social worker explained to Sally the family that let him stay with them the night before changed their mind. Having the police in their home that morning after Carl had been discovered missing was not a healthy situation for their own children. The news spread throughout the neighborhood, which made any other family that might have considered putting Carl up reluctant.

She went on to explain there was a county run home for children in this situation, "Boys Town."

Sally thought, "That would be so easy! The perfect, perfect, perfect solution!" Out loud She said, "I have plenty of room here and there's absolutely no way I'll allow my nephew to be placed in an institution the likes of that. I'm sure its very nice, but, I'm sure you understand."

The principal and social worker felt the snooty and "better than thou" attitude pouring off Sally and tried not to be offended. But, at the same time they shared a sense of relief. The principal had his hands full with only a day left in the school year and the social worker was overwhelmed with work. The thought of being able to end this problem by handing it off to someone else was fine by them.

It was agreed by all that when the boy was found he would be escorted to Sally's home. Pleasantries were exchanged and hands shook.

Ruth had been there for the entire meeting and was in shock. She had to sit down in the fear that she might faint. She could not believe what she had just seen. Sally caring for another? Willing to let a teenager into her home? Live there?

"Ruthy! Can you hear me?" The shout brought her out of her trance. "Yes, yes. Sorry."

"Well let's get on with it. I have a feeling that they'll find him soon and there's still a lot to do," Sally said as she walked toward her study.

She instructed Ruth to bring her another brandy. Her nerves were still rattled so much that the whole bottle might not have helped. Sally sat in her chair feeling confident she had pulled it off. Everyone, including the maid and Ruth, believed she had genuine feelings and concerns for the boy, which in part may have been true. A microscopic part. Sally's real motivation was Sally.

One disadvantage the town had over the city was that news traveled faster. When she was in her trance after hearing the news of the accident she could visualize the gossip mill going into overdrive. The phone lines would buzz and the echoes off the country club's walls would be filled with chatter of how the rich old bitch had turned her back on her recently orphaned nephew. She would never again be able to go out without hearing whispers behind her back. Selfish, cruel, cold hearted, these were not attributes she wanted pinned on her. But if she did not take the boy in she knew that was exactly what was going to happen. She would be ruined and there would be no recovery.

Sally was always a problem-solver and was adept at finding ways to make things work out. Work out for her, at least. She was at her desk thinking hard on how to do that. There had to be a way. She had no desire to have a teenager invade her privacy, but she knew she could not shun him either. She was stuck between the proverbial rock and hard place. The more she thought about it the more she realized that for the first time in a very long time she had absolutely no idea what she was going to do.

At eight P.M. Carl thought he should go back to his house. He knew curfew was ten o'clock and if he left now he could use the cover of darkness and get there just in time.

He sat in the dark theaters for over eight hours concentrating on what to do and it was a complete waste of time. He was no closer to figuring things out. He thought about asking for help, but there was nobody to ask. He was going to turn fourteen soon; is that still a kid? He knew he would not be considered an adult, but maybe he could convince the powers that be he could take care of himself. How long could he sneak into the house before being caught?

He thought about his mom and dad. Did they suffer? Were they thinking of him when they died? Were they watching over him now? All of his questions just led to more, and it was driving him out of his mind.

Although he came no closer to figuring out what he was going to do, he did learn things. You do not have to be alone to be lonely. He was surrounded by hundreds of people most of the day, but never felt more alone. And he was introduced to grief. The sense of complete loss and knowing the hole it left was never going to be filled. All day he had sudden, uncontrollable bouts with tears that wrenched him, followed by a sense of bewilderment. It was relentless and it hurt.

At the age of thirteen he could not grasp the concept of time like adults. At that age forever meant waiting for a vacation from school or anticipating a special event and it was only his impatience that made it feel like it was forever. Now he had a much clearer understanding of what forever was. He was never going to see his parents again.

There was the gut-wrenching fear. He had been scared plenty of times before for hundreds of different reasons, but nothing like this. Having to bring home a report card for his mom or dad to sign with a poor grade in English. Sitting in anguish waiting for his dad to come home so his mom could tell him that Carl had done something bad. That moment riding his bike when he realized he was going to crash and there was nothing he could do to stop it. This new fear came from deep within and was paralyzing. And then there was the guilt...

As Carl approached his house he carefully looked around. "Looks like the coast is clear," he thought as he went to the back door and stopped dead in his tracks. Someone fixed the window he smashed out the night before. They did not replace the glass, they had taken two sturdy boards and covered the hole on either side and bolted them in place. Carl could see the shiny, smooth heads of four bolts imbedded in the board, which meant the nuts were on the inside, impossible for him to reach. He tried to move them, just in case, but they might as well have been welded in place.

He thought about breaking out a window, but was afraid it would make too much noise and have the neighbors calling the police in no time.

He stood trying to come up with something, anything he could do to gain entry to the only place on earth where he could be safe. He drew a blank and walked around the house. As he rounded the corner and stepped onto the front porch he saw the policeman from the night before sitting in the chair. "Hello, Son. I had a feeling I might be seeing you here tonight…"

"Ruthy, get over here right now, they're on their way!" Sally screamed into the phone and hung up. She was a nervous wreck. She spent the afternoon thinking herself into circles. She realized she had to at least try to make the boy feel welcome, maybe even happy. What if he didn't like it here and told the social worker he would rather live at Boy's Town? It would be a complete disaster. Her status would be completely destroyed and she would be laughed out of the country club. But, she HATED kids. She had no idea how to talk to them and did not like being around them. In her mind they were not really people until they reached their mid-twenties. The time before that was just a nuisance everyone had to put up with.

Sally felt like she was walking on a tightrope over a pool infested with sharks with their jaws snapping at her feet.

Fifteen minutes later Ruth and Sally were waiting in the living room. Ruth had never seen her boss so agitated, which was saying a lot. "Sally, I'm sure it will all work out. Things like this happen and people get through it."

"SHUT UP!" Sally screamed as Ruth sank back into her chair wondering if the paycheck was worth it.

A few minutes later the silence was shattered by the doorbell. Ruth left the iron gates open in anticipation of their arrival and as she opened the door she saw Carl surrounded by the social worker and the cop. "You must be Carl, I've heard so much about you," she lied. "I'm so, so sorry for all you must be going through. I'm your aunt's assistant and I'm sure we'll be seeing a lot of each other. I hope we can become friends."

Carl was silent. He was not trying to be rude; he just did not know what to say.

As the four entered the living room, Sally gave Carl an awkward hug, "There you are, I've been worried sick about you; are you okay?"

"I think so."

Over the next hour there were forms that had to be signed and questions asked and answered. Carl was tired and was not paying attention to the adults discussing his fate until something the social worker said caught his attention. "I'm obligated by law to inform you that Carl has the option to be place at Boy's Town if he wishes when he turns fourteen," she said scanning the room and continued, "I'm sure that won't be an issue in this case."

At the end of the meeting the social worker handed Carl her card, "That has all my numbers. Anytime you want somebody to talk to or if you need anything at all, you can call me. I mean it, Carl; I'm here for you." Sally watched Carl stick the card in his pocket and made a mental note to burn it.

"Thanks."

"I'll come by and check on you from time to time." Sally was thinking, "Wanna Bet?"

The policeman put clothes on a table, "We got these from the place you were staying, or at least was supposed to be staying last night. This should hold you over. In the next couple of days we will take you back to, well uh, your old house to get your things."

The cop and the social worker let themselves out and Ruth handed Carl another card. "I take care of your aunt's details and I'm sure I'll be helping with yours, too. These are my numbers and you can call me anytime," she said hoping that middle of the night phone calling did not run in the family. Then she thought,

"This is a good time to demand a raise!" and made a mental note to bring it up the next day when her boss should still be the most vulnerable.

With that, Ruth said goodnight and left, leaving Sally and Carl alone in a room together for the first time in their lives. Sally looked at Carl, trying to have a look of loving concern on her face. It almost worked. "I thought you might be hungry, so I had the maid make a plate for you. Do you like spaghetti?"

"Yea, that'd be great. Thank you," It sounded good. When he was in the theaters earlier and saw hot dogs cost five bucks, so he decided on extra-large popcorn. It came with unlimited refills, so he would be set for the day. The problem was when he went for the third refill he noticed the girl behind the counter looking at him funny. It had been four hours between the first tub and the last. Movies are only two. He decided not to push his luck.

Sally pulled a plate from the oven and poured a glass of milk. They sat and Sally, as gently as she could, started small talk with some power points mixed in. Again, Carl had to endure the "how sorry for your losses" and "I'm here for yous." But overall Sally was making him feel comfortable.

She showed him his room after he finished his meal. She noticed he rinsed his plate and put it the dishwasher without having to be asked. A good sign. She did not know he never did that before, his mom always cleaned up. He felt obligated.

On the way to his room, she showed him the bathroom; it was bigger than his old room and he noticed the shower had at least six shower heads in it. She showed where the towels and hamper were and explained the maid would take care of all of the laundry. "Just make sure you always put your dirty things in this hamper. I don't like clutter."

His new room was bigger than his mom and dad's. In fact, it might have been larger than his living room. Well, his old living room. He saw the TV. "That looks pretty new."

"Just bought it today; I thought you might like it. Plus I think you'll be spending most of your time here, so I want it to be as fun and comfortable for you as possible." Translation: "I don't want you in the rest of my house."

Things were going well. Sally had calmed down, thinking this might not be as hard as she thought. Carl started to relax too, but his head was still spinning.

"I'm not going to pretend I know what you're going through, but, like I said, I want you to know I want to do everything I can to make it easier. This is a big shock for me too, but I'm sure we can work things out in a way that's best for both of us. We'll have plenty of time to talk about it in the days ahead, but I had Ruthy make up this small list of rules to start us off on the right foot."

As soon as she put it in his hand only one thing stood out, and it stood out large. No Pets.

"What about Mutt!?"

"Who's Mutt?"

"My dog, I want him to be with me. I've had him for a long time!"

Sally's act was in trouble as she lost a little control. "No, no, no. Absolutely not. There are to be no dogs, cats, or any other kind of animals on this property. Do you understand?"

She regretted her harsh tone right away. The tension increased tenfold and she could see a small tear on his cheek. Sally had had enough, "I don't want this anymore than you do, but we have to make the best of it and the only way to do that is to make and follow the rules. Get the message?"

He got the message, loud and clear. He wanted to respond, but was afraid he would embarrass himself by breaking down.

Sally knew she made her first mistake and wanted to leave before she made another. "Okay then, get some rest and we'll talk more tomorrow. I'm sure we'll feel better then."

Carl thought quickly, "Tomorrow's the last day of school, I think I should go."

"I'll have Ruthy take you."

"That's okay; I know where the bus stop is. I can get myself there and back," he called after her. "Goodnight."

"Yes, goodnight," she said as she continued walking and not turning around.

Carl was grateful to find an old fashioned clock. It was the round kind that had to be wound up every day and set by hand. To turn on the alarm, he had to pull a pin in the back of it until he heard a loud and satisfying click. He liked this clock very much.

He was not sure he was going to like it here, but he was not sure of anything for that matter. The house was nice and his room incredible. All of his friends would envy it. But the vibes he got from Aunt Sally were not sitting well and he was upset about Mutt. "Maybe I just need to get used to things," he thought. "It's got to be better than Boy's Town. I hope."

It had not been two full days, but he felt like he had lived a lifetime since the accident. Exhausted, he stripped to his boxers and crawled into bed. He was asleep before his head hit the pillow and he did not cry. His body did not have the energy to produce tears.

Sally made a detour on the way to the master suite. She stopped in the kitchen and poured a healthy shot of brandy. Her third of the day. After she got into bed, she thought about the day. It was going so well, and then boom. It was not that big of a deal, but it could have ended better. She was angry with herself for losing control. She was more upset for the reason why. It had nothing to do with the boy questioning her rules. She expected that. It was because of the rule he wanted to break. The woman who was once a girl dreaming of becoming a veterinarian and helping dogs and cats because she loved being around them so much now could not stand the sight of them, even the thought of them. She had no explanation. But, on a subconscious level there was one. It reminded of her how much she lost when she made that horrible life-changing decision years ago.

Sally did not sleep well that night.

CHAPTER 5

ARMOR

Carl was used to being gently awakened by a calm beeping that would start out low and slowly grow louder until he lazily reach over and hit the snooze button when he was good and ready. Not this time. He was jolted from deep sleep to wide awake instantly with the explosion of a loud and very annoying clanging of bells. He went into a panic as he reached to hit the snooze button that was not there. His fear went through the roof when he looked around and had no idea where he was. Then he remembered and grabbed the clock and pushed the pin that stopped the little hammer from hitting the bells. "Maybe I don't like this clock so much, after all," he thought as he sat up and soaked in his unfamiliar surroundings.

He sat on the end of the bed waiting for his heart rate to go back to normal as he thought about the coming day. Normally this would have been one of the best days of the year, the last day of school and the beginning of three months of freedom. But the joy was replaced with anxiety. He did not know what to expect, how his friends were going to treat him, or what kind of freedom he was going to have at the end of the day.

For a moment he thought about skipping school but remembered why he decided to go. He went into the bathroom. On the counters were brand new toiletries: Toothbrush and paste, combs and brushes, deodorant, and everything he would need to get cleaned up. It reminded him of when his parents had taken him on a vacation and stayed at a fancy resort when times were better. When they entered their room in the hotel, he saw the same thing in that bathroom and told his mom, "I can get used to this!" Now he was not so sure.

He walked into the shower. Literally walked in. It was big enough to hold half a dozen people with room to spare. He stood naked studying all the valves and switches trying to figure what they were for. He pushed one button and blinding lights came on and as he hit the switch again they dimmed. After pressing it four times, the light was at a level where he did not have to squint. He hit another and could hear the blast of a fan and feel a rush of warm air.

The valves really confused him. This shower alone had more knobs than his entire house, and it took him awhile to learn how to work them. It was his habit to get in and stand to the side while turning the knob so the blast of cold water would not hit him. He looked up at the multiple showerheads and figured out where to stand. He turned a knob and was blasted with ice cold water on his sides from jets embedded in the walls. This was his second heart-stopping moment of the day, and he had not been up for ten minutes.

He got the hang of it. One knob created steam and another controlled the water flow to the showerheads. The other big surprise was when he turned another knob and water came at him from everywhere, the top, the sides and a couple of jets from the floor. He felt like he was stuck in a carwash, and the jets were strong enough to sting. At the end of his adventure he dried off and had to admit that it was a very cool shower.

After he got dressed he went downstairs and realized he did not have his own room, he had his own wing. He heard a voice calling, "Carl, I'm in the kitchen. Join me."

After a couple of wrong turns he saw Sally sitting at the same table where he ate the night before. "Good Morning!" Sally beamed, "How did you sleep, my dear?" Carl could tell she wanted to sound nice and he was skeptical but decided to give her a chance.

"I slept good. I was tired. That's quite a shower you have in there! It took me awhile to figure out how to use it."

"I thought you would like that, you should see mine," she said, immediately regretting not catching herself. She forgot that one of the rules on the list was he was not allowed in her area of the house. "You must be hungry. Can I have the maid make you some breakfast?"

"That's okay. I don't want to miss the bus, and I'm already late."

"With all the confusion yesterday I forgot today was Friday and Ruthy's day off. But if you want breakfast, I can have the maid take you to school afterwards."

"Thanks, but I want to take the bus so I can see what kids live around here."

"Not many," she thought.

"Suit yourself and have a good day. When you get back we can talk," she said as he walked to the front door. "Use this one, Honey," pointing to the door at the back of the kitchen. "The front doors are only for guests." She did not want him near her expensive furniture or add wear to her Persian rugs.

It took two attempts for Carl to leave. He could not figure out how to open the iron gates at the end of the driveway so he had to go back to get the maid's help.

He knew where the bus stop was because his old stop was the first on the route and it passed by this area on the way to school. He was surprised how far it was from Aunt Sally's house. He was more surprised to see only two kids at the stop and he did not know them. "What time does the bus usually get here?"

"Should be here in five minutes, maybe ten if it's running behind. I never saw you here before."

Even though it was not a question, Carl felt like he should respond. But how? He had not answered many questions up to this point since being called to Yoda's office. Everyone had been talking at him, not to him, and as he tried to come up with something to say he got stuck, so he just shrugged his shoulders.

Another new experience. There had been too many of these over the last couple of days, and Carl suddenly felt like he had made a big mistake going to school today. There were going to be a ton of questions, and either he did not know how to answer them or did not want to. He was trying to figure out what he felt and did not have energy to care what others thought. His fear began to rise again. It was then the first change in his core began. He would not allow anyone in and would not give a crap about what they thought. He did not have to be mean, but it was okay not to answer every question, and there was absolutely no reason to care. He was the one suffering. They should care about how he was. Not the other way around.

The revelation helped him cope, enough to give him the resolve to get on the bus and go to school to complete his mission. But, it also made him feel guilty. He always cared about people and what others thought about him. The thought he would have to change that did not sit well. But he had no idea how else he could defend his fragile emotional state without it.

The bus came to a stop and Carl could feel eyes on him the moment he got on. He saw Joe and sat in the empty seat next to him.

"How's it going?" Joe asked.

"Not sure, yet. It all seems crazy right now. All I know for sure is that I miss my mom and dad. Does everyone at school know?"

"That's all they talked about yesterday. That, and the fact that you snuck out of my house the other night. My mom was pretty upset. She didn't know all those cops would show up after she reported you missing."

"I'm sorry I caused trouble. I just wanted to be home," he said. He then thought to himself, "Great, now I'm a troublemaker."

At school Carl could sense how uncomfortable his friends were as he walked up the steps. It strengthened his resolve to build a wall. He was putting on a suit of armor that would protect him from the outside world. The problem was it also was keeping the bad things inside.

Carl endured the morning classes. The only reason he decided to come today was going to happen at lunch. Some of his classmates were nice and told him how sorry they were, and there were not as many questions as he thought there would be. However, most avoided him. Carl had always gotten along with everyone and was social, now he was an outcast.

When the bell rang signaling the lunch break Carl rushed to the open area where the students ate their lunches. He scanned the tables and became worried his plan might be in trouble until he saw them. He did not know the two boys sitting at the end of one of the tables very well. They had a few shared classes and would play basketball during the breaks once in awhile, but it was important to talk to them, and this might be his only chance.

"Hey," he said as he walked to them.

"Hey, back."

One of them recognized him and said, "Sorry about your folks. I know what its like and it sucks."

"Thanks and you're right, it *really* sucks. I know you live at Boy's Town and I'm hoping I can ask you some questions."

For the entire break they sat and talked. One of the boys lost his parents a couple of years before. The other was a product of the foster family program before being placed in Boy's Town. "Let me tell you, some of those foster families are mean," he said. It had been a couple of days since Carl had actually "talked" to someone, and it felt good, although he was not thrilled about the subject.

They explained what it was like. The food was horrible, and the rules were not as bad as they could be. They both hated sleeping in dorms and wished they could have their own room, even if they had to share it.

They told Carl when they left school and went back to Boy's Town it felt like they were going to another school. Carl noticed when they referred to it, they never said home. They either said "The Place" or "Boy's Town." From their descriptions, Carl could tell that there was no privacy. Watching television, eating, showers and everything else was a group activity.

As the lunch break was coming to an end, Carl had two more questions. "Do you like living there?"

"It doesn't feel like I'm living there. More like staying. It could be worse. I don't want to live on the streets, but I do miss having a place I can call home," one said as the other nodded his head in agreement.

Then, Carl's last question, "Do they allow pets?"

They both laughed and shook their heads, "Not even a goldfish!"

Carl spent the rest of the day in his own world. He did not want to talk. He knew Sally would let him live at her house, but he also knew that she did not want him there. In fact he could not figure out why she made the offer in the first place. He remembered her brief and infrequent visits. She was happier to be leaving than arriving. And last night he felt her vibes, and they were not welcoming at all. But the house was cool. Maybe if he just stayed out of her way it could work. After finding out about Boy's Town it sounded like Sally's was a better choice, but not by much.

In the last class everyone was talking while waiting for the final bell and the start of summer vacation. One of the boys Carl did not know came up to him. "Sorry about what happened."

"Thanks."

"I hear you are going to be living at that big house up the hill. I know about that place, and it's awesome."

"I'm still not sure. It's only been a couple of days," Carl said as he walked away.

"Man, you're one lucky kid if you get to live there!"

In an instant Carl turned and punched the kid in the face. As the kid fell down, he jumped on top of him, pinning him with his knees and grabbing his shirt and pulling his face up to his. "LUCKY!" My parents are dead. I don't have a home. I don't have a dog. I don't know what's going to happen to me, and you say that I'm lucky, Asshole!"

As Carl pulled his fist back to strike again, the teacher grabbed it.

Ten minutes later Carl was sitting in front of Yoda's desk for the second time in three days. The second time ever, for that matter.

He had never been in a fight before and this was the first time he aggressively cussed out someone. He could not believe what he had done, but what surprised him most was how good it felt.

"Have you calmed down?" asked Yoda.

"Yes. I'm sorry. I don't know what came over me. I was walking away and then…"

"Well, I talked to the teacher. There isn't a good excuse for what you did. But, under the circumstances, and with it being the last day of school, I'm going to cut you some slack. You've never been in trouble before. Plus, the other kid seems okay."

Carl was relieved, but still wanted to get out of there. He felt like the walls were closing in. "Thank you. Do you want the citizenship plaque back?"

Yoda laughed, "No, you earned that. But I do need to call your aunt and tell her what happened. I have no choice. The social worker, too."

"Can I go now?"

"Yea, get out of here, and I hope things get better for you. Have a good summer."

Carl stood when Yoda said, "What happened this time won't go into your file. In fact, I'll forget all about it. But, I'm going to check up on you next year, and the headmaster and I are good friends, so if it happens again, I might remember what happened today."

Carl half walked, half ran out of his office, through the halls, out the doors, and past the bus stop. He kept it up until he got to his house, or what used to be his house. This time however, he had no desire to go in. Just the opposite. The thought of being inside now terrified him.

He went to the side and grabbed his bike, hopped on it and started to ride with no destination in mind. And, his armor was slightly thicker.

Sally was startled as the phone rang. Five minutes later she hung up after being informed by the strange looking man that was in her living room the day before about Carl's outburst. She was not sure what to make of the fight, but it did bring to mind that she did not know Carl. Not really. He seemed like a nice enough kid on her past infrequent visits, but maybe he was on orders from his parents to be on his best behavior. Was he a delinquent or a troubled young man?

The principal told her Carl was one of the best behaved kids at the school, so much so that he was awarded best citizen of the class award. But, maybe he was trying sell her on the idea so he could get the problem off his hands.

This revelation magnified her trepidation about allowing him into her house. But, it was too late. She already called her friends and received nothing but praise and support. Sally knew the news was quickly spreading throughout the gossip channels and it was proving to be very good for her image. Kind, thoughtful and stepping in to help the boy when no one else would. It was almost heroic, and Sally knew she would soon be basking in the glory of praise in her tight-knit social circle. If things went badly now, well, she did not want to think about that.

She was also frustrated that it was Ruthy's day off. Her assistant had been with her for years and served her well. She only had one condition; no Fridays. It worked out for Sally because the weekends were when most of the events and gatherings would take place, but sometimes she wondered, why Fridays?

Ruth had taken care of the details the day before. Funeral arrangements were in motion and seeing to Carl's parents' assets and personal affairs began. There was not anything Ruth needed to do at this point, but Sally wished today was not her day off. She needed to abuse someone, so she went in search of the maid.

After finding her and demanding she rearrange the pantry, which did not need rearranging, she felt better and was left to her thoughts.

Sally was not concerned about Carl's feelings or well-being, and the only reason she wasted any of her energy thinking about what she could do to help him be happy was how it affected her. She somewhat recovered from the shock of the bad news the day before, but was still confused about how her future changed. This was not an annoyance she could ignore and would go away, this was a life-changer. But Sally did not want to change her life. She liked it just the way it was. In the end, she decided she would do what she had to do to appease the boy. She could buy him anything he needed or wanted, what kid wouldn't be thrilled with that? Money and status were what made her happy, so with her spoiling him he should be happy too, right?

Sally also thought about the house. It was large, and it had been months since she had been to the part of the house where she placed Carl. "We might not see each other for days at a time!" she thought with triumph. It was not like he was a baby. He was old enough to take care of himself and surely he had his own interests. He was going to be in high school and young men that age wanted independence. The more Sally thought about and spun the situation in her mind, the better she felt. All she had to do was provide a place for him to stay and the essentials. Room and board. So he would just be a tenant. Not so bad after all.

When the phone rang again, Sally was to experience the first challenge to her plan. The social worker wanted to see how things were going and talk to Carl. Sally made her first mistake when the social worker asked where Carl was and she said that she had no idea. "I'm very concerned about Carl. I've talked to several of his friends and teachers, and his behavior has been very unusual. I want to make sure that you understand he's in a critical stage, and with this tragedy it's even more important he be in a stable home full of love."

"Love?" Sally thought. The only thing she loved for many years had been herself.

The social worker continued with suggestions on how Sally could help Carl, but Sally forgot every word of the advice as soon as she hung up the phone. The one thing she did remember was she needed to know where he was at all times. Ever the problem-solver, Sally formulated a plan and sent the maid on an errand.

There was a massive difference between Carl's armor and the one Sally had been forging for years. Carl's was in its infancy and still allowed him to feel and care. Sally's had been forged into an impenetrable shield that did not let anything in or out. She did not mean to be cold-hearted and uncaring; she could not help it because of the person she allowed herself to become.

As Carl rode past Joe's house he stopped to apologize to his mother for the commotion he caused with the police. He knocked on the door and Joe said, "Hey, Slugger!"

"Cut it out."

"I heard you hit that guy but good! Everyone was talking about it on the bus. By the way, why weren't you on it?"

Carl rolled his eyes and said, "Because I figured everyone would be talking about it. Is your mom home? I want to tell her I'm sorry for the trouble I caused."

Joe stepped aside to let Carl in and as he passed by said, "Just don't hit anyone!"

"You know, you really can be a jerk sometimes."

He did his best to apologize and was surprised to find out that she knew about his fight at school. He figured his buddy filled her in and the look in her eyes might have been one of concern, but also of condescending judgment. "Does she consider me one of the bad kids now?"

Joe tried to talk him into staying and playing video games, but Carl declined. He was uncomfortable after the exchange with his friend's mother and wanted to get out of there. "Maybe I'll stop by tomorrow, and we can hang out."

"Okay. So you're staying at your aunt's now?" Carl nodded his head. He was afraid his voice would crack if he talked. "That's okay, it isn't that far away. By the way, what's the phone number there? I'll call you later."

"I don't know," he said with embarrassment. To himself he thought, "I don't even have a phone number anymore."

"Carl, this has to be hard. If you ever want to talk, well, we have been friends a long time, and we are good at keeping each other's secrets."

He realized Joe was right. Neither one ever betrayed the other's trust. In fact, there were many times they covered for each other, hoping to stay out of trouble. So he opened up. Carl told him about the conversation he had with the kids from Boy's Town. Then he told Joe he thought his aunt did not want him at her house. "I know it was just one night, but I can feel it. She doesn't like me or any other kid for that matter. She tries to be nice, but I think she's about to explode if I make one mistake. You should see the list of rules she gave me. It filled a whole page."

"It's only been a day. Give her a chance. Besides, I hear that house is amazing! I can't wait to check it out."

"Well, it might be a long wait. One of the rules on that dumb list is that I can't have anybody over. It's crazy. She has a pool that's bigger than the one at school and I thought it would be cool to have you guys come over to swim, but noooo."

"Wow," was all his friend could say. He wanted to ask what other rules were on the list, but saw talking about it was upsetting Carl. "Come over tomorrow and we'll do something. Don't worry about my mom. She likes you and will get over the other stuff soon. You going home now?"

"What's home?" Carl said as he got on his bike and rode away.

He did not go to Sally's. Instead he did something he needed to do and wanted to get done before dark. His mind was blank as he peddled his way past the school. It took him another thirty minutes to reach his destination. The closer he got, the faster his heart beat, and it had nothing to do with the exertion of riding his bike. He rode into the parking lot of the convenience store on the corner, walked out to the edge of the intersection and looked at the remains of the crash scene.

It had been cleaned up, but there was still evidence of the accident. A few pieces of broken glass were scattered on the road, and in the gutters was debris that could have come from a car. He waited for the traffic to pass and dashed into the middle of the intersection and looked down to see large dark brown stains. Blood. His mom's and dad's. A car horn blasted him out of his trance and he ran back to the sidewalk where a man was looking at him.

"Are you out of your mind? You're going to get yourself killed pulling a stunt like that," the stranger said. Carl noticed he had on a name tag and asked, "You work here?"

"I do."

47

"Did you see the crash?"

"I did. I was out here putting up sidewalk signs for the store when it happened. Most terrible thing I've ever seen," he said as he walked to the sidewalk. "I was standing right here and could see the truck coming from over there and the car from this way." He was pointing to the two different directions.

"I knew it was going to happen. Neither one was slowing down. I screamed, trying to warn the drivers, but it all happened so fast. They didn't stand a chance. The only good thing that is no one lived long enough to suffer; they had to have died instantly. At least I hope so. Look over here," he said pointing again to the middle of the intersection. "No skid marks. Neither one of them hit the brakes." Carl stared at the spot. "The worst part was the aftermath. They had to do a lot of cutting to get the bodies out, worst thing that I've ever seen and hope never to see again."

The stranger looked at the boy next to him and saw he was upset. "Did you know any of the victims?"

"Yea. I knew them," Carl said as a tear ran down his cheek.

CHAPTER 6

LINES

Carl was glad he had forgotten his keys to his woodshop. The extra time helped him relax. He was also glad because he had forgotten to kiss his wife in his rush and made up for it when he went back to the house. He still felt a sense of urgency as he unlocked the padlock and opened the double doors. He walked in, turned on the coffeemaker and sat at his desk. With the open doors facing east, the sunlight illuminated the space and the wood he laid out the day before. It was beautiful. He poured a cup of coffee and as he walked to the worktable and looked down, he smiled. The grains and colors of the wood danced as they shimmered in the natural light and it reminded him of a glimmering surface of a pond at sunset.

He pictured the finished project and sorted the boards. He visualized where each should be placed, then put them on the table accordingly. The process took over three hours, trying different variations until he had a result that satisfied him.

He searched for the only tool he would use today. He pulled out a drawer and rummaged through dozens of carpenter pencils until he found the right one. If the lead was too soft the lines would be too thick and not precise. Too hard, it would score the wood, damaging its surface. Secure with his choice, he bent over the worktable, studied the plans and started to draw the lines on the Santos Mahogany that would later be used to guide the cuts. It would take him all day and maybe a good part of the next, but that was fine. He had plenty to think about as he worked.

Carl stood at the intersection a long time. The stranger went back to the shop sensing the boy wanted to be left alone. When Carl decided to leave he turned towards his bike and saw a flower shop next to the mini-mart. He went in, pulled the remaining money he had taken from his parents' room from his pocket and put it on the counter. "How many flowers can I buy with this?"

"What's the occasion?" the perky clerk asked.

"To say goodbye."

The clerk sensed his somber mood and gave him a lot more flowers than he could afford. She watched through the storefront window as he went back to the intersection and put the flowers on the sidewalk, got on his bike and rode out of sight.

Sally was going out of her of her mind. The social worker called twice and she still had no idea where Carl was. As soon as the maid returned from the errand, she ripped into her for taking too long. After five minutes of the banter the maid handed Sally the keys to the house, took off the nametag Sally insisted she wear and threw it on the floor. She jumped in the air and landed on it to crush it several times screaming, "I quit, I quit, I quit." After her tantrum she turned to Sally, calmly made a hand gesture, and walked out.

"What the hell is her problem?" Sally thought. She didn't have clue.

Carl was leaning on his bike outside the iron gates a half hour after sunset with a sense of understanding and dread. He did not have any place else to go. As he looked at the house he felt strange. Any other kid would love to live there. He remembered how incredible the house was and caught himself wishing his parents could afford something like that. He then turned to admire the view.

Lights were starting to come on and he saw his old school and high school further in the distance. He thought it was beautiful until he noticed he could make out his old neighborhood. Then he did not like the view.

He also remembered seeing Sally's house from the valley. His friends were amazed when he told them it was his aunt's house and he had brunch there once in a while. Once in a great while…

Now, he was at the front gates of his new house and he did not know how to get in. He looked at the keypad on a pole and pushed a button that had a picture of a telephone on it. The speaker crackled with a few ring tones then he could hear Sally's voice, "Is that you, Carl?"

"Yea, I don't know how to get in."

After a loud tone a mechanical voice said, "ENTER," and the gates slowly opened. As he walked to the backdoor he asked himself, "Do I just go in or do I have to knock?" He did not need an answer; Sally was standing at the door.

"I've been worried about you! I thought you'd come back right after school," Sally said in a voice that barely covered her agitation.

"I thought I should get my bike."

"Well, next time call. It was very selfish of you to make me worry like that," she said, again trying to sound gentle but sounding harsh.

"Selfish?" he thought. Out loud he said, "I never had to check in before. As long as I was home in time for dinner it was okay with my mom and dad. Besides, I don't know the phone number."

"As you can see, its past dinnertime, otherwise I wouldn't have minded," she lied. "And I put the number on the list I gave you, so that's no excuse. But the good news is I have a solution. Come inside and I'll show you!"

They walked into the kitchen and she picked up a box, "I have a gift for you, go ahead and check it out. I think you're going to like it."

He opened the box and removed an item. It reminded him of the handheld radios he saw in old war movies. "What is it?"

"It's a cellular telephone. It's just like the phones you're used to, but it's also like a radio or walky talky. You can make calls from anywhere. Now if I need to check up on you I can call!"

He heard of them but had never seen one. As he looked over the brick-sized device he asked, "I'm supposed to carry this with me? It's kind of bulky and I don't see how it can fit in my pocket. How am I supposed to ride my bike and hold this at the same time?"

"Now look Carl, I'm responsible for you and I spent a lot of money on that thing, almost fifteen hundred dollars and the monthly fees are outrageous! The least you could do is to show some appreciation," she said, realizing things were already turning out badly and he had not been in the house for more than a few minutes.

"I'm sorry, I do appreciate it. I'm just not sure how I'm going to carry it around, but I'll figure something out. Maybe I can rig up some kind of carrying case," Carl said, hoping it would calm her down.

"That's more like it!" Sally said victoriously. "Now, are you hungry?

He nodded.

"I had to fire the maid today. I'll have Ruthy find a replacement tomorrow. But in the meantime I thought I'd take you to a nice dinner and we can talk. Sound good?"

He nodded again.

"Great, grab that list I gave you last night and meet me at my car. If you like steak, you're going to love this place."

Carl watched as she left the kitchen and realized this was the first time in three days he had something to look forward to. He loved steak and it had been a long time since he enjoyed one. Tuna casserole and hamburger helper had been what his parents' budget allowed on the dinner table for quite awhile.

As he walked to the car with Sally already in the driver's seat he felt like he was going into a spaceship. It was huge and looked futuristic. He opened the door, got inside and saw all of the gauges and buttons. The seats hugged him as he closed the door and heard the music. "This is a nice car!"

"I've had it for almost a year and am thinking of getting a new one. I'm getting tired of it. Don't touch any of the buttons."

They pulled up to the restaurant's valet stand. When Carl saw the valet attendant drive off he asked, "Do you always let strangers drive your car like that?"

"He's just parking it for me, dear."

As they walked through the entrance she was thinking, "This kid has a lot to learn…"

They were seated and ordered their dinners. He realized this was the fanciest place he had ever been to. For the first time in his life he felt uncomfortable with what he was wearing. His blue jeans and t-shirt did not fit in with all the suits and ties. He also noticed he was the only kid in the crowded room. Carl got the biggest steak on the menu and when it was placed on the table he was wide-eyed.

Several people came to the table to say hello and have conversations with Sally as the evening went on. Carl noticed they did not talk like the people he was used to. If he had to put a name to it would have been "fake." Their words and smiles. Some tried to talk to him, but he was uncomfortable and could not think of anything to say, the only exception being when offered their condolences about his parents. He would respond with a little, "Thank you."

He did not know how to handle the sympathy of strangers and was wondering how they knew in the first place. He was also wondering why Sally was acting differently. Her voice changed and she was nice.

Sally tried her best to get Carl to open up, but his resistance was firm. "I think you might need more time to feel better. Maybe you'll talk then. There are a couple of things we need to cover now, though. That strange looking man from your school…"

"Yoda," He interrupted.

"What?"

"That's what we call him. Because he looks like, well, Yoda!"

"Whatever. He told me that you got into a fight today."

"It wasn't even a fight; I just hit the kid once. Yoda told me that he wasn't upset about it and was going to let it slide."

"I hope you didn't hurt the boy. I don't want to get sued. The other thing I need to talk to you about is that nosy social worker. She keeps calling wanting to talk to you. When you do, you tell her you are very happy living with me and everything is fine, okay?"

"Sure, I'll just fib a little," he thought as he nodded his head.

"It would be much more polite if you answered instead of just bobbing your head up and down."

"I'm sorry Aunt Sally, I just don't know what to say."

"Call me Sally, let's drop the "aunt" stuff. It makes me sound old." She talked about the rules and spent the most time on the "lines." Places in the house where he was never to go. It was most of the house. He could use the backdoor, spend as much time in his room as he liked and the kitchen for meals. That was it. She did say he could swim as long as he did not disturb the patio furniture.

On the drive back the car was silent with the exception of the music playing in the background, cutting through the tension.

As they entered the kitchen Sally said, "I hope you enjoyed your steak."

"Yea, it was great. Thank you. It was the best I've ever had."

"Maybe next time you can be more polite to my friends. They were just trying to be nice."

Carl felt the same as he did right before he punched the kid. Part anger and part fear, and hoped he could control it this time. He looked at her trying to figure out why he disliked her so much. She was a bitch, no doubt about that. But he could see that she was trying and he started to feel guilty for not trying himself. "I'm sorry, Sally. You've been nice and I'm thankful for what you're doing. I just miss my mom and dad."

"Like I said before, it will take time. As long as you follow the rules and not cross the lines it will be okay."

It was not what she said, but the way she said it that bothered Carl. He nodded his head as a tear ran down his cheek.

"Carl, what's wrong, dear," Sally asked, surprising Carl by sounding sincere for the first time he had known her.

"I'm really, really scared," his voice cracked and more tears flooded his eyes.

And then it happened. It was only an instant, but for the first time in a decade Sally's world changed and she did not like it one bit. She had compassion and a genuine concern for him. It had been so long since she cared for anything but herself that she did not understand the brief bout of emotions. She stiffened as she tried to process everything, quickly recovered and said, "Why don't you go up to your room. Maybe you'll feel better tomorrow." Then she walked away.

Unfortunately, Carl did not see Sally's revelation. He heard the cold words which added to his new armor.

Sally was shaking. Although it was just a second or two that she experienced compassion for the boy, it left an impact on her. She grabbed the bottle of brandy and poured a healthy shot. As she sat down she was hit again by unusual thoughts. She had been so consumed with how to handle the situation with Carl and how it was affecting her that she never took time to realize what happened. "My sister is dead," she said to herself. It only lasted a moment, but the grief was real.

She noticed her hand shaking as she raised the glass to her lips. As the brandy took effect she felt herself getting back to the same old selfish bitch that she wanted to be. She thought about the upcoming days and planed for the best possible outcome. She had an image to maintain and nothing was going to stop her from keeping it. But for those two seconds, she was almost human. The first minuscule crack in her armor.

CHAPTER 7

OPTIONS

Sally endured another night of fitful sleep. Although the brandy helped, she could not shake off the alarm from the momentary emotional slip. It was more than just uncomfortable, it scared her.

"Ruthy! We need to hire a new maid right away!" she screamed into the phone.

Ruth looked at the clock seeing it was six a.m. "Well, it could have been worse," she thought. "What happened to the old one?"

"I didn't like her attitude, so I let her go. We need a live-in this time, with Carl being here."

"I have a list of candidates. I'll bring it over in a few hours. Is that okay with you, Sally?" Ruth always kept a list as Sally had a habit of "letting go" maids often.

"That's fine, but I need one right away. I don't care if it's Saturday," Sally said as she slammed down the phone.

A few hours later, they were looking over the list of potentials. With such short notice it did not look like they would find one as quickly as Sally demanded. Then Ruth got lucky. She contacted one that had just become available and wanted to start right away. The interview was set for that afternoon.

As they looked over her qualifications, the gate bell sounded. It was the social worker. "What is it with this woman?" Sally thought as she pushed the button to remotely open the gate and went to the front door. The social worker was not alone. Walking up to the entrance next to her was the strange looking man from the school carrying a backpack. "There's no need for me to come in. Carl left this in my office and I wanted to drop it off," he said as he handed it to Sally, who then handed it to Ruth.

"Find some place for this thing, Ruthy," Sally said and then turned to the man, "Thank you Mr. Yoda, I'll see that Carl gets it."

The man flinched. Sally tried to recover by saying, "I thought that was your name, that's what Carl told me."

"I know the kids call me that, but no, it is not my name," he said as he turned and walked away.

"I was wondering if I could talk to Carl," said the social worker as she walked through the door.

Sally had not seen Carl all morning and assumed he was sleeping. "He's still in bed, do you want me to get him up?"

"If you don't mind. I'm behind schedule."

"This lady is starting to get on my nerves," Sally thought as she went to get Carl. As she approached his room, she saw the door was open and the room empty. She checked the bathroom to find that is was empty, too, except for the cell phone standing on the counter. Sally's blood pressure rose.

"I'm so sorry, I completely forgot he was going to see his friends early today. We had a marvelous dinner last night and everything went very well. I think he's going to love it here."

The social worker gave Sally a perplexed look, then shrugged her shoulders and said, "Maybe I can call or stop by later. I do need to see him."

Sally answered a little too quickly. "Just call. My assistant is interviewing for a new maid today. I didn't think the old one was a good fit for Carl, so it is going to be a little hectic around here. I don't want to put any undo stress on the boy," she said as she guided the social worker to the front door.

"I'll do that."

Ruth put the backpack in a hidden corner of the pantry. She made a point to cover it with shopping bags. Sally hated clutter.

Carl was in front of Boy's Town. As he looked at the large industrial looking building he thought, "This place could pass for a prison." Then he noticed one of the boys he talked to the day before coming out the main door.

"Hey."

"Hey, what are you doing here?"

"I wanted to check it out, any chance of showing me around?"

"Sure. We have to check-in at the main desk, but I don't think they'll have a problem. We don't get many visitors here..."

Carl explained to the staff what happened to his parents and that he was turning fourteen soon.

Again, he had to endure the "Sorrys" and "We're here to helps." He was sick of hearing it. He understood people were just trying to comfort him, but it kept on reminding him that his parents were dead and that his life had been torn apart.

Carl was surprised one of the counselors already knew. He explained he was contacted the day of the accident in case Carl had to stay there that night. Over the next couple of hours Carl was shown every square inch of Boy's Town. The dorms were exactly as described. He had a hard time picturing himself being able to sleep surrounded by dozens other young men. The showers were open with no privacy. At lunchtime he saw the kids line up to have their trays filled and sit at the bench-style seats. The food looked and smelled awful and he thought about the big steak he enjoyed the night before.

At the end of the tour he sat down with the counselors and talked about what it was like to live there. "We do our best to provide a safe and comfortable environment. Unfortunately we have a limited budget. I think most of them wish they had a real home," he said, then added, "I can't blame them."

"Me neither," Carl thought.

Carl left Boy's Town confused and defeated. Last weekend he was looking forward to his summer vacation. Now he did not know where he was going to live. Sally's house would be the obvious choice; but the tension that poured off her was so hard to deal with.

He could not picture himself being happy at Boy's Town either. The more he thought about it the more he realized his choice was not where he would be happier; it was where he would the least miserable.

He also missed his parents desperately. It had only been a few days but he thought he would have started to feel a little better. Carl hoped when he placed the flowers on the sidewalk he could say goodbye, but it was proving not to be that easy. The grief came in waves and always unexpected. One minute he was trying to think about his future, and then reminded of the pain of his recent past. It felt like part of him had died in the car crash also.

Carl thought about what to do next. He could go to Joe's house, but he was not sure if his mom was comfortable with him yet. So, he made a plan to go to Sally's and hide in his room the rest of the day. Glad that he made a decision, but not with it, he started his long bike ride back to the house with the iron gates.

"Well hello, you must be Carl!" said the stranger with a warm and kindly manner as he walked through the back door. She had on a maid's uniform and a smile. "My name is Matilda. Your mother.., sorry, your aunt hired me to take care of things around the house and to do the cooking. So, we'll be seeing a lot of each other!"

"Nice to meet you, I'm Carl," he said as she took his hand into hers. It was not a handshake; more of a kind gesture.

"Have you eaten?"

He shook his head.

"Well then, you must be starved. Let's see what I can whip up for you, it won't take long at all."

Carl sat while Matilda made him a sandwich. She asked him what kind of foods he liked, how he liked to have his clothes put away and made small talk. The conversation was pleasant and it was the first time Carl was comfortable being around another human being the last few days. Carl looked at the food as she set it on the table. At first he was not sure he would like it. It looked funny with all the different ingredients, but when he took a bite he rolled his eyes.

"This is good!"

"I'm glad you like it. I can do better after I go to the store and get the right ingredients." They continued their conversation as he ate and it struck Carl that she did not mention his parents.

"Do you know why I'm here?"

"I do and I'm very sorry, but I thought it would be better for you to talk about it when you're ready."

Carl was getting to like this lady. But then his heart sank when he thought about how Sally treated the other maid. "How well do you know Sally?"

She smiled at the question then explained she knew other maids who worked for Sally. Matilda was not derogatory in her description of Sally but at the same time explained she was fully aware of her reputation. Carl could tell she knew what she was in for and she seemed like see could handle it. It made him like her all the more.

Sally walked into the kitchen and looked at Carl, "Where've you been?"

"I went out."

"I know that, but where? I have been worried sick about you!" she said, meaning she was concerned what the social worker was thinking.

Carl tried to get the courage to tell her the truth. "I went to a friend's," he lied. The good citizen was nowhere close to being the perfect kid. He lied to his mom and dad on a few occasions and always felt guilty when he did. Not this time, not telling the truth to Sally felt good.

"What about the cell phone I gave you, why didn't you take it with you?"

"I forgot," he lied again.

"Well, don't do that again!" she said trying to calm herself. "We have a lot of things to go over."

She sat down across from Carl and explained that Ruth was going to take him to the men's shop to pick out a suit. "A suit? What for?" he asked.

"We've been working on the funeral arrangements and it is set for Monday. I didn't think you had a suit and thought it would be appropriate."

"I don't want to go to the funeral." As far as he was concerned he already had his funeral when he placed the flowers on the sidewalk.

Sally was going into a panic. She had set the gears into motion to make the funeral and reception a social event. It was a perfect chance to show off what a great humanitarian she was by parading the boy she was saving. "It wouldn't be right for you not to go, Carl. I've already invited a lot of people."

"I don't want to. I already said goodbye my way. I want to be left alone."

Sally was at a loss. "Well, maybe we can talk about it later. Ruth is on her way to pick you up and take you to your house to get your things."

"My house," he thought. "Okay, I'll wait in my room?" he said, feeling strange to say "my room."

"That'll be fine," she said as he walked out the door and up the stairs. She turned and looked at Matilda who was wiping down the counters. "What do you make of that?"

"Just give him a little time and space. I can see there is a good boy inside that shell."

"Where?"

The ride in Ruth's car was silent. They pulled into the spot where his parent's car should have been. Ruth reached into her bag and pulled out a set of keys that Carl immediately recognized as his mother's. She unlocked the front door and they went into the house. "This is the first time I used the front door for a while," Carl thought.

The house was more eerie than before. It felt like it had also died. In his room, Ruth helped Carl pack up his belongings. "Maybe this'll make it feel more like home for you at Sally's."

"I don't think so."

They loaded her car and as they were pulling out of the driveway Carl said, "Wait, I forgot something. Let me see the keys and I'll be right back. You won't even have to turn the car off." He ran up to the front door, unlocked it and stood in the entryway. "This might be the last time I'm ever in here," he thought, his way of saying goodbye to what had been his home for as long as he could remember. He went to the mantel in the living room and took a framed picture of him with his mom and dad.

In the car he reached back and laid the picture on top of the boxes and handed her the keys. Ruth asked, "Did you make sure to lock the door?"

"Yes," he lied. Just in case.

It took a lot of gentle persuasion, but after explaining the wrath she would endure from Sally if they did not come back with a suit he reluctantly agreed. Ruth seemed like a nice lady and he did not want to put her in a bad position. He still wondered, "Why does everyone put up with Sally? I wouldn't if I didn't have to."

He hated every minute at the men's shop. The clerk made him try on several suits, ties, shoes and belts. The process took forever and with his mental state being so fragile he was becoming agitated. Finally the last decisions were made and the purchases bagged. "Thanks for doing that, I know you didn't want to," Ruth said. "But I do have to say, you looked pretty good all dressed up!"

"I'm just glad it's over with. I want to go back to Sally's and be left alone."

As she pulled into the driveway Carl was opening the door and getting out of the car before it came to a stop. He reached into the back and grabbed his things and walked through the back door. Sally was talking to Matilda explaining exactly the way she wanted things to be done around the house. "There you are! Did you get the suit?"

He looked at her and nodded, itching to run up to his room.

"Great! You have to try it on for me. I'm excited to see how it looks on you."

"Can we do that tomorrow? I'm tired and just want to relax."

"Well, I have to make sure that it fits. If it needs any adjustments, we only have tomorrow. The funeral is Monday, you know."

"I told you, I'm not going to go to the funeral."

"Carl, dear, I have already invited a lot of people and they're looking forward to meeting you. Besides, you have a nice new suit now, so there's no reason for you not to go!" she said trying to sound cheery.

"The only reason not to go is because I don't want to! Can't you understand? I don't know any of those people and they don't know me. They're going because of you. I bet none of them even knew my mom or dad!"

"They want to show respect," she lied. "It wouldn't look good if you weren't there."

"For you or for me?" he yelled. "Because to tell you the truth, I don't care what those people think and I don't care what you think about it either!"

Sally wanted to say something but he was out of the kitchen and halfway up the stairs before she had a chance. She did not like to be challenged. She found it infuriating that this boy did and there was nothing that she could do about it.

"Maybe you should just let him be for now," Matilda said.

Sally was startled, forgetting her new maid was in the room. She wanted to lash out. But it was the way the woman was looking at her. She did not have to say a word to convince Sally that she was right. "Give it time, I think we can bring him around."

"We?'

"Yes, we. Now what can I get for you? Maybe a little something to settle your nerves?"

"To tell you the truth, that sounds nice right now," Sally said as she collapsed into a chair, feeling she was losing control.

The next morning Carl woke to a gentle knocking and Matilda's voice, "I have breakfast for you if you're hungry."

"Yes, come in."

Matilda was carrying a tray with pancakes, milk and syrup. "Have you ever had breakfast in bed before?"

"No. Have you?"

Her smile was heart-warming as she shook her head and said, "You know what? No and I think someone should serve me breakfast in bed someday. It would be very nice."

"Well if you teach me how to cook, maybe I can do the same for you sometime," he said as he started to devour the food. "How did you learn to cook like this?"

"I have been doing it for so long I don't remember. It's just what I do now."

They talked while he ate and Carl forgot why he was waking up in his new room. He just woke up being a kid and just a kid. Not an orphan. But soon he remembered and his body stiffened.

"It's okay, you're safe. Everything will be fine."

Her words were calming but he still dreaded the rest of his day. "Is Sally up?"

"Yes, she is waiting for you downstairs. I have a feeling you already know what she wants to talk to you about," she said. "It's up to you, but some of my biggest regrets came from things I thought I was right about only to find out that I wasn't so right after all," she said as she left.

"Is she telling me I should go to the funeral? Or not?" he thought.

He did not want to go. That did not change. He also thought his reasons were right. The only other family member would be Sally. Everyone else would be strangers and he did not want to play a roll for them. But what Matilda said sparked a question. "Would I regret it later if I didn't go?" He knew he had the option, but then realized that he really didn't.

He showered then he reached into the closet and took out the suit. "Maybe this will make Sally happy. At least calm her down," he thought.

Sally was surprised, "You look wonderful! Does this mean that you will go to the funeral?"

"I'll go, but only if I don't have to talk to anyone and be left alone."

"You're making the best decision. It'll help you and I have a lot of friends who want to meet you!"

"I just tell her I want to be left alone and now she's talking about me meeting her friends? What is it with this woman?" he thought as turned to leave. As he did he saw Matilda smiling at him. He shrugged his shoulders.

"You'll see, it's going to be a very nice time," Sally said after him.

Carl organized his room. He stayed there all day with exception of having lunch in the kitchen and talking to the counselor on the phone with Sally hovering over him as he said how happy he was. "This lying deal is starting to become a habit," he thought. But, overall it was a pretty good day. He only had to see Sally twice.

CHAPTER 8
CONFRONTATIONS

He was right. Sally was the only person Carl recognized at the funeral and reception.

It was a day of firsts for him. The first time he attended an event worthy of wearing a suit. The first time he had ridden in a limo. The first time he wanted to physically hurt everyone in the room.

The funeral itself was alright. A few people sat in the pews in the chapel located on the mortuary property and whispered among themselves. Carl was seated in the first row next to Sally. He looked at the two closed caskets wondering which was his mother's and which was his father's. But he was thankful he did not have to see the bodies. He remembered the store clerk said they had to be cut out of the wreckage. He found comfort in the fact the last time he saw his parents things were good. His dad talking about fishing, and his mother saying that she loved him.

As the short service began Carl became uncomfortable. A man he had never seen began speaking about his mom and dad like he knew them well, but it was easy to tell it was a rehearsed speech with "fill in the blank" parts for this particular occasion.

Carl was hurt and confused, and he wished he could go back to Sally's to hide. "This is going to be a very long day," he thought.

Sally was acting differently. She insisted on putting her hand on his shoulder and pretended she cared. For outsiders it looked like she was kind and motherly, but for Carl it was as if he was in a drama class.

They rode in a limo following the hearses which carried his parents to their final resting place. Sally said, "I think that was a nice service. What did you think?"

"I don't know, I've never been to one but it seemed fake to me. And to be honest, I think you're acting different too."

"What do you mean by that?" she said with that now familiar demeaning manner.

"You don't act like that when we are at your house."

"We're not going to have any problems or outbursts today, are we?'

"No, as long as everyone leaves me alone."

"People are going to want to talk to you and they mean well. I hope you behave better than you did at dinner the other night."

There was another brief service at the gravesite, the only audience being Sally and Carl. Then machines lowered his mom and dad into the ground. "Do you want some time alone?" Sally asked, surprising Carl. She seemed sincere and no one else was around. "I can wait for you in the limo if you like."

"I think I do."

"Okay, just don't take too long, I'm sure there are already guests arriving for the reception."

"So much for being nice," he thought as he stood over the graves. He wanted to cry so much so that it hurt. But the tears would not come.

He reached in his pocket and took out a fishing lure. He caught the biggest fish in his life with it on one of his dad's fishing trips. He bent down and gently tossed it on the casket. He pulled out a card he made for his mother for one of her birthdays. It was her favorite and he remembered she cried when she read it. At first he thought he did something wrong, but she explained they were "good tears." He tossed it on her coffin and stepped back. Moments later the limo horn blasted and Carl walked towards it. But just before he turned and whispered, "I'm sorry."

As the limo pulled away Carl said, "Sally, I don't think I can do this."

"Do what?"

"This reception thing. I don't know anyone and I'm not in a good mood. I don't want to embarrass you in front of *your* friends," he said, trying to sell his point. "I think it would be better for everyone to let this guy take me back to your house."

Again, after several panic attacks over the past couple of days, Sally thought she was going to blow a gasket. She got him to the funeral, unbeknownst to her with Matilda's help, and now was going to be the payoff for all the work and planning. Everyone at the country club would see firsthand how she rescued this poor child. She would be the center of attention and it would be glorious. Now this kid says he cannot go? It would be a disaster. Instead of singing her praise, there would be gossip why the new prince was not there.

"Carl, honey, I know this isn't easy. But I think it would be good for you to be around people who care for you…"

"They don't know me, how can they give a crap!" he interrupted.

"Well, maybe being around people who are happy will make you feel better. Besides, there's going to be great food and the club has a pool table and a theater. I'd like you to see it. We might be spending time there," she said. Translation, "I still might have to show you off."

"We can check it out later."

Her persuasion was not working. "Look, I don't ask you for much. But I'm asking you to do this for me. I won't ask you for anything like this again," she said, enraged that she had to plead.

He chuckled, thinking about the full page of rules not "asking for much." But he could see it was important to her. Maybe it would be easier to just give in. If it got too uncomfortable he could sneak out and hit some balls on the pool table. Besides, it might be nice to have Sally's favor in his back pocket for later. "Okay, I'll go. But don't expect me to be in a good mood because I'm not."

"Just fake it," she said, and he knew this was the most honest statement she had ever made to him.

He could not believe his eyes when he got out of the limo and looked at the Country Club. It was incredible and reminded him of fancy places he had seen on television. The building was huge and surrounded by ponds and waterfalls. Trees and plants transported him to a completely different world. As they entered it was more spectacular. Seeing the fountains and art-filled the walls, he was impressed.

"It's this way, I reserved best banquet hall here, I think you'll like it," Sally said as she walked toward a large corridor with Carl in tow.

It was a long walk to the reception hall and as they reached the door Carl saw a picture of his mom and dad on an easel. He read the words below it and noticed that his last name was spelled incorrectly. He thought about telling Sally, but then thought better of it. "What's the point?"

At first things went well. Sally introduced Carl to dozens of her friends and he did not have to say much. She was in her full-on fake compassion mode and doing it so well that Carl started to take the bait. "See. This isn't that bad now, is it?" Sally whispered in his ear.

"Yea, this is kind of cool."

"I'm going to work the room. Why don't you get something to eat and check out the place?" she said pointing to the enormous buffet table.

He walked to the table and again was blow away. There were fountains flowing with chocolate with strawberries for dipping and others that had soda flowing. He saw people filling little glasses in the streams and putting in a splash orange juice. He could not believe the rows of appetizers stretched down the long table. He discovered he loved shrimp cocktail and lobster claws and he really liked the soda mixed with orange juice. He thought caviar was disgusting. After shoving a big spoonful into his mouth it took several times to rinse the taste out after running to the bathroom.

He found a secluded table and made several trips to the buffet. His mission was to try everything at least once. He realized his mistake on the last experiment. A tray was filled with something pink and he did not have a clue what it was. Carl placed the thin slices on his plate. It did not look like it would taste good and he was still leery after his bout with the caviar, but he did like some of the other stuff that looked gross, so he decided to give it shot. On his way back to the table he stopped at the soda fountain. He looked at the little glasses and decided to use a bigger glass this time. The last four did not last long enough. "Save a trip," he thought as he filled the water glass from the fountain and topping it off with a little orange juice.

Carl sat and smelled his new experiment. It was smoky. It took him time to gather courage to try it so he sat back and looked at the people in the room.

They were different than the down to earth types he was used to. The women had stuff on their faces that made them look funny and wore more jewelry than he had ever seen. One woman had so many bracelets he was surprised she had the strength to lift her arm. And the way they talked… it was English, so he could catch the words. But the way they said them reminded him of old-time movies. Even things they talked about were strange. He noticed most were talking about others and not being complimentary. Carl remembered his dad telling him he should never talk about people behind their backs and now Carl understood. He grew tired of people-watching and looked at his plate.

"Here goes nothing…" he thought as he took a big bite. His stomach immediately revolted as he tasted the lox. He wanted to spit it out, but was afraid people were watching. So, instead, he grabbed his glass and chugged every last drop to wash down the mouthful of salmon. Carl was afraid he was going to be sick. He rushed to the bathroom and bent over the toilet hoping to throw up, but could not. The queasiness would have been bad enough but now his head was feeling funny. He tried to concentrate. "What was that pink crap?" he wondered.

As he stood the walls were moving and he realized it was because he was swaying. He put the toilet lid down and sat. He wanted, needed, to get better soon. Real soon.

Sally was in all of her glory. Things were going exactly as planned and she had a hard time holding in her excitement. Everyone, absolutely everyone, made her the center of attention and she was soaking it in like rays in a tanning bed. As she walked through the room, eavesdropping on several conversations, she could hear talking about one thing, her. She was climbing the social ladder each passing moment and she intended to never come back down. "This might work out well, after all," she thought with self assurance. Then more of the guests were asking to meet Carl.

Sally was frantic again. She could not find Carl. "Did he sneak out?" she wondered. As a last attempt, she asked one of her friends to check the men's room.

"I think he's in there, but the stall door is closed and doesn't answer when I ask if he is okay."

"It's been a difficult day for him; he must want to be alone," she said relieved he did not skip out and, more importantly, she had a good excuse for people wanting to meet him. She had dodged a bullet, again.

Carl was feeling better but nowhere near normal. When he heard the man walk into the restroom and ask him through the stall door if he was okay he became too confused and scared to answer. He dared to stand up and was in somewhat more control of his body. But he still felt like he was on a slowly spinning merry-go-round. He walked out of the stall, a little wobbly, and splashed cold water on his face. It seemed like the right thing to do. The splash was a shock, but it helped, so he did it a few more times. He lost track of time and thought he should be leaving soon, so he gathered up his courage and went back to the banquet room.

He saw the picture of his mom and dad and something snapped. He was having a difficult time concentrating but knew he was angry. Angry at Sally, angry at himself, angry with the whole messed up situation. "I don't want to be here!" his mind screamed.

"There you are, I have been looking all over for you!" Sally said. "There're people who would like to meet you."

"No, I'm not going to talk to anyone else, I want to leave. Right now! I already kept my promise, now you keep yours."

"We had a deal and I expect you to keep your word. It won't be many, just a few. After that you can leave," she said as she turned and looked at him, "What's wrong with you?"

"I don't feel well and I want to leave. I don't know what's wrong, but I think I ate something that's making me sick. Please, just take me to your house."

"Please, Carl. Just a few more people and then I'll have the limo driver take you back."

"Promise?"

"Promise."

"Okay, but just a few. I want out of here."

Relieved, Sally grabbed Carl's hand and he immediately pulled it back. He could not bare her touch anymore. "Follow me. This'll be over soon."

"Not soon enough," he thought through the haze.

His next introduction went well. Mainly because Sally did the talking but he was still having trouble standing with out swaying. He noticed Sally's friend looking at him strangely. "I ate something that didn't agree with me." The stranger nodded his head like he understood.

The next meeting did not go as well. Right after Sally made the intros the woman looked at Carl's bloodshot eyes. "Look Sally, this poor lad has been crying."

"No I haven't," Carl slurred.

"I'm sorry, your eyes look like you have been."

"I haven't been," Carl snapped, feeling his adrenaline level increase.

"That's okay, I'm just so sorry for the loss of you mother and father."

"Did you know them?"

"No, I'm afraid not."

"Then how the hell can you be sorry about a couple of people getting killed if you didn't even know them?" Carl asked with a smirk.

The woman was shocked and Sally stepped right in, "You have to excuse him, this has been such a trying day."

"I can stick up for myself!" Carl snapped. "None of the people in this room knew the first thing about my parents and now they want to tell me how sorry they are? The first time any of them even knew what my mom and dad looked like was when they saw their picture at the door! Hell, they didn't even get the spelling of our last name right and you are going to tell me they give a sh...."

"Carl!" Sally interrupted just in time. "Excuse us for a moment," she said to her friend as she ushered Carl to an empty table. "Sit down right there, young man."

"No!" he yelled loud enough for everyone to hear.

"What are all of you looking at! Why don't you just get back to your little party so you can talk crap about each other?"

Sally heard gasps and saw looks of surprise. "Carl, please come out to the hall with me."

"I want to leave and I want to leave right now! I don't belong here and I don't belong with these people!"

"Okay, you win. I'll have the limo driver take you back right now, but I need you to do just one thing for me," Sally growled.

"What?"

"Please Carl, apologize to my friend. If you do I might be able to salvage this mess you caused."

He went to the first lady he offended, "I'm sorry if I was rude."

The woman shook her head with an approving smile.

Then Carl went to the door and yelled, "Don't blame my outburst on my Aunt Sally. She wants all of you to be impressed with me, but today is not going to be the day. It is my fault and not hers. Well, maybe a little of hers." Then he stumbled, catching himself on the doorframe.

Sally was in shock, but it could have been worse, she thought she might be able to salvage the situation and began planning how. Play the sympathy card. It would help explain Carl's behavior and make her look even better making her guests believe how committed she was to helping the poor, helpless boy. "Yes, this can work!"

she thought. But, she needed to get Carl out of there. "Come on Carl, let's go. Thank you for doing that, for me."

"I didn't do it for you, I did it for me."

Sally did not care who he did it for but she had to admire him for making the "almost" apology. That was until Carl picked up the picture of his parents, tore it in half as he walked down the hall and threw the remains on the floor.

Carl stumbled twice as they walked in silence to the limo. As the driver opened the back door Carl stopped him, "Can I ride up front?" The driver shrugged his shoulders in the universal "why not?" gesture and opened the front door.

"Sally, I'm sorry. I don't know why I said those things. You know I didn't want to be here. But I thought I could handle it, I think something I ate messed me up."

"What did you eat?"

"I tried everything."

"What about to drink?"

"The soda from the fountain next to the orange juice. That stuff was pretty good, but that pink stuff," he said shaking his head.

"How many?" her interest peaked.

"How many what?"

"How many glasses?"

"Well, I had three or four little glasses then filled up one of the big ones. I had to chug it down to swallow that pink guck. That pink stuff made me feel weird."

Sally wanted to be outraged at the boy but could not help herself, and she experienced another one of those pesky little cracks in her armor and smiled a real, warm, caring smile. "The driver will take you back now. I'm pretty sure you'll feel better soon, but I have to warn you, tomorrow morning might be tough."

"Why?"

"We'll talk about it when I get back tonight," she said as she went back to the banquet room. She had some major damage control to handle.

CHAPTER 9

GETAWAY

A s the limo rolled along swaying on its soft suspension Carl got queasy. He had never been carsick before, but he knew he was going to lose it. "Pull over!"

"What?"

"Pull over, I'm going to be sick!"

The driver parked and Carl rolled out and lost all of the contents of his stomach. He leaned over with his hands on his knees, trying to catch his breath. As he stood the driver was holding papers towels and a bottle of water. "You done?"

"I think so."

"Here, use this to wipe your face and the water will get the taste out."

Still shaky he leaned on the fender and wiped his face before slugging down the water. "Thanks. You always carry this stuff around?"

"In my line of work it's a necessity. How much alcohol did you drink?"

"I drank soda."

"Uh huh."

After Carl recovered he was dropped off at Sally's house and walked into the kitchen where Matilda was doing housework. "How did it go?" she asked, then saw him, "Oh my, you look terrible!"

"I bet I feel worse than I look."

They sat down and Carl told her everything that happened. Matilda smiled, "I don't think that was soda, Carl. They usually use those fountains for Champagne."

"What's that?"

She pulled a corked bottle from the cabinet. "This is Champagne."

"Booze! That stuff was booze?"

She made him a mixture of tomato juice, spices and hot sauce. Carl asked, "What's that?"

"You're not going to like it, but it'll help you feel better. Now and later."

"I tell you one thing, I have no idea why anybody would drink booze. I feel terrible."

"A lot of people have said that. Now drink that down all at once. It'll be hard to believe, but it helps."

It burned all the way down his gullet. He shuddered, "I don't ever want to have to drink that again, either."

He went to his room to rest but every time he closed his eyes the room spun and he thought was going to get sick again. So he got up and decided to take care of something that had been on his mind. Still wearing his suit, less the jacket, he got on his bike and started to Joey's. Matilda watched as Carl rode off.

He nearly crashed a few times and fell over once while waiting for a light to turn green but he got to Joey's in one piece and knocked on his door.

"Look at you! Why are you all dressed up?" Joey asked.

"The funeral was today."

Joey twisted his head and took a closer look at his buddy, "You don't look so good."

"I know, I know. Can I come in?"

Joey walked inside and Carl followed him into his room. They sat down and Carl told him about the Champagne fountain. "I thought it was soda..."

"Man, if it makes you look and act the way you do, I'm going to stay away from that stuff!"

"Trust me on this one, stay away from it."

They played video games and talked. Carl said, "I need to ask you a big favor."

"What?"

"Can you take care of Mutt for me? Sally won't let me have him at her house. If you have him here at least I can see him once in a while. Plus, I'm scared what will happen to Mutt if you don't."

"I don't think my folks would have a problem with that, he's a great dog. I'll ask when they get home. Might be a good idea for you not to be here when they do. Mom is just getting over the cop thing. But if she sees you like this... it wouldn't be good."

"I get it."

They played video games for a couple of hours. Even though Carl was feeling better, he was still in rough shape. He knew he was off because he lost every single game, badly, and that never happened before.

When Joey's parents were due to be home Carl got on his bike to go back to Sally's, but the thought of the ride discouraged him. He was tired and did not think he had the strength to make it. He went back to his old house and the front door was still unlocked. He walked into his old room, collapsed on his bed and passed out.

Sally was exhausted. Her salvage operation at the reception used up every bit of her energy. She relentlessly worked the crowd and as people were leaving she could tell she accomplished her mission and her social status was on an upward swing even though Carl had almost destroyed it.

As she sat in limo she thought, "What next?" She had been so occupied with making arrangements for the reception that she had not given thought to the real problem. She had a thirteen year old living in her house and it was very, very uncomfortable. She enjoyed years of living a completely self-serving existence. When those brief pangs of heartfelt compassion hit her it reminded her of parts of her life that she wanted to forget.

The limo drove to the grand entrance of the house. As the driver opened the door he said, "I think that boy of yours had too much to drink. He got sick on the way back."

"He is not my boy!"

"Whatever, he's still pretty young to be drunk."

She shrugged him off and went into the house to the kitchen. She noticed the light was blinking on the answering machine.

The social worker's voice crackled through the speaker, "Hi Sally. I'm calling to see how Carl is doing, I'm sure it must've been a difficult day. Have him give me a call."

"Difficult for him, what about me?" Sally thought as she hit the delete button.

She poured a brandy and went up to her suite. She turned on the large television more for noise than entertainment. Her mind was still swimming with the unease of how she might not be able to maintain her life the way she liked with a teenager in the house. "I need more time to figure this out," she thought. But there was no time, it already happened.

Then it hit her. "Why didn't I think of this before? It's so easy!" she thought and reached for the phone as the eleven o'clock news was wrapping up, "Ruthy! I need you to find a summer camp for Carl right away!"

His head was pounding as he opened his eyes. Carl could tell someone was in the room, but his mind was too fuzzy to know who and he was too sick to care. "Carl, we need to get you up. Rise and shine you party animal!" Matilda said in a cheery voice that grated on his nerves.

He sat up and saw her at the foot of the bed. He looked around and realized he was in his old room. "What are you doing here? And, what am I doing here?"

I saw you ride off yesterday and when you didn't come home I figured you might be here. I got the address from Ruth," she said. "I brought you a change of clothes."

"My head is killing me."`

"Goes with the territory. Get up and put these on and we'll get some breakfast. I don't see any reason for your aunt to know you were gone last night. I'll just tell her I took you to an early breakfast. It can be our little secret!"

As the haze wore off he vaguely remembered riding his bike to Joey's and asking if he could take care of Mutt. But, that was the last thing he remembered. He did remember his outburst at the reception and figured Sally would be upset. "That might be a good idea. I think I blew it yesterday and Sally's probably pretty mad at me right now."

He got up and changed. As they walked out the door he stopped. "I think this really is the last time I'll be here," he thought. He locked the door and slammed it shut.

They went to a small café and Carl devoured his breakfast. "I don't think I've ever been this hungry before."

"That's a good sign. You're on your way to recovery!"

"Thanks for getting me. I can't imagine what Sally would think if she knew."

After breakfast, Matilda drove him to Joey's where he learned that Mutt could stay with his family. Carl was relieved to the point of tears. He was also relieved that Joey's mom liked him again.

Sally was in the kitchen when Matilda and Carl walked in. "Where the hell have you been?"

"He got up early so I took him out for breakfast."

Sally wanted to be angry but thought better of it. Maybe having a maid that could take on some of the duties taking care of the boy could come in handy. "Next time let me know. That damn social worker keeps calling and if I don't know where Carl is she acts like I'm not a good parent, or custodian, or whatever…"

"I thought you might like to sleep in. It must've been a trying day for you yesterday. Now, what can I get for you?"

"Just scramble me some eggs," Sally barked as she turned to Carl. "I have some wonderful news for you! I think you are going to be very, very excited!!"

Carl's guard went up. He was expecting to get chewed out for what happened at the reception, not for her to be perky. "What?"

"I had Ruthy find a fantastic summer camp for you, Camp Big Lake. You're going to love it! There'll be a lot of kids there. I just know you are going to have the greatest time! It'll be your little getaway!"

He had never been to a summer camp before but heard some of his friends talk about it with mixed reviews. Some thought it was great. Others said they were being dropped off at a glorified babysitter. "Let me think about it."

"Think about it? What's there to think about? I already had Ruthy set it up and she's dropping you off Friday. It'll be the best two months of your life!"

"Two months? Friday? What if I don't want to go? Did you ever think of that? I want to hang out with my friends, not be around strangers."

"Now Carl, we have already made the arrangements. You're going on Friday and that settles it. Besides, after your behavior yesterday it might be good for you to have some time away from here," she said as she left the room.

"It might be fun," Matilda said.

"I don't know. It would've been nice if she asked instead of forcing it on me. My parents would have. I was looking forward to hanging out with my friends. I won't know anyone there."

"Might be a chance for you to make new friends and experiences."

"I have enough friends and believe me, I don't need any new experiences right now," he said as went to his room.

Matilda watched him and thought, "This is not going to end well."

The next day Ruth took Carl to the kennel. As the handler gave Carl Mutt's leash the dog was spastic, jumping all around and then laying on his back so Carl could rub his tummy. Ruth thought, "That's the ugliest dog I've ever seen in my life!" As they walked to her car she told Carl, "That's a nice dog you have there!"

"He's not mine anymore."

He purposely avoided Sally. His plan was to show her he could stay out of her way. He realized her choice to send him to camp was not for him to have fun, but rather to get him out of her hair.

The plan was set for Ruth to take him on the two-hour drive and drop him off. The night before, Carl steeled himself to talk to Sally. They had barley seen each other the last couple of days and he thought he had a chance to talk her out of making him go. The problem was the few times they did see each other the tension was overwhelming. Ignoring the rules, he went to Sally's office. She saw him standing at the door, "What are you doing, you're not supposed to be in this part of the house!"

"I know, but I wanted to talk to you for a minute," he said shyly.

"Fine. What?"

"Well, I was thinking. I've stayed out of your way, and I think you'll see having me here won't change things for you. So, I don't have to go to that camp."

"You are going."

"Sally, I really don't want to. I promise I'll stay out of your way. You won't even know I'm here. Please, don't make me go," he pleaded.

"Carl, you are going. I'm in charge of you now and know what's best for you. It's a very exclusive camp. Consider the matter settled, and make sure you're ready first thing in the morning," she said. "Now leave me be, I have things I need to attend to." Translation: "I don't want you here."

"This isn't fair. I don't want to go! I can hang out at Joey's and I won't bother you at all. I promise!"

Sally stood up and looked in him in the eye. "You are going," she ordered as she slammed the door in his face.

As Ruth steered through the curves on the mountain road that led to Camp Big Lake Carl was silent. She tried to start a conversation with no luck. When signs showed they were getting close he asked, "How can you stand working for Sally?"

Wanting to be careful with her answer she thought then said, "I'll make you a deal. Whatever you tell me will stay with me and you do the same, okay? I don't want to have problems getting between you and Sally."

"Deal."

"Sally is just Sally. She's never going to change. She is selfish, self-serving and I don't think I've ever met anyone so shallow. But she pays very well and after awhile you learn not to let her attitude affect you."

"How do you do that? I get frustrated just being around her a couple of minutes."

"Has it always been like that?"

"I knew she didn't like kids. We didn't see her often, but she was always the same," he said. "I never imagined living at her house and now that I do it's worse than I thought."

"I noticed you stayed out of her way. Maybe if you keep doing that it can work out."

"Yea, but it's the feeling I get around her. She doesn't even have to say anything. I can tell she doesn't want me there," he sighed. "Maybe I would be better off at Boy's Town."

"You would rather live at Boy's Town than at Sally's?"

"I think Sally would be happier if I did."

Twenty minutes later they were unloading his gear at Camp Big Lake. The grounds were beautiful. "Maybe this won't be so bad," he thought as he turned to Ruth. "Thanks, I know you don't like to work Fridays."

"That's okay, I was able to bargain a weekend off, so it was worth it. Maybe you can relax and feel better."

"We'll see how it goes," Carl said as he picked up his things.

Ruth checked him in at the main office and said goodbye. "I'll see you in a couple of months."

Carl nodded and followed the camp staffer to his temporary home. He saw boats on the lake and passed by stables filled with horses. He also noticed something strange: no kids. The place seemed deserted.

"This is your cabin, your folks…"

"My folks are dead," Carl interrupted.

"Oh, sorry. Well, whoever made the reservations made sure you got the deluxe one, you only have to share it with three other boys and it has its own bathroom. For showers you still have to go to the main cabin."

"Almost as bad as Boy's Town," Carl thought. He saw two sets of bunk beds and put his stuff on one of the lower ones. "When do the other boys get here?"

"Monday. You get it all to yourself for the weekend! In fact, you pretty much have the whole place to yourself!"

"Why?"

"You're the only one arriving early. We had to make special arrangements for you. Normally no TV allowed, but we're going to let you watch the one in the staff lounge this weekend if you get bored and you'll be having your meals with us. The other kids get here Monday"

"Sally couldn't wait to get me out of her house," he thought. He also wondered what was going to happen after camp. The more he thought about it the more his spirits sank. "I really am screwed."

It was the longest weekend of his life. The camp was a ghost town and Carl was bored to death. With nothing to do the downtime allowed him to think way too much and he did not have good things to think about. His depression came across as a bad attitude and became apparent to the staff. After lunch one of them said, "We're going to have to keep on eye on that one."

Sunday night Carl sat on his bunk. He did not like self-pity, but he could not help it. "Sixty days to go," he thought. After he washed up he crawled into his sleeping bag hoping things would be better after the other kids arrived. But at that moment he never felt so alone in his life.

As he closed his eyes he whispered, "Happy Birthday to me…"

CHAPTER 10
BULLIES

Examining his work, he enjoyed deep satisfaction. To outsiders the Santos Mahogany looked like a pile of planks covered with haphazard lines. Not to Carl. What normally would have taken a day had taken several. He measured and re-measured and the painstaking work produced exactly what he wanted. Now, time to cut. He would use hand tools. His shop was filled with the most advance power tools available, but he needed to feel every stroke of sawing the boards by hand this time.

He looked at the clock with its second hand loudly ticking. It was getting late. "First cut tomorrow, then as long as it takes…" he thought as he closed up shop and walked home transforming into Carl the husband and father. And then a tear rolled down his cheek.

It took Carl a month to get kicked out of Camp Big Lake.

It started well. Almost. On the first day when the rest of the kids filled Camp Big Lake, Carl was sitting on a dock watching new arrivals say goodbye to their parents. He was jealous watching them hug their moms and dads.

He stayed out of the way of staffers who were showing everyone the campgrounds. He already checked it out and did not want to be around people yet. He leaned on a pole and watched from a distance as a slight breeze whipped at his hair.

His spirits rose with the hum of activity. Laughter and excitement from other kids was contagious. But he missed his old life terribly and was confused every time he pictured his new one.

He walked into his cabin and saw two boys setting up sleeping bags. They introduced themselves and Carl saw they were twins. "You guys look like exact copies of each other!"

"We get that all the time," one said. "But we never dress the same or any of that crap; you'll be able to tell us a part."

Their names were Skip and Sam and they were cool, to his relief. They told him about the missing roommate. They had been coming to Camp Big Lake for years and always had the same cabin. That also applied to the boy who had not arrived yet. His name was Max and the way the twins described him made Carl worry. "Max is a complete jerk! He loves to stir things up."

"Maybe I can stay away from him if he's that bad."

"Good luck with that. If he doesn't like you he'll go out of his way to get to you," Sam said.

"It can't be that bad, can it?"

"You'll see. Just try to stay on his good side."

After the twins finished unpacking they went to the main cabin for lunch. Carl noticed the crowd was like his friends had described. A lot of the teens were excited, already having fun. But there were also some that obviously had been dumped off. He could see in their faces they were not happy campers. Carl knew he was part of the second crowd at that point but made a vow to become part of the first.

After lunch the new roommates went back to their cabin and Carl saw whom he assumed was Max. The kid was big. He had a good four inches on Carl and his arms were twice the size as his. Carl saw Max holding his sleeping bag. "Hey, what are you doing, that's mine."

"I'm moving it for you. This is my bunk."

"I got here early and picked that one out. I've been sleeping there for a couple of nights."

"You take the top one, I don't like the top. That's why I get the bottom, understand?"

Carl remembered what the twins said about Max and how it would not be a good idea to get on his bad side. He wanted to keep the same bunk, but if it could keep the peace by letting Max have his way, so be it. "That's fine. You take the bottom and I'll take the top," Carl said as he took his sleeping bag from Max.

"That's more like it," Max said in a belittling tone then turned to Skip and Sam. "Well, if it isn't Twiddle Dee and Twiddle Dumb! How you two little runts doing?"

"Hey."

"I have to get my trunk. No one messes with my stuff," Max said as he walked out.

"You weren't kidding! He's a piece of work."

"We warned you and you haven't seen nothing yet. And, just wait till tonight!" Sam said.

"What?"

"You'll see. You were smart to give up on the bunk. Maybe that'll keep you on his good side. If he has one…" said Skip.

Max walked back in dragging a huge trunk. It was bigger than the other three boys' bags put together. He slammed it on the floor and opened it. Carl never saw so much candy in one place. Every different kind and all shapes and sizes. Then Max pushed some of it aside and Carl saw packs of cigarettes and tiny bottles. "Have the Runts explained the rules to you?"

"What rules?"

Max told Carl. Don't touch his stuff. What happens in the cabin stays in the cabin and how painful it would be if any of his rules were broken.

"Great, more rules," Carl thought.

The rest of the afternoon was filled with first-day orientations. Carl's spirits improved as he thought how much fun it sounded. He had never been sailing or horseback riding and he started to look forward to the coming weeks. "Plus I don't have to worry about Sally," he thought.

After dinner there was a bonfire. Carl met other teens and started to get settled. He could tell there were still two types of groups. The ones that wanted to be there and the ones that did not. He was beginning to feel he was part of the happy crowd and decided not to tell anyone why he was there. He did not want to endure the sympathy about his mom and dad and had no idea how to explain his relationship with Sally.

After the flames died it was time for lights-out. Carl had not seen Max the entire afternoon and forgotten about him. But when he walked in he was quickly reminded.

Max was sitting on the floor with another kid. Both were smoking and sipping from Max's little bottles. "That stinks; can't you smoke those outside?"

"Right, and get caught by the staff? Don't worry, you'll get used to it like the Runts did."

Carl went outside, sat on a tree stump and listened to the noises from other cabins. The soft laughter calmed him. He did not think about the bad stuff, his mom and dad, Sally and giving up Mutt. He thought about what he was going to do the next day.

Later the twins walked up the path and saw Carl.

"Hey," one said.

"Hey! Max has a friend in there and they're smoking. It's stinking up the cabin, so I came out here."

Skip said, "The good news is they take turns, so we don't have to put up with it every night. Plus it is getting late, his friend should be leaving soon and then we can try to get some rest."

"Try?"

"You'll see."

After Max's friend left they went in to get ready for bed. Carl was climbing up the ladder to his bunk when he heard Max, "Don't forget the rules. What happens here stays here. You wouldn't want to know what I do to snitches."

"I won't say anything."

Carl was dozing off when he heard it. At first it sounded like a low rumble then got louder. "Could that be a bear?" he wondered. He swore he felt the bunk shake with every burst of the low organic noise. And it was getting deeper and louder. He got out of his bunk and took the steps on the ladder to the floor. It was coming from inside the cabin, he was sure of that. But what the heck was it? He turned on the lights. The twins were on their elbows looking at him. "What's that noise?"

They pointed at the bunk below his. Max was on his back with his mouth open. Carl had never heard anyone snore so loud. "Does he snore like that all night?"

"Not all night, but a lot of it. We tried to warn you!" Skip said.

"This is crazy! I'm taking my sleeping bag outside," he said as he grabbed it and his pillow. A few minutes later the twins joined him and then they knew what it felt like to be really camping.

Ruth walked into the kitchen and saw Matilda. "Good morning. How was your weekend?"

"To be honest I thought it would be quieter around here with Carl gone. Now I realize how little work he is and how much Sally is!"

Ruth told Matilda how impressed she was that she could handle Sally. "She drove all of the other maids crazy. You seem to be immune to her."

"Sally's like a tire that's over-inflated. I let her take out some of the air and it releases the pressure," Matilda said. "How did it go with Carl?"

Ruth told her about their talk. They agreed Carl was a great young man. They also agreed how much he changed when he and Sally were in a room. It was different people living in the same body. Ruth wrestled whether or not she should tell Matilda about what Carl said about Boy's Town. She did not want to betray his trust, but it concerned her.

"The social worker told him he could live at Boy's Town if he wanted when he turns fourteen."

"When will that be?"

"I'm not sure. I'm going to check. You two get along. I was wondering if you think he'd do it?"

"I don't know. He seems fine enough when he is on his own, but like you said, Sally agitates him."

Sally walked in and ordered coffee from Matilda and told Ruth to meet her in her office. Ruth told Matilda that she had to tell Sally about Boy's Town, and sooner would be better than later. "Wish me luck," she said to Matilda.

"I can put a shot of brandy in her coffee if you think it would help."

Ruth shook her head and smiled, "I can handle it."

They sat on opposite sides of Sally's desk. "Here goes nothing," Ruth thought as she steeled herself.

When Sally learned Carl was actually considering going to Boy's Town the tension in the room became unbearable.

"He would prefer that place! It doesn't make any sense. Look at this house! Any one of those boys at that orphanage would love to live here!"

"Look Sally, your home is beautiful. But that's not the issue. Carl thinks you don't want him around," Ruth said in the softest tone she could. "Maybe if we could figure out a way for you to get along better it would help. I think he turns fourteen soon so it might not be in your control anyway. Besides, he's a good kid."

"No such thing."

Ruth rolled her eyes realizing there was no way she was going to get through to Sally. Instead she took notes on how Sally was going to take care of the problem. "Find out when he turns fourteen and let me know right away," Sally demanded as she shooed Ruth out.

Later, Ruth endured her second dreaded trip to Sally's office of the morning. She stuck her head in and Sally looked up. "Well?'

"Yesterday."

Sally sat back in her chair. There was no way she could allow Carl to go to Boy's Town. She would be the laughing stock of the club. She called the social worker to get all of the information she needed. As she hung up she looked at Ruth and said, "Have my attorney call me right away."

Ruth stood dumbfounded after hearing the conversation.

Carl was having a blast. At least during the days. He loved the water activities and made friends. He also liked being around horses and shooting bow and arrows. Although they were still there, the strange and uncomfortable feelings Carl was enduring since his parent's death were kept in check. The only things he was unable to control was his anger with Sally and an unexplainable guilt.

He figured out the real reason Sally wanted him at her house. He remembered the reception and the things she said and it added up. But why should that bother him? At least she wanted him there. But he knew she really did not want him there, not for the right reasons. However it was more than that. He was feeling bad about his anger towards Sally. At least the days at Camp Big Lake gave him a distraction.

The nights, however, where entirely different. Max made the cabin a living hell. If the snoring was not bad enough then it was the smoke and his attitude. He developed a habit of pestering Carl every night when he tried to fall asleep. He put his feet up and push up on Carl's bunk saying, "Good night Carly boy. Sleep tight."

Carl was scared of Max. But his anger intensified with every night of the torment. On the bad snoring nights he slept outside until a staff member stumbled upon him and said he had to stay inside the cabin. "We're in the middle of nowhere and there are wild animals. You don't want to get eaten, do you?"

"You don't understand. Follow me and I'll show you something. Listen to that kid!"

He listened to Max's bellowing snores, shook his head and thought, "Man oh man!" but said to Carl, "Sorry kid. Rules are rules."

The beginning of the fourth week things got worse. It was on a night when Max was at his buddy's cabin. When he came back he saw Carl and the twins sitting on the floor joking around. "Hey look, a floor full of runts! How ya doing runty boys?" It was clear the he had more to drink than usual. "You know where runts come from? Runt parents! That's where!"

Carl wanted to let it go. But it had been a hard day. He missed his mom and dad more. Now this jerk was going to call his folks runts? Not tonight. Carl slowly stood. "Look, how about we just stay out of each other's way? You do your thing and we do ours. We don't have to make fun of each other's families."

"What's the matter? You all butt hurt because you have runts for parents?"

"Come on Max, let it go."

"The poor little runt is embarrassed because he has runts for a mommy and daddy."

"Look Max, my mom and dad were killed in a car accident just over a month ago, maybe you can cut me a little slack on this one," Carl said, trying to be calm and hoping it would end the standoff.

Max started to laugh and then spat, "So you're an orphan runt! Look at this Twiddle Dee and Twiddle Dumb! We have a Little Orphan Annie runt!"

It was over in seconds. Carl became enraged. He knew that if came to a fight, he was going to get his butt kicked. He realized he had one shot. He looked at Max dead-on, then over his shoulder. Max saw Carl's glance behind him and turned his head saying, "What?"

Carl brought his leg back as far as it would go then moved it forward as fast and hard as he could. Right when Max turned his head back, Carl's foot landed squarely in his crouch lifting the bigger kid nearly half a foot into the air.

The sickening scream could be heard several cabins away and within minutes the staffers were bursting into the cabin. They saw Max squirming on the floor, holding his privates and crying like a baby. Then they saw Carl standing over him with a big smile.

Ten minutes later Carl was standing in front of a desk that reminded him of Yoda's. Max was seated behind him. He was having trouble standing. The nameplate on the desk told them this was the head of the staff of Camp Big Lake, like a principal. Carl was reminded of when Yoda first broke the bad news just over a month before.

"Neither of you want to tell us what this is all about. Sam and Skip are not saying anything either," the staffer said. "So we have no choice but to find you both in the wrong. We have a policy that everyone gets one chance. But if anything like this happens again we'll kick you out of this camp. Understand?"

They nodded their heads and walked out. "Stay out of trouble. I mean it. One more problem from either of you and you'll be packing your bags."

Max was limping next to Carl. "You got a cheap shot in, runt. You won't be so lucky next time."

"Just leave me alone and I'll stay out of your way. If you keep on picking on me, well, I don't care what happens," Carl said with all the bluster he could muster.

Max stopped and put his hand on Carl's shoulder. "You think you're getting off that easy? I can promise you this, runt. I'm going to get you."

Carl pushed the big kid back, turned and walked away.

CHAPTER 11
GUILTY

Days following his super-human-force kick Carl worried about repercussions, but there were none. He figured Max took heed of the camp master's warning. So he became a normal summer camper doing normal summer camp things again and met a girl and developed a crush on her.

It had been a week since Max's warning, but Carl forgot about it. The only reminder was when kids gave him high-fives. A lot of them did not like Max.

Everyday before lunch was mail call. It was one of the few times the entire camp was in one spot the same time. The first couple of times Carl hated it. "Who's going to write me?" he thought. But on the third day he was surprised to hear his name. He opened the large envelope with three birthday cards. One from Ruth, one from Matilda and one from Sally. He noticed the one from Sally was not signed and figured it was sent on her behalf. A few days later his name was called again, this time he got a package the size of a shoebox. He opened it he and saw Matilda sent him homemade cookies. He shared them with Sam and Skip and they rolled their eyes.

"I wish my mom could cook like this!" Skip said.

"Me too…" Carl whispered to himself.

Matilda sent care packages often, so Carl looked forward to mail call. It was Saturday and Carl loved Saturdays. The food was always good but on the weekends they went all out. Last weekend it was turkey legs, the biggest he'd ever seen. The week before, the best barbeque ribs he'd ever eaten. The rumor was it was going to be nice big juicy steaks today.

As the kids crowded in hoping to hear their names called, Carl felt a tap on his shoulder. He turned to see Max. "Just remember what I told you how I deal with snitches. In your case it will be double pain for your runt buddies, Twiddle-Dee and Twiddle-Dumb." He walked off. Carl was alarmed but then calked it up to Max just being a jerk, again.

He heard his name and was excited, but was handed a note saying to report to the head of staff right away.

He walked into the main office. On top of the same desk he stood in front of the week before he saw his bag. "Is this your stuff?"

"It looks like it."

"Well, do you have anything you would like to tell me?"

"No, what's going on?"

The staffer stood and turned Carl's bag over, emptying its contents. Mixed with his personal effects were several packs of cigarettes and little bottles. "Well, what do you have to say now?"

"Those aren't mine! I never smoked! Not once in my life and the only time I drank it was a complete accident."

"I'm hoping you have an explanation."

Carl froze remembering what Max told him minutes before. If he told the truth he might get beat-up badly. But he knew for sure his friends were going to pay a bigger price and there was nothing he could do to protect them. "Believe me sir, I wish I could tell you. But, I can't. All I can say is that those things are not mine."

"Well, Carl, I told you about our one chance policy. If you can't provide an explanation I'm afraid we will call your parents and have them pick you up right away."

"My parents are dead."

"Then we call whomever is responsible for you. I'll give you one last chance to explain, otherwise consider yourself kicked out."

Carl thought hard. He knew what happened and exactly who did it. It would be easy to tell the truth. He would be able to stay a month longer and have fun. He could hang out with the girl he met. But, he could not because he knew Max was out there and was sure he would keep his promise to hurt the twins right away if he got called to the main cabin. "I guess I'm leaving then."

They made him stay in the staff cabin so he did not get to say goodbye to his new friends or whom he hoped would become his girlfriend. He was getting used not being able to say goodbye to people he cared for.

Sally was enjoying dinner with her friend in city. She was upset with Ruth because she did not get the table she wanted. She had not told Ruth until four o'clock that afternoon to make the reservations.

They talked about plans for the upcoming trip to France. Her friend noticed every time a waiter walked by Sally talked louder. You have to keep the staff impressed... Then the conversation drifted to the subject of Carl.

The gossip reached the city, and it was very favorable. Sally could not have been happier. She loved being the center of attention and should be able to milk this one for all it was worth. And then some.

After finishing their after dinner drinks, plans were made to meet one more time to shop before the big trip. You have to know how to shop for a trip where you are going to do nothing but shop. They said their goodnights and Sally went to her room.

She was in bed reading the society columns when the phone rang. As she listened to Ruth, Sally clinched her fist, and by the end of the conversation the newspaper was smashed into an unrecognizable mess. She did not say goodbye or goodnight, just slammed the phone and steeled herself for a sleepless night.

On the drive home the next day, Sally's head was spinning. Her planning and scheming worked out perfectly, even after the close call at the reception. Summer camp made it all the better. She was able to reap all the benefits of the appearance she wanted and not have to deal with the boy. She felt like she hit the jackpot without having to put a quarter in the slot machine. Now her standing was in real trouble. He got kicked out of camp? For cigarettes and alcohol? Her friends sent their offspring there. When she was at the club next time she would be surrounded by parents, grandparents, aunts and uncles of kids who were at the camp right now. She cringed as she thought about the scuttlebutt. No matter how hard she thought, she could not come up with a plan for damage control.

And what about all the things she heard about him being such a good kid. Was it all a load of crap? It had to be. In less than two months he had gotten in trouble for fighting, running away and now getting kicked out of camp. She started to wonder if the Champagne fiasco was really a mistake.

"I can pull this off if he's decent, but if he is a delinquent I have a real problem," she thought.

On the drive back to Sally's house the day before, Ruth tried to find out what happened, but Carl was not talking.

She picked up Carl and the head of staff handed her a report explaining why he had to leave. "This has to be a mistake. I've only known him a short time, but this seems completely out of character. Did he have any other problems?"

"Well, there were a couple of things. When he first got here a couple of the others on the staff had an uneasy feeling about him. But up until last Monday he was fine."

"What happened Monday?"

He gave the details of the conflict between Max and Carl. "We can't read their minds, they have to tell us what is going on, but they clammed up. Same with their cabin-mates. I'll be honest, I don't feel good about it, I think he's a good kid. But if Carl doesn't talk my hands are tied."

"Carl, I hope you're okay and want you to know that I'm here for you," Ruth said as she was steering down the mountain.

"I don't want to talk. I'm sure I'll get grilled by Sally when we get back. Besides, it doesn't matter anyway."

"Sally's in the city. She'll be back tomorrow."

"One more day of peace," Carl whispered. "Have you told her yet?"

"No. I wanted to talk to you first."

"Maybe when we get to her house."

Matilda was waiting. "You both must be starved. Let me whip up a little something for you."

"That sounds good, the drive back was a nightmare," Ruth said. "Carl, I have to call Sally and tell her what happened. You sure you don't want to talk before I do?"

"Like I said, it doesn't matter. Do what you have to. I don't feel like talking about it."

With that Ruth walked to Sally's office. As she did Carl looked over to Matilda and said, "Thanks for all that great stuff you sent. Everyone said you should've been a chef!"

"Who said I wasn't?"

They talked as she made dinner. Carl felt better and thought maybe he should open up. Then Ruth walked back into the kitchen and sat across from Carl. "Well, that's done."

"How did it go?" asked Matilda.

"Just Sally being Sally."

"That bad, huh," said Carl.

Ruth noticed Carl was relaxed. She looked at Matilda and thought to herself, "How does she do that?" She looked at Carl and asked, "Given any thought about letting us knowing what happened?"

"Yea, maybe. I just hope you believe me."

"Try us," Matilda said as she put a casserole on the table.

"Okay, this is how it went." he said as he took a bite of his dinner. He leaned his head back and said, "You're right! This is good, you are a chef..."

As they ate Carl told them everything, leaving nothing out except for how good he felt when he kicked Max. "I was pretty upset when I found out I was dropped off three days early."

"Sorry about that. Sally's idea," said Ruth.

When he finished the women looked at each other in an unspoken agreement. Ruth was the first to speak. "There is no way Sally can be upset with you. But, wait a minute, it's Sally. I'm sure we can figure something out."

"I'll make sure I'm close by when you tell her. Give you a little moral support at the very least," said Matilda.

Relief washed over Carl. But it was strange that his allies were old enough to be his mother, or older. "When will Sally be back tomorrow?"

"My guess is around ten," Ruth answered.

"Okay. I'm going to take my stuff to my room and call it a night. Sorry you had to pick me up, but thanks. And Matilda, thanks for this awesome dinner. It was great!"

It had been a month since his sleep had been shattered by a blast of annoying bells. It took him a couple of seconds to remember how to turn off the old time alarm clock and a longer for his heart rate to slow. "I hate that thing," he thought.

He made his plan the night before. Carl showered in what he now called the carwash and felt cleaner than he had in four weeks. As he brushed his teeth he saw the cell phone Sally bought him on the counter. After he dressed he went downstairs where he saw Matilda. "Good morning."

"And to you. Sleep well?"

"It is nice to sleep in sheets instead of a sleeping bag. I'm going to my friend's house."

"How about some breakfast?"

His first reaction was to decline but he looked at the clock and realized there was time. Besides, it was hard to turn down her cooking. She made him an omelet. "Is there anything you can't make taste great?"

"No," she said with a smile. "Why such a hurry?" she asked already knowing the answer.

"I want to see my buddy and my old dog. I shouldn't be too long."

"The rush wouldn't have anything to do with Sally being here in about a half an hour, would it?"

Carl did not respond. He started toward the door and heard Matilda, "I'm supposed to tell you to take the cell phone with you."

"I forgot it."

"Maybe I forgot to tell you."

Joe was surprised to see him. "What are you doing here? I thought you were at summer camp."

"Long story, can I come in?"

They went into the house and Carl asked if Joe's mom was home. "I need to talk to her."

"She is in the kitchen."

Carl explained everything that happened at the Camp Big Lake. He did not want her to hear it from someone else and have another reason not to like him again.

"I'm glad you told me and am sorry you went through that. You're welcome here anytime, Carl," she said. "We are going on vacation next week, but I hope to see a lot of you around here until then."

The boys went to the backyard. When Mutt saw Carl he lost all control. With tail wagging and tongue licking he knocked Carl onto his back with excitement. Joe and Carl sat in the lawn chairs and Carl asked, "Can I talk to you about something?"

Over the next hour Carl opened up to Joe. All of the feelings he was going through with the loss of his parents, the tension with Sally, his uncertainty about his future, and how he was changing. "I gotta tell you, I've never been so confused."

"You've been through a lot and it hasn't been that long since the accident. I miss your mom and dad, too. They were nice. Maybe if you give it more time you'll feel better."

Carl explained he was starting to relax at Camp Big Lake. But the minute he found out that he had to go back to Sally's house he slid back into the dread. "I can't explain it. The house is nice. Matilda and Ruth are too. It's when Sally and I are together I go out of my mind. I think I do the same to her. I wish I could explain it or know why it happens. If I could, well, maybe I could fix it."

"You sound like you are mad at her or something."

"I don't know what it is. I just know when we are together my skin feels like it is crawling off my bones."

"What can you do about it?"

"I'm thinking it would be a good idea to go to Boy's Town."

"Boy's Town! Come on, things can't be that bad!"

"Yes they can," Carl said with defeat.

"You haven't even seen Sally since you got back. Maybe things will be better now."

Carl explained why he thought Sally had taken him in in the first place and how the camp was probably filled with kids from families that Sally knew. "I don't know, but I'm scared. Sally is going to be furious."

They talked more and Joe convinced Carl to wait to make his decision. "Maybe it won't be as bad as you think, it has to be better than Boy's Town..."

Carl hopped on his bike and decided to ride by his old house. As he turned the corner his heart sank. In the middle of the front yard was a big "For Sale" sign.

"Well, that's that," he thought as he turned around.

Carl was leaning on his bike in front of the gates trying to get the courage to go in. On the ride back he remembered times like this when he had to come home knowing he was in trouble. But it was never like this. Now he was truly scared.

He got the nerve to punch the gate code and ride his bike up the driveway. The house seemed empty as he went into his room and sat on his bed. A few minutes later Matilda came in and asked, "How was the visit with your friend?"

"Okay. She here?"

"Yes, I'm supposed to tell her when you get here."

"Might as well get it over with, I'll go to the kitchen."

"Just tell her what happened, she'll understand."

"Where the hell have you been!" Sally screamed. "You know you are supposed to take the cell phone if you leave!"

Carl's armor magnified as her negative energy filled the room. "I don't want to carry that thing around. It's embarrassing and I have no way to carry it."

"I don't care. You are to do what you're told. With the stunt you pulled at summer camp I'm starting to see you are not the young man I was told you were. Cigarettes! Alcohol! What is it with you? Do you have any idea how embarrassing this is for me?" she yelled. "How am I supposed to explain this? Plus, that place cost a fortune and that's how you thank me? By being a thug!?"

"I didn't do anything to embarrass you."

"Now listen here you little…"

"Sally!" Matilda interrupted. "Maybe you should hear what the boy has to say."

"Maybe you should mind your own business. I don't need your help with this!"

"I think you do. Now let's just settle down and I'll make you some tea to settle your nerves," said Matilda as she turned on the stove.

"I don't want any tea!"

"Yes you do."

Sally could not figure out what was enraging her more, Carl or the fact this maid had a way of taking control. "Okay. Make the damn tea. But I'm going to talk to this boy and let him know the way things are going to be."

"That's fine, but first you are going to listen to the boy and know how things are," Matilda said in a soft voice.

Sally was speechless. "How does she do this to me?" she thought as she sat, calming down.

Carl was speechless as well. He watched the maid give Sally orders and it was working. "Sally, I can explain what happened at Camp Big Lake. If you still want to be mad, that's okay."

Sally sat in silence while the water was heating. When it was ready Matilda poured it into a cup with a teabag and served it. "This should help."

Sally said, "All I know is what Ruthy told me. And it doesn't sound good. I'm going to be a laughing stock at the club because of you."

"Listen to him," Matilda said.

Sally looked at her, then at Carl. "Okay, say what you have to say. But know that as far as I'm concerned there's no excuse for your behavior."

Carl took a deep breath and went into detail again about what happened with Max and the set-up.

Sally sat and listened. "That's what happened?"

"Exactly."

"Why didn't you just tell them! That would have taken care of everything. Do you have any idea what they'll be saying about *me* at the club?"

"I didn't want to see Skip or Sam hurt. They were nice and it wouldn't have felt right."

"Why?"

"I just wanted to do the right thing."

"Why?"

"Because it's the right thing to do."

Sally sat in silence. She had no concern for Carl. All she cared about was the impact on her image. The more she thought about it the more the frustration dug in. Her anger at Carl had been heating up all day and now reached a boiling point. "I can't believe you let this happen! You have to be the most...," she said stopping midsentence. Then said, "Wait a minute, I can fix this."

Without a word she jumped up and ran out.

"That was a little strange," Carl said.

"More than a little," Matilda responded.

Awhile later Sally walked back into the kitchen a changed woman. Matilda and Carl watched her as she was almost dancing. "You alright Sally?" Matilda asked.

"Never better! Did you unpack?" she said looking at Carl.

"Yes, last night."

"Well, go re-pack. You're going back to Camp Big Lake. Ruthy will take you first thing in the morning!"

Carl was in shock. "What happened?"

Sally gave Carl the edited version. It only took a few phone calls. First to the camp to find out who the families were of the boys involved and she hit pay dirt. The twins were members of one of the most established families at the club and with Sally's second call she set the plan into motion. Nobody knew anything about Max, so his family could not have been in any important social circles, thus Sally did not care about him. Then it was a game of telephone. She called the twins' father who called Camp Big Lake, talked to his sons and the head of staff. Then Sally called the camp back and with a series of demands and threats she closed the deal. The fact that the twins' father was one of the most respected lawyers in town did not hurt.

Sally not only saved the day by keeping her image intact, she improved it. Now the social circles would be filled with buzz of how she and Carl saved the twins from the bully. They would be heroes! This time she hit the lottery without buying a ticket.

"Wow!" was all Carl could say.

"Go get packed."

Later Sally went to the kitchen and poured herself a brandy. Carl walked in to get a glass of milk. The tension was a fraction of what it usually was. But, neither knew why.

Sally was exhausted from a day of stress, thinking, planning, executing and winning. Carl was just plain tired. "Sally. I don't know if I should apologize or thank you."

She smiled as it happened again, that little tug at her heart. Only this time it was comfortable. Well, almost. "Maybe a little of both. Besides, it must've been pretty hard on you too."

"I've had better experiences, that's for sure," he said feeling uncomfortable actually being comfortable around Sally.

"For what it is worth, I'm proud of how you handled it."

Carl grabbed the handle on the refrigerator to stop falling. Sally actually complimented him. Maybe it was the brandy.

When he opened the door the light illuminated his face and Sally saw the hair on his chin. "Looks like you could use a shave."

"I don't know how."

"What?"

"No one taught me."

Then it happened again, another chip out of her armor. "Well, I have been shaving my legs for decades. It can't be much different. Maybe I can teach you."

Carl was speechless. Was this the same woman who hated him a few hours before?

Sally said she would meet him in his bathroom. The truce had been good for both of them. But they had no idea the worst was yet to come. But for right now, it was a good night.

Sally brought shaving cream and a razor to Carl's bathroom and had him practice. She showed him how to apply the foam and had him scrap it off with the guard still on the razor. "Just a little pressure and never side to side."

Then the real test. Carl took the safety cap off and shaved for the first time in his life. When done he wiped off his face and looked in the mirror. He saw his smooth face and Sally standing behind him smiling. He smiled too.

And with that, Sally taught Carl to shave.

Chapter 12

Control

Carl was sleeping the sleep of the dead. So when the alarm went off it was more, well, alarming. He fell out of bed franticly grabbing the clock to stop the clanging. "Maybe I should get one with smaller bells," he thought as he picked himself up off the floor.

He enjoyed an extra long shower in the carwash. He remembered the showers at Camp Big Lake had weak streams and on a good day the water was warm, on most just above cold.

He breathed in the steam as the powerful jets massaged his back. He thought about the night before. Sally was human and it should have made him feel better. But it did not.

As he got dressed he decided to keep the truce going. He was not sure it was possible, but it would make things easier. It would also make the decision he made about Boy's Town harder.

Sally was numb. Two nights of fitful sleep did not help, but it was more. On the drive back from the city she convinced herself he was a problem child. And who could blame her? Every bit of information pointed to the only logical conclusion. So, she was not wrong, just mistaken. Right? But when she found out the truth she was blindsided. She did not like being wrong. Especially when her staff was in the room to wittiness it. She was humiliated. "How can I keep control of things when they see me like that?" she thought as she was getting dressed.

What bothered her more were the emotions. They controlled her for a moment. She felt sorry for the boy, so much so that she was compelled to help him. Where the hell did that come from? What was more troublesome was she felt good doing it. And that smile on his face after the shave, she was smiling too and they were both honest to God heart-felt smiles.

She did not like the change and had to put a stop to it right away. "I can do this. It was just a momentary lapse! A fluke, that's all," she decided as she went to the kitchen.

Sally and Carl walked in at the same time. Matilda was cooking and Ruth was sitting at the table. Carl looked at Sally and said, "Good morning, thanks for the help last night. All of it."

"You're lucky it out worked well. That could've been a real problem for me. As for the shave, well, we can't have you looking like a bum."

The tone of her voice told Carl that Sally was Sally again. "So much for the truce," he thought. "But I want you to know I appreciate it," he said hoping it would revive the Sally from last night.

"Just make sure you don't do anything to embarrass me at the camp. That's all the thanks I want."

"I won't. I promise," he said realizing that any hope things might be better between them was a fantasy.

Sally looked at Matilda. "I have things that need to be washed right away. I left them in my bathroom. Drop whatever you're doing and get them right now."

"No."

"Excuse me!"

Matilda turned to her and said, "These two have a long drive ahead of them and you need breakfast, too. I'll see to your things when I'm done here."

Carl and Ruth tensed in anticipation of the blow-up Sally was sure to have. But it did not happen. Sally looked at her maid and said, "Right afterwards then, bring my breakfast to my office."

Carl and Ruth were shocked. "How do you do that?" Ruth had to ask.

"Just letting her release some of her pressure without raising mine."

Carl and Ruth shook their heads in disbelief and were jealous. Either would have loved to be able to handle Sally like that.

Matilda put plates on the table. "I made something special for you, Carl. I'm sure you won't be having anything like this at summer camp."

They took a bite, and let out a sigh of satisfaction.

As Carl was loading his things into Ruth's trunk he laughed. Last time he headed to Camp Big Lake he was angry with Sally for making him go. Now he was thankful. "What a difference a month makes," he thought.

As they drove, the farther Carl was from Sally's the more he was relieved. At first he and Ruth did not talk. But Carl sensed he could trust her. "Sally and I got along last night."

"What do you mean?"

Carl told Ruth about the night before and admitted he enjoyed Sally's company. It seemed so real then, but now the words were awkward. "I don't know. She was just so… different. I've never seen her like that."

"Me neither."

As they pulled onto the campgrounds Carl said, "You had to do a lot of driving on my account the last couple of days, sorry."

"No problem. It gives me a break, besides, I'm glad it worked out for you."

Carl grabbed his stuff. They walked to the main cabin to check in. As they entered they saw Max sitting in a corner surrounded by his belongings. Seated next to him was one of the staff. The biggest.

"That's Max," Carl told Ruth.

"That's the kid you kicked? He's huge!"

"He looks bigger when he stands."

"Carl, the more I get to know you the more I'm impressed. I can't believe you stood up to that kid!"

"You had to be there to understand."

The head of staff came into the lobby and greeted them. "Carl, I'm glad this worked out. I didn't feel good with how things ended last time."

"Thanks. I'm glad it worked out, too."

As Ruth signed the paperwork a police officer came into the room and walked over to Max. "This the kid?" he asked the head of staff.

"He's the one."

"Come on kid. I'm going to take you to a much different type of camp."

Carl was amazed. "The police?"

"He had more than cigarettes and alcohol in his trunk. When we got the calls yesterday we searched his cabin. We brought him to the staff cabin right away and he slept here last night. He's the only one that did. Man, that kid snores like crazy!"

"Believe me, I know!"

"I'm glad he didn't plant that stuff in your bag or you might have faced the same fate."

"Me too."

Carl watched as the police officer made Max stand and turn so he could put the handcuffs on. He led the kid toward the door and as they passed by Max said, "So runt, you think you won this one?"

"Well, yea. You're the one in handcuffs."

"You go ahead and have fun with your little runt friends you jerk. If I ever see you again I'm going to rip you apart."

"Go suck an egg!" Carl fired back feeling brave with the big kid in cuffs and a police officer holding his arm.

Carl and Ruth said their goodbyes, "I'll be here to pick you up in a month. Have fun!"

"Thanks," Carl said as he picked up his things and started the hike to his cabin. When he got there it was empty and he realized it was almost time for mail call. He put his sleeping bag on the top bunk out of habit then remembered. He smiled as he set up on the lower bunk.

"Carl!" Skip said as he saw his friend walking up the path.

Sam told him about the night before. "It was crazy! The head staff guy came in and went through Max's trunk and found a bunch of drugs."

"I just saw him get arrested. He didn't seem to be a very happy camper," Carl said with a smile.

"We had no idea you were coming back!"

The three boys continued talking as mail call was winding down. As they walked to lunch Carl looked for the girl he liked and saw her sitting with her friends.

He walked up behind her and said, "Hi Kim."

She turned around and her eyes went wide. "Carl! You're here! I can't believe it, you're here!" she said as she gave him a hug.

That caught him by surprise. He was not sure she liked him the way he liked her, the hug removed all doubt. It was the first time he had a real hug since his mom and dad died. But he knew that was not the reason why it felt so good.

The rest of the day Carl and Kim hung out. They went horseback riding then sat on the dock. Before he would get nervous, but now was comfortable. He told her what happened with Max and how Sally saved the day so he could come back.

"That Max guy was a creep. He tried to pinch my butt a couple of times," she said. When Carl heard that he wished he kicked the bully harder.

"I'm happy you're back. I missed you."

"Really?"

"Really," she smiled.

As Carl crawled into his sleeping bag he reflected on the day. The twins ribbed him about Kim. "Oooh, Carl has a girlfriend!" But it did not bother Carl at all. If Max had said it he would have wanted to punch him. He thought it was strange how two people can say the same thing and have totally different results.

He was happy to be back. But having seen Kim and understanding she liked him made it all the better. He fell asleep happy.

Sally knew the clock was ticking. She had not fully recovered from the troubling experience the night she taught Carl to shave. She had two weeks to figure something out. But what? She could not stand having him in the house, but he had to stay there. It was a real problem. "What if I slip up again?" she thought. She realized it was not the boy. It was how he made her feel on those rare occasions the pesky tugs at her heart popped up. She became a master of masking her feelings, so much so she thought they were dead. But the kid had reawakened them.

She even let herself slip and thought about her life before she made the choice to delay collage and marry the wrong man. The choice that ruined her life. It hurt as she remembered being happy and having people care for her. It seemed like so long ago because it was. It took years to build the armor. To feel again would mean she would be in a position to be hurt again and the memory of that pain drove her into her shell.

"How does that boy do that to me?" she thought in a moment of weakness. She remembered Carl did it before on those rare visits with her sister and her family. Not as strong as now, but still unsettling. Being in a house surrounded with love was not a good way to keep her happy memories buried and she remembered the need to escape. Then she found it easier to make excuses why she could not visit. It was easier than having to fight off the hidden demons.

The dock became "their spot." Every night after dinner they met there. It was perfect, beautiful with incredible sunsets but mostly because no one else was there. As Carl was waiting for Kim he thought about what happened a couple of days before.

Sitting on the dock with their feet in the water Kim said, "I like you Carl. I like the way I feel when I'm with you."

"Me too."

"I was wondering about something."

"What?"

"Have you ever kissed a girl?"

Carl felt nervous again. "Uh, no."

"Well, I never kissed a boy. I think we should try it to see what the big deal is."

Sounded great to him! But instead he said, "You think we should?"

She leaned into him and Carl experienced another first in his life as he thoroughly enjoyed the kiss. And he thought it was a very big deal.

He learned Kim lived a couple of towns over from his. Close enough to be tempting. But far away enough to make it impossible for them to see each other after leaving Camp Big Lake. The days were going by faster and he started to dread the time when summer camp was over, it would be over for them too. He decided to tell Kim about his parents. Up to this point he had not said a word about the accident or Sally. But he was not sure if he was ready to tell her about his decision to go to Boy's Town.

"Hey!" he heard Kim from behind.

"Hey, back!" he said as he stood up and she kissed him. "I can get used to this," he thought as they took off their shoes and put their feet in the water.

"I need to tell you some things."

Kim's face filled with alarm, "Is it about us?"

"No, not anything bad. Well, it *is* bad, but not like that."

He told her about the car accident. "I know it sounds strange, but sometimes when I'm in the cabin alone I can almost hear them." When he was done he looked up to see Kim's tears. "Oh man, I'm sorry. I didn't mean to upset you!"

"It's not that. I just can't believe how much I hurt for you. I had a friend who lost her dad to cancer last year. It was sad but it didn't hit me like this."

"Like what?" he asked, still upset he made her cry.

"Let's just say I'm starting to realize how much I like you."

"I know what you mean."

The next two weeks flew by. He thought about his mom and dad every day, but it was easier. There was still grief and sometimes when he was alone it overtook him. He was also becoming more uneasy about having to confront Sally. He had plenty of time to think about it and, even though it did not sit well, he was getting used to the idea of Boy's Town. "At least I can still see my friends at school and live someplace where I'm wanted," he thought.

The one thing that he could not figure out was why he had a deep-seated anger towards Sally. Sure she was a bitch, but he should be grateful. She sent him to summer camp and gave him a place to live. The one time they got along was great, but it was the only time. Between the tension and the unexplained anger, he thought he was making the right decision. Besides, the social worker said it was his choice. He liked having control of his life.

On the last night of camp Carl and Kim were sitting on the dock enjoying one of Matilda's brownies. "She sure knows how to make things taste good," Kim said.

"You have no idea…" he said as they were holding hands. "I'm going to miss you."

"I'm going to miss you, too," Kim's voice cracked. "Are you going to be here next year?"

Carl doubted Boy's Town would pay for a place like this. "I'll do my best."

"I promise to write all the time if you do."

"Just try and stop me!" he said trying to sound brave.

They sat not sure of what to say. Carl decided not to mention Boy's Town. Part of it was he was embarrassed. But the main reason was he did not want to have to explain about his Aunt Sally.

The next day, cars were streaming into Camp Big Lake's parking lot. Sam and Skip were the first to go. They shook hands with Carl and thanked him again for taking care of Max. "You made the last month a heck of a lot better than the first!"

Then Kim came up to him. "I want to introduce you to my parents."

"You sure?"

"Yes I am," she said as she took his hand. They said their goodbyes the night before thinking that mom and dad might not be thrilled to see their little girl kissing her new boyfriend goodbye.

"Mom, Dad, this is my friend Carl." she said as they walked up to her family's car.

Carl shook their hands, said how nice it was to meet them and how wonderful he thought their daughter was. Kim's dad raised an eyebrow. As the time came to say goodbye Carl and Kim hugged causing her dad to raise his other eyebrow. As Carl left her mother said, "He seems like a nice boy."

Kim turned away so her mom and dad could not see her brush away a tear. "He is."

Carl was wiping away his own tear. The first he cried that was not for his mom and dad since they died.

Carl loaded his stuff in the trunk. "How are things at Sally's house?" he asked Ruth.

"It'll always be the same."

Carl told Ruth about Kim.

"How cute! Your first girlfriend!" she gushed, making Carl blush.

The drive was filled with Carl telling her about the things he did at camp. But as they got closer he was less talkative as the feelings only Sally could bring out rose to the surface. He did not know when he was going to tell her. Probably not tonight, but he had to soon. He wanted to get it over with and get settled into Boy's Town right away.

CHAPTER 13

LEVERAGE

R uth and Carl got back to Sally's and noticed her car was gone. He was relieved, needing time to recover.

Near the end of the drive his mind was all over the place. He thought about his mom and dad. He also thought about Kim. He knew he was going to miss her, but this soon and this much? Although Camp Big Lake was fun it was over and Carl was forced to think about things other than horseback riding and meeting Kim at the dock.

He wondered about Boy's Town. He shared the cabin at Camp Big Lake and thought sleeping in the dorm might not be that bad. Unless a dorm mate snored like Max. He realized it really was not a decision. It was an escape. He remembered what Joe said and wondered, "Am I crazy?" Sally's house was nice, even though he was not allowed in most of it. One thing he was getting a handle on was the grief for his mom and dad. It was still loud and clear, but he could now remember good times with them instead of just the car accident.

As he was pulling his things out of the trunk Matilda came out. "Welcome home!"

"Home?" he thought. "Hi Matilda, thanks for the care packages. That must've been a lot of work."

"Cleaning your things is going to be a lot of work. Don't you dare bring that stuff in. Leave it by the door and I'll take care of it," she said as she laughed while plugging her nose.

Carl was embarrassed as he put his things down noticing they did smell pretty bad.

"Sally went to the city and wanted you to make reservations for dinner. She said you knew which one," Matilda said to Ruth.

Ruth looked at her watch and realized she was going to get chewed out again for not getting the exact table Sally wanted. "I'll be right back, I need to call them right away if she's even going to get in," she said, running inside.

"There have been changes around here."

Carl's guard went up. He was not at summer camp anymore where change meant good. Now he was at Sally's where it never was.

Matilda sensed his unease. "Not to worry. Go check out your room and I'll start cleaning up this heap."

"Sorry," he said sheepishly as he went in the house.

"Not to worry! All part of the job!"

Carl went into his room and could not believe his eyes. It was like a genie had given him a bunch of wishes. The new television was replaced with one twice the size. There was a top-of-the-line stereo and a stack of new records. In the corner was a small refrigerator and when he opened it he saw it filled with all of his favorite snacks and drinks. He noticed a micro-wave oven. The biggest surprise was in the middle of the back wall. It was a door. This confused him because his room was on the second floor. He opened it and walked onto a balcony with stairs that led down to the backyard. There were chairs and a table and as he sat he thought, "WOW."

He was in a daze realizing this was not going to be his room much longer and started to have doubts about Boy's Town.

After he recovered he walked back into the room. He noticed a new clock radio next to the cell phone, the old windup noisemaker nowhere to be seen. He unplugged it, took it downstairs and looked for Matilda. He found her on the side of the house hosing down the stuff.

"Do you know where the old clock is?"

"I put it away. I thought you'd like this one."

"No thanks, I want the old one."

"Up to you, it's your ears. What do you think of the digs? Ruth and I picked out a lot of the things for you."

"Incredible. I've never seen anything like it and have no idea why Sally went to so much trouble with…" he stopped himself realizing why she had. With the improvements he would have less reason to be anywhere else in the house. He had his own private entrance so the chances of running into Sally were close to zero. At first he wanted to be angry but after thinking about it he calmed down. "Maybe I can make this work," he thought

Matilda looked at the boy. She had no idea about his decision to go to Boy's Town but remembered Ruth mentioning it. "I think it'd be hard to find a room as snazzy as that one."

"No argument there," he said in a faraway voice.

"You seem like you are someplace else. Everything alright?"

"Yea, just a lot on my mind."

"Wanna talk?"

"Not right now," he said as he handed the new clock to her. "I don't want this."

"Why?"

"I don't know, I just don't."

Matilda decided not to push. She knew he was not going to give an explanation and suspected he was not sure himself. They walked into the kitchen and Matilda dug the old clock out. "Here you go, back to the Stone Age as far as timekeeping is concerned."

"Thanks," he said as he went back to his room.

She watched him, convinced something was bothering him. She planned to find out what before Sally got back. Matilda did not want to think how things could turn out if Carl was acting like this when Sally returned.

The new clock did not fit where she stored the old one. She went in the pantry, saw large shopping bags in the corner and moved them aside seeing the backpack and rested the new clock on top of it.

A few hours later Carl came into the kitchen, his hair wet from spending a long time in the carwash. Ruth was going over notes and Matilda was making dinner. "What are you cooking? It smells amazing!"

"I thought I'd make something special tonight. Call it a welcome home dinner."

There it was again. That word. Home. Carl was starting to understand the difference between the words "home" and "house." This was a house and he believed he would never have a home again. "Thanks."

"Seems like something's bothering you," Matilda said.

Carl became so used to holding the bad things inside that it bothered him when anyone asked about them. Part of him wanted to run to his room and hide, but another wanted to explode. Matilda sensed the turmoil. "You know, you're among friends and I'm sure Ruth would agree if there's anything you'd like to talk about... You're safe with us."

"I know when something's bothering me it helps to bounce it off my friends," Ruth said.

It was bad enough to have to think about it, but to talk about it? He was not even sure he wanted to. He stood struggling and a tear ran down his cheek.

Matilda gently held his hand, "It's okay. You don't have to go through this alone, whatever it is, we can help."

He spilled his guts.

He had trouble finding the words, but it became easier and almost impossible to stop. He talked about the unease and it was because of the anger he was having toward Sally. It was also because of the dislike he knew Sally had for him.

"I look at that room and feel guilty. Any kid in the world would be thrilled. But, I don't know, as nice as it is, I just don't belong here."

He told them he was better at summer camp. But on the ride back to Sally's house the discomfort came back stronger than ever.

"What bothers you so much by being here?" Matilda asked.

"That's just it! I can't explain it. I just know I don't want to be here and Sally doesn't want me here, either. At least not for the right reasons."

He looked at Ruth and said, "It's like I told you when you drove me to Camp Big Lake the first time. I think it'd be better for everyone if I went to Boy's Town. Everyone would be happier, or at least not as unhappy."

Ruth's heart skipped a beat. She remembered but did not want to believe he would actually move to the orphanage. She also remembered how she betrayed Carl's trust. The guilt consumed her and was only outweighed by the dread of what was going to happen.

"Carl, maybe with the way your room is now it can work. You won't have to see her much and it has to be better than Boy's Town."

"You don't understand. The house is great and I like you both. Sally makes it seem like I don't belong here. In fact the more I talk about it the more I'm convinced," he said as he got up. "Matilda, everything smells great but I'm not hungry. I'm sorry."

He stopped at the door, "Thanks for listening. I feel better. I'm going to tell Sally tomorrow."

Now Ruth thought her heart was exploding. Matilda looked at her, "You look like you've seen a ghost. What's wrong, dear?"

"We have a problem. There's no way to fix it and it is completely my fault."

That night Carl slept well. The talk with Matilda and Ruth exhausted him. Matilda's sleep was fitful with concerns for Carl. Ruth lay in her bed staring at the ceiling all night knowing the next day was going to be a very bad day.

Carl decided to see Mutt. He could tell Matilda wanted to talk, but he had had enough. His mind was made up, but he was not sure how he was going to explain it to Joe.

After he told Joe's mom about summer camp the boys went to the back yard and the dog went spastic at the sight of his old master. "He looks great!"

"Yea, he's a great dog. The only problem is my mom is a cat person, but she tolerates Mutt. I think he's growing on her."

"I'm thankful you guys took him in. There's no telling what would've happened if you didn't," he said, then thought, "Kind of like me right now."

After playing with the dog the boys talked and Carl told Joe about his decision to tell Sally when she got back.

"I can't believe it. The room sounds awesome and you still want to go to Boy's Town," Joe said. "Sally must be awful."

"I wish I could explain it. I just know it will be better. I was feeling better at summer camp. But on my way back to Sally's I got scared again."

Carl explained that Boy's Town was pretty far and he would not be able to visit as often. Joe said, "Maybe you can stay here on weekends. My mom wouldn't mind. Do they allow that at Boy's Town?"

"I don't know." Carl said realizing he had not thought of everything.

They goofed off, played video games and talked about the upcoming school year. "Can you believe we'll be in high school?" Joe said.

"I know, it's crazy. It'll be good to see everyone again."

As time grew near for Carl to leave he got nervous and his friend could tell. "Are you sure you want to do this? You might be able to make it work at Sally's and not be so far."

"I'm sure."

The bike ride to Sally's seemed forever and over in a flash at the same time. Part of Carl was dreading the confrontation and part was looking forward to getting it over with. He punched in the gate code and rode his bike up the driveway. He saw Sally's car and knew the time had come.

Sally thought she came up with the solution. She also believed it was far easier to deal with the situation with her checkbook than her effort. The room had to be a kid's dream and with the added door to the outside she knew she would not see him hardly at all.

She thought of making a new rule. He would only be allowed to use his new door, but thought that might be a little much, even for her standards.

As Sally pulled onto the driveway she saw Matilda putting Carl's gear in the garage. "Is he here?"

"No, he went to see his dog. Well, his old dog."

"Fine. Did he take his phone?"

"I didn't notice."

"I gave you strict instructions that he was to take it with him if he went anywhere," Sally barked.

"I'm sure he'll be home soon."

Sally wanted to continue brow-beating her maid but looked at her and thought, "What's the point." She was still unaccustomed to how the maid controlled the conversation. "Let me know when he gets home and bring my things up right away."

"I will when I am done here."

Sally turned and glared as Matilda finished putting the gear away.

Carl leaned his bike against the wall and saw Matilda. "Looks like she's back."

"She got here an hour ago. She wanted me to tell her when you got home."

"That's okay. I'll find her."

"Are you going to tell her?"

"Yes. I want to get it over with."

"You're absolutely sure?"

"About as sure as I'm ever going to be."

"She's most likely in her office with Ruth. But I have to warn you, she's already on edge."

As Carl went to Sally's office he could hear her chewing out Ruth. Something about a table at a restaurant. He stuck his head through the door and Sally looked at him, "Well, at least you stayed out of trouble this time."

"Thanks for sending me. I had a good time. I need to talk to you."

"Can't it wait? Ruthy and I are going over details for my trip right now."

"It'll only take a minute."

Ruth stood up, "I'll leave you two alone. I have to make some calls and can do it from the kitchen." She wanted to be anywhere but near Sally at that moment.

"Sit down Ruthy. The boy said it wouldn't take long and I have a lot to go over with you."

Ruth sat and steeled herself for what she knew was coming.

Sally looked at Carl, "Well, what is it? I don't have all day."

He decided just to go for it. "Sally, I appreciate everything. The things you've done to my room are great and I'm thankful for Camp Big Lake. When I was there I got to thinking. I know you don't want me here. To be honest I'm not comfortable here either. So I think it would be best if I went to Boy's Town."

Sally raised her eyebrows and looked at Ruth and then at Carl. "You would rather live at an orphanage than here? Do you have any idea how that would look to my friends? I'd be the laughing stock of the club. Did you think about that?"

"Sally, I know what your friends think is important to you, but I can tell you don't want me here and it's best for both of us if I leave," Carl said trying to sound mature.

Sally sat motionless and the silence was disturbing to Carl and Ruth. Then Sally looked at Carl, "Well, you are right. I'm not thrilled having you living in my house. But what is done is done and you don't have a choice. I don't either. I'm not allowing you to destroy my reputation and humiliate me like that."

"Why would it humiliate you? You don't want me here, you just said so. I don't see what the big deal is!"

"You are too young and naive to understand. If I allowed you to live at that Godforsaken orphanage word would quickly spread and my reputation be destroyed," Sally scowled.

He had been getting ready for this moment for a long time. It was not going as planned. "Well, I don't give a crap about your reputation! You don't want me here. I don't want to be here, so what's the problem? I leave, problem solved. I stay, it gets worse. It's that simple so I'm going to Boy's Town and there's nothing you can do to stop me!" he said believing he had the upper hand.

"No, you're not."

"How are you going to stop me? I heard the social worker tell you when I turned fourteen it's my choice. Well guess what? I'm fourteen and I choose not to live here!"

Sally was calm. "You don't have a choice. I'm your legal guardian and have complete control of you until you are eighteen. Ruthy told me you were thinking of going to that hell hole. So I called my lawyer. We had the inspections and the paperwork is complete. The judge agreed with me being your only relative and with the things I can provide that the obvious choice is for you to be with me."

Carl was floored. "Is that true?"

Ruth looked at the floor when she answered. "Yes."

"We had a deal!" he screamed. "I don't want to live here!" he looked at Sally, "You don't want me here! Can't anyone see how crazy this is besides me?"

"Now just calm down. You can scream all you want but it won't change a thing. You're living here and that's that. I've spent a lot of money to make your room nice. You can spend your time in there. But I'm going to warn you right now, young man, you are going to follow the rules and the first rule is to do as you're told. Now get your butt in your room and let me finish making these plans!"

Carl was not sure who he should be angrier at, Sally for being the bitch that she was or Ruth for betraying his trust. In either case he understood he lost. He had thought it through and spent time and energy deciding what to do and now he knew it was all wasted effort. He was trapped. He opened his mouth to scream but nothing came out.

"Go on now Carl, go to your room so we can finish up here," Sally said.

"I don't want to be here."

"You have to so you might as well get used to the idea. Now leave us be."

Carl walked away and Ruth followed him, "Carl, wait!"

He stopped. "I'm never going to talk to you again"

He went in his room and saw the cell phone. He picked it up and marched through the new door to the balcony and threw it as hard as he could. And it flew very far.

CHAPTER 14
CONFLICTED

The old-time alarm did not startle Carl awake the next morning because he was too upset to sleep. He had felt better believing he had a say in his life. Now he had none and was subject to Sally's rules whether he liked it or not.

He had rules when his mom and dad were alive, but it was different. Before, they were made by people who loved him, cared for his happiness and had his best interest at heart. Sally's only purpose was to appease her.

He sat up and looked around the large space filled with all the gadgets any kid would love, but no matter how hard he tried he could not picture himself being happy here. "I can hide out in here all the time," he thought. But not being able to have friends over and knowing Sally was close made it a prison.

He looked at the picture of his parents. "I miss you so much," he said out loud. When Yoda told him about the accident he knew that his life had changed. Now Carl was starting to realize how much. The grief would have been enough. But with all of the uncertainty he was starting to greave for himself, too.

After getting dressed he went down to the kitchen and saw Ruth sitting at the table with a stack of papers. "Good morning," she said in a sheepish voice.

"We had a deal."

"I know and I feel terrible. I hope you can forgive me."

"Why'd you do it?"

Ruth explained she was worried and believed he was thinking about moving to Boy's Town without considering the ramifications. "I know Sally's a handful but do you hate her so much that you would rather live in an orphanage?"

"I don't hate her. It's like I told you before. When I'm around her I get this knot in my gut that drives me out of my mind. I thought living at Boy's Town would be worth it if I didn't have to deal with that."

Ruth explained Boy's Town was never a real option. Sally could have pulled him right back out. Her lawyer explained everything. "I'm not trying to make excuses, but it would've never worked out even if I had not said anything to Sally."

"You still shouldn't have. I trusted you. Now I wonder if you're my friend or are a spy for Sally."

That hit Ruth hard. She had grown fond of Carl and felt sorry for him. He was going through enough hardship and the fact she added to it was difficult. "Carl, I was completely wrong and again, I'm sorry. If you don't want to trust me I understand. But please know that I'll never do anything like that again. It's not just a deal, it is a promise."

He saw her eyes tearing up. "Awe man," he thought. He wanted to be mad at her. The problem was he liked her and to see her upset brought on guilt. "I don't know…"

"I promise to be *your* friend if you give me this chance," she said trying to smile.

He put his hand into hers and she gave him a hug. The only other person to do so besides Kim for months. "Thank you, Carl. It takes a special person to be able to forgive."

He did not understand why he was relieved. Then he realized it was a lot easier to forgive someone than to be angry at them. Besides, he still had plenty of anger left for Sally. "Wait a minute…" he thought. He stood looking into the distance. "Carl, what is it?" Ruth's voice brought him back.

"I just thought of something, but lost it"

"What was it?"

"I don't know. I think it had something to do with Sally but I can't remember. Strange, huh?"

"It'll come back to you. So we are good now?"

"Yea."

Matilda walked in, "How about some waffles?" They both quickly nodded.

They made small talk as the meal was being prepared and enjoyed. As he finished Carl asked Ruth, "What's up with Sally today?"

"She plans to go to the club. In fact, she should be coming down soon,"

"Then I'm going up. Let me know when she leaves. I can't hear from my room."

An hour later Ruth walked through Carl's open door to let him know Sally had left but did not see him. She noticed the new door was opened a crack, so she stepped onto the balcony. She saw Carl rummaging through the brush surrounding the property. "What are you doing?"

He looked up and yelled, "I'm looking for something."

She went down the stairs and to the brush and could see him pulling back plants. "What are you looking for?"

"We still have that trust deal, right?"

"Yes we still have the trust deal!"

"I was pretty upset last night. When I got back to the room I saw the cell phone and threw it."

"Where?"

"That's the problem. I'm not sure."

"You're not sure?" she said becoming nervous about what would happen if Sally found out. "Carl, this is a lot of space to cover. You have no idea where it landed?"

"Believe me, I wish I did."

"Maybe I can help you find it."

They searched for hours digging into the scruffy plants. They were frustrated when Matilda saw them from the balcony and came down. She saw Carl was covered head to toe in dust and grime and Ruth's hair was a filled with twigs and had smudges of dirt on her clothes. "What on earth are you doing?"

Carl explained his predicament. "I've been looking a long time. So has Ruth. I think it's lost, and I'm sure its not going to go over well with Sally."

Matilda looked around for a few seconds then walked up to a shrub, reached into it and pulled out the cell phone. "Here it is," she said as she handed it to Carl and went back into the house. Ruth and Carl stood dumbfounded.

Carl had to take another shower then went downstairs. Matilda was folding clothes and looked up. "You clean up good!"

"Thanks. I learned my lesson on that one. How'd you find it so fast? Ruth and I tore up those plants for a long time; it only took you a few seconds."

"Just dumb luck."

"For me...I still have a problem, though," Carl said.

"What?"

"I think it's broken. It doesn't look that bad but it won't turn on."

"Go get it and let me see."

"Why?"

"Just do it."

He retrieved the cell phone and handed it to her. She looked it over and tried some buttons. "Yup, this one is a goner."

"Sally is going to be upset."

"I'll handle it."

"How?"

"Let's just say that I forgot to check your laundry and it got washed by mistake. Solves all problems! It'll clean up and no one can expect it to work after that."

"Sally is going to blame you! I can't let you do that. She will be furious!"

"Don't worry, I can handle it. Besides, we need to do everything we can to keep the peace between you two now you are back to stay."

He could not argue with that. Not even a little bit. But he also was not sure he cared either way.

Over the next few days Carl developed a routine of hanging out with Joe and their friends during the day and staying to himself in his room at night. For the most part it worked. There were a few times when Sally and Carl would be in the kitchen at the same time and the tension was intense. In the times when Matilda or Ruth were there they could sense it and agreed there was no way the two could sustain it. Something had to give, but what and when?

Matilda was right in saying she could handle Sally as far as the phone was concerned. When she told Sally she accidentally washed it with Carl's clothes Ruth could see Sally approach her boiling point. Then Matilda gave her a look that made Sally's bravado melt away. After Sally left the room Ruth looked at Matilda, "You're going to have to teach me how you do that."

Carl started to relax about everything except Sally. He and Joe talked about the upcoming freshman year. However having something to look forward to did not solve the problem. Every time he let his guard down it immediately went back up during the few times he saw her.

He came back to Sally's after spending the day shooting hoops with his buddies and saw Sally's car was gone. He walked into the kitchen and saw Ruth and Matilda. "Speaking of the devil!" Matilda said.

"If you're talking about me, I'm sure Sally would agree," Carl said, only half jokingly.

"That's exactly what we've been talking about. We need to find a way for you two to get along," Ruth said. "There has to be something we can think of to release the tension."

"I'm all ears, but I wouldn't bet on anything. I can tell Sally is as uncomfortable around me as I am around her."

Matilda said, "Well, we just have to figure out why. Can't fix a problem if you don't know what the problem is."

"That's just it. I don't know. All I know is when we are near each other I can feel it. And I don't even know what 'it' is. It's like you said, you can't fix the problem if you don't know what it is. I know I should be thankful. It's just…"

"Tomorrow's another day," Matilda said as she walked into the pantry and came out holding the new clock and his backpack.

"I don't want that clock."

"Why?" Ruth asked.

"I don't know, I just don't."

Matilda put it on the counter and held out the backpack to him. "How about this? School starts soon and I thought you could use this."

"Good idea."

"I'm going to serve dinner soon, go ahead and put that away."

Carl loved her cooking and was excited, so instead of taking his backpack to his room he put it down in front of the stairs and rushed back to the kitchen. He broke one of Sally's rules.

Sally came in as they were finishing cleaning up and when she saw Carl, she tensed. She saw the clock on the counter. "I can't believe you don't use that one. It cost a lot of money, why don't you use it instead of that old one?"

Carl went from being happy with a full stomach of Matilda's cooking to a mixture of depression, anger, and an urge to escape. "I don't know."

"That isn't an answer. I want you to tell me right now!"

Ruth and Matilda glanced at each other.

"I don't know. I like the other one."

"That's silly. I want you to use this one."

"I'm fine with the old one."

Sally shook her head with disgust as she started toward the stairs and saw the backpack on the floor.

"What this?"

Carl walked to where Sally was looking at the backpack. "I'm sorry! I was going to take it up after dinner!"

"You know the rules! Nothing on my floors but feet and furniture! I can't believe you would leave this laying around!"

"I was going to take it up; it was only there for a little while," Carl said. He was trying to keep his voice calm but it was not working.

"I can't believe this! You know how I hate clutter. And you leave this on the floor? You know better!"

"What do you want me to say? I'm sorry. It won't happen again!"

Sally noticed the difference in his voice and looked at him, "Are you talking back to me, young man?"

"No! Well at least I'm not trying to. I made a mistake."

"Go put this where it belongs right now and never, ever, leave anything on my floors again. Understand?"

Something snapped inside of Carl. He had never been comfortable around her, with the exception of the night she taught him to shave. But this time it was different. The anxiety in his gut magnified and took control. He picked up the backpack and ran up the stairs. Sally called after him, "And you're going to use the new clock!"

"No, I'm not!"

Carl's defiance caught Sally off guard and she lost control of her temper. She grabbed the new clock then followed him up to his room.

When she went in she looked down to see the backpack on the floor spilling its contents, then saw Carl glaring at her. Sally reached down and pulled up his good citizen plaque. "Why can't you do this for me?"

"Because I don't want to!"

She looked at the clock, then at him and demanded, "Use this one, the other one is too old."

"No!"

"Oh yes you will, young man!"

He took it from her and threw it into the wall. Sally took a step back. "What's wrong with you? It's just a clock!"

"No it's not. It's not just a clock! The only reasons why we're stuck with each other is because you care what others think and that damn clock."

Sally was taken aback by what he said and the intensity in which he said it. "What in the world are you talking about?"

He picked up the clock and stuck it in her face. "You see this. This little button? That's why you and I are stuck with each other. It is completely my fault!" he screamed as tears flooded his face.

Sally was stunned and trying to make sense of what he was saying. Carl could tell she did not understand and became more frustrated as he threw the clock into the wall again. Then he turned to her holding his hand up with the thumb and index finger almost touching. There could not have been more than a fraction of an inch between them.

"That's all it took, just this much and here I am. And it's my fault!"

"What on earth are you talking about?"

"It's my fault mom and dad are dead! Don't you get it! It's my fault! I didn't mean for it to happen but it's still all my FAULT!"

Sally was in shock that instead of being upset she was concerned for him. Her armor was starting to crack again. "Carl, you're not making sense. How could it be your fault and what does it have to do with a silly clock?"

"If I had pushed the button just this much more," he said holding his fingers up again with a look of pain on his face, "The alarm would've gone off. I wouldn't have overslept! They wouldn't have had to take me to school! They wouldn't have been late and had to rush…" he stopped in mid-sentence and sat on the floor and put his face in his hands. Between the sobs Sally could barley hear him say, "The crash was my fault."

A large sledgehammer had smashed it into her armor. Now instead of just cracks there were gapping holes and her emotions surged as she looked at the boy. She could see the guilt he was suffering. It had been over a decade, but she understood the pain he was going through and now cared for someone other than herself.

She wanted, needed to help him. "Carl, you can't blame yourself for what happened. It was an accident."

"Yes I can. Because it is!" he said between sobs. "And it's your fault, too!"

That caught Sally by surprise. "How's it my fault?"

"I heard my parents talking. They asked you for a loan and you said no. If you'd helped them out they never would have had to go to the bank in the first place! So see, it is just as much your fault as mine. That's why you are stuck with me! Don't you get it?"

She remembered the call when her sister told her about the financial troubles they were having and asking for the loan. The amount was less than Sally spent on one of her shopping trips in the city. But the timing was bad. Sally was in the middle of something and could not be bothered, so she said no. She remembered that later she decided to call her sister back to tell her that she would lend her the money, but one thing led to another and she simply forgot.

"Carl, honey, this isn't anyone's fault. Not yours, not mine. It was just a horrible accident. No one is to blame. Especially not you." Sally had become the Sally from years before. Truly compassionate and wanting to help someone she cared for. She involuntary knelt down and put her arms around Carl and he collapsed into her embrace.

Carl might as well have been on the moon. He was unaware of his surroundings. The nagging emotions he tried to figure out over the last couple of months had exploded into waves of guilt and were overwhelming. Up until this point he tried to figure out a way to deal with them, but now he did not care. He had a complete understanding of what his situation was and why he was in it. A stupid button on an alarm clock. The fact that he did not slide it all the way resulted in his parents' death and there was absolutely nothing he could do to change it.

Although he wanted to be mad at Sally, he began to understand that shifting part of the blame to her was an attempt to relieve his pain. But it did not work. The pain was relentless, and he felt it physically.

Sally was afraid. Not for what Carl was going through. More because she was experiencing emotions she had buried. And they only surfaced when she was around the boy. But she had been able to control them. Not this time. She had a need to reach out to the boy and help relieve the pain. She was shocked when she touched her cheek and felt a tear for the first time in over a decade. "Carl, honey, you need to listen to me. You can't accept any of the blame for this; it's not your fault! You have to see that."

Carl did not say a word. He stood up and collapsed on his bed face down and sobbed uncontrollably. Sally sat next to him and put her hand on his back, "Listen to me, please. I don't want to see you put yourself through this. It's not your fault Carl. It's no one's, things just happen."

Neither one of them moved or spoke a word. Carl's sobs subsided and he sat up and saw Matilda standing in the doorway holding a tray. "I thought some hot cocoa would be in order."

"I don't want any."

"I think you might. I'll set it on the table in case you change your mind." She then looked at Sally and said, "I set a glass of brandy in your room for you."

"How long have you been standing there?" Sally asked.

"Long enough."

Sally looked at Carl and asked, "Are you okay?"

"I don't think so."

"Do you want to talk about it?"

"No."

"Sure?" Sally coaxed.

"Very sure. I just want to go to sleep," he said as he lay on his side with his back to her.

As she stood and started towards the door she looked back and said, "It's not your fault, Carl. Maybe tomorrow we can talk about it. I want to help you with this." She then went to her suite and sat on her bed surprised that she still had tears running down her cheek.

Carl had nothing left. The waves of guilt, anger and a total sense of loss had stolen his energy. He could smell the cocoa and tried it, and finished it. Then he fell fast asleep.

"Well?" Ruth asked Matilda as she walked into the kitchen.

"Maybe a start."

Chapter 15
Cuts

The woodshop was chilly making the mahogany harder. Without diligence there was a greater chance for a mistake with the cutting.

Carl was a couple days into sawing and stacking the finished pieces. The uncut stack was still larger. He received calls from paying customers asking when their orders would be completed. But they had to wait. He was not going to work on anything else until this project was finished, no matter how long it took.

He picked up the old saw he sharpened the night before and continued. He loved the feel and sound the tool made as it bit into the wood.

Sally was sitting in the kitchen when Carl walked in. Matilda was making breakfast and said, "How are you this beautiful morning, Carl?"

"My head hurts."

Matilda thought, "That's what happens when you cry all night..."

As Carl looked at Sally he was embarrassed. Sally was still in shock. She had not recovered from her emotional rollercoaster.

Matilda served breakfast and said, "I'm going to leave you two alone." She went to the living room, out of sight but still within earshot.

This time it was not tension that filled the room, it was discomfort. Sally said, "How are you?"

"I've never been so embarrassed. I feel like a fool."

"Why?"

"I don't know what came over me last night. It was like something took over and I couldn't stop it."

"It seems you've been holding in a lot of things and they needed to get out."

Carl was confused. The woman sitting in front of him was closer to the one that cared for him the night before and when she taught him to shave, but he could sense the Sally who only cared for herself was right under the surface.

"Sally, I can't begin to tell you how sorry I am. I must've scared you to death with all that yelling and throwing the clock."

"Well, maybe we can figure out a way to help."

"I don't hold you responsible for what happened to mom and dad. I don't know why I said that. I think I just wanted to hurt you," he said looking at the floor.

"Why?"

"I think I figured out one of the reasons it's so hard for us to get along" He looked up. "I never realized how much you look like mom. Maybe when I see you it reminds me she's gone forever."

Sally was quiet as she thought about it. She could see how that could trigger those feelings. But what concerned her most was the real problem. "Carl, you can't blame yourself for what happened."

"Part of me knows that. But every time I think about it I remember that clock. If I had only slid the switch all the way mom and dad would still be here. I'd give anything to have that moment back."

Sally was at a loss. It was a challenge because she understood. She wished she had loaned her sister the money. They would not have been driving to the bank that day.

"Carl, maybe we can find someone to help you to deal with this."

"No."

Sally sensed his anxiety. "Okay! It was just a thought. Just know this. What happened to your parents was an accident."

"How do I stop thinking I caused it?"

"That's what we're going to have to figure out," she said. She did not like being in situations she could not control. She started to revert to her habit of shutting down her emotions. "Let's give it some time."

She needed to get away from Carl and he sensed the tension. She quickly stood and started toward the door. "We'll talk about this later."

Matilda came into the kitchen, "How's the head?"

"Hurts pretty bad."

She made him an icepack. "Put this on your forehead for awhile then switch it to the back of your neck. Keep doing it until it feels better, shouldn't take too long."

"Thanks. I'm going back to bed. I didn't sleep last night."

"Sounds like a good idea to me!"

Sally was a wreck. Years before she resolved never to allow herself to care for anyone ever again. It was the only way she knew how to avoid the pain. It was a cancer and she wanted it cut out. If she were able to control it, it would have been one thing. But now it controlled her for a few moments and she knew it was because of the boy. She found herself cursing the accident. Not for the loss of her sister, but for putting her way of life at risk.

She was becoming agitated wondering if she made the right choice allowing the boy to live at her house. Her scheme worked out exactly as planned and she could not be happier with the results at the club. But what was going on inside the house, and of her, was driving her nuts. She wondered if it was worth it.

She needed to escape, so she decided to go the club and catch up on the latest gossip. Talking about other people's problems was always a good way to ignore your own.

She walked into the kitchen to get her keys and saw Matilda looking at her in the way that Sally found unsettling. It was all-knowing, judgmental and soothing at the same time. "What?"

"I think you and Carl might've made a little bit of headway."

"What do you mean by that?"

"Maybe now you'll keep things civil between each other."

"I was fine with the way things were and have every intention not to change a thing. This is my house with my rules. He'll just have to get used to it!"

"We'll see."

Sally wanted to explode. We'll see? What the hell was that supposed to mean? She opened her mouth to yell but then saw that look that disarmed her. She sighed and said, "I'm going to the club."

Sally relaxed the moment she walked through the entrance of the country club. She saw her friends and they decided to have lunch and catch up on the latest *news*.

The conversations always started the same, "You can't repeat this to a soul, but I heard..." On this particular day there were some extra juicy secrets to betray. One of the girls who was not as high on the social ladder as Sally's crowd was said to have had a botched plastic surgery procedure. "I wondered why I haven't seen her around," Sally said. She was secretly thinking, "Good! I don't have to worry about her looking better than me."

The rumors of money troubles and other embarrassing situations filled lunch and Sally felt better. Then one of her friends asked, "How's Carl doing?" Sally felt herself slip. She wondered how he *was* doing. But she recovered quickly by saying that he was adjusting well and she could not be happier. She enjoyed all the praise saying what a wonderful thing she did for the boy.

One of the girls saved the best story for last. A prominent family had a problem. The husband had been caught having an affair with a younger woman and the wife was on the warpath. As Sally listened to the details she became uncomfortable again. Her friend was describing exactly what happened to her years ago. As the story went on Sally became agitated and excused herself.

As she looked at her reflection in the mirror in the ladies room Sally thought, "What's wrong with me?" She heard stories like that before and it never bothered her. But now listening to her friend describe the events that might as well have been her own, she slid back and remembered the betrayal and pain she endured during her divorce and the years leading up to it. It was not the memories that were so unsettling; it was that she could not push them back.

It took her several minutes to regain her composure and she rejoined her friends. "Tell the wife that I have a very good attorney. Believe me, he'll rock the cheating husband's world," she said remembering the look on her ex-husband's face when he realized how screwed he was and how it gave her a sense of satisfaction.

Sally spent the rest of the afternoon playing cards and enjoying cocktails. She did not think about Carl once and only focused on her image. Sally was becoming Sally again, the careless bitch that she was and in the only state where she could be truly comfortable.

"How's the head?" Matilda asked as she saw Carl walking down the stairs.

"Better. That ice trick worked."

"That's why I wanted you to do it."

"Where's Sally?"

"She went to the club. I don't expect that she will be back anytime soon."

"Good."

"Good? I thought things might be better with you two."

"Maybe, not great. I thought about it and I'm going to stay out of her way. School starts in about a month, that'll keep me busy."

"Maybe you should give Sally a chance. I could tell she was concerned about you last night. I know she can be difficult, but maybe this can be the start of things getting better."

"I thought so too. But this morning didn't end well. She was like she was before and I don't want to deal with that. It would be better if I stay out of sight."

"This is a big house, but that still might be hard to do."

"All I can do is try."

"One day at a time. Let's go make you some dinner."

Sally could not believe it. She was feeling great at the club and was back in control. Time with her friends revitalized her and the armor was as strong as ever. But on the drive home her emotions began to surface again. It was so much easier when the boy was at summer camp. She enjoyed all the benefits and did not have to deal with Carl. She made a mental note to have Ruthy sign him up for summer camp the entire summer next year. "Year?" she thought.

She parked and went into the house. It felt bigger than before and empty. It never bothered her, but now she was lonely. She knew Carl was most likely in his room and Matilda was close by but she still had a sense of being completely by herself. She turned on the light in the kitchen and saw a note on the table. Matilda left her a plate in the oven in case she was hungry. But Sally had no appetite.

She poured a healthy shot of brandy and went to her room. As she got ready to retire for the evening she was trying to think of ways to get control back.

Although it was getting late she needed a diversion so she went into her office and shuffled papers. She looked over the itinerary of her trip and thought, "At least I'll get a break from him then." She sat for more than an hour tinkering, but no matter how hard she tried she could not get her mind off the situation with the boy. "I'm in real trouble," she thought as she closed her eyes. Just when the frustration was becoming overwhelming it came to her.

"Why didn't I think of this before? It's so easy and it solves everything!" she thought. Sally got giddy with excitement and picked up the phone not caring it was after midnight. "Ruthy…"

CHAPTER 16

BOARDERS

"*BOARDING SCHOOL!*"

"Now just calm down, Carl," Sally demanded.

"This is crazy! I promised I'd stay out of your way and I have kept it. Why do I have to go to boarding school?" Carl was trembling.

It had been a fairly smooth few days. They only saw each other a couple of times, and for brief periods. Carl was becoming comfortable. That is why he was confused when Ruth told him Sally wanted to see him. With fear and trepidation he walked down the hallway to her office. He had no idea what to expect. But boarding school? Sally's revelation completely blindsided him, and any chance to have any control of his life was thrown out the window. He knew Sally had already made her mind up, but he had to try.

"Sally, everything's set at my high school. It starts in a few weeks and I won't be here hardly at all. Joe and I have been talking about it and we're excited. Please don't do this!"

"It's for your own good. I have to think about your future and this is one of the best prep schools in the state. You'll be able to see your friends during the vacations," she said. Translation: this will be best for me because you'll be out of my hair.

"Vacations? You mean I'm going to be there on the weekends?"

Sally nodded.

Carl wished he could persuade her but over the last few months he learned wishing accomplished absolutely nothing. "Please Sally.

Don't do this. I'll do anything if you let stay and go to my high school," he said realizing that his high school was not his anymore.

"No, Carl. You're going and you'll thank me someday. Only the best of the best attend and I pulled a lot of strings to get you in on such short notice. You should be thankful."

Thankful! His life was being torn apart again and he should be thankful? He remembered when she dropped the bomb about summer camp and that turned out well. But this was not like that in any way, shape or form.

"Please, Sally…" he said with a tear running down his cheek. "Don't do this to me."

"Everything's set. Ruthy and I are taking you Saturday and your classes begin on Monday."

"Saturday! That's only a few days away!"

"I know and we have a lot of things to take care of. Ruthy is going to take you today to buy your uniforms…"

"Uniforms!" he interrupted. He closed his eyes and thought, "Man, this just keeps getting better and better."

Sally explained she arranged a going-away party for him at the club. There was no way she was going to pass up an opportunity like this. She would be able to parade the boy and brag on how she got him in the prestigious school. It should be worth at least a few weeks of positive gossip.

"Can my friends come?"

"No. This party is for adults."

"Then why do I have to go?"

"Because the party is for you, silly!"

Ruth took Carl shopping. He looked at the list and noticed the requirement of a sports coat and several ties. "I'll have to wear ties?"

"This is a pretty exclusive school. Their mission is to groom boys and turn them into proper young men, so yes, you'll be wearing a tie most of the time."

"Do they have sports?"

"They're big on golf and tennis."

"What about baseball?"

"They don't believe that's a sport that's appropriate."

"Great, my new school doesn't even have my favorite sport. This sucks. Do you think I can change Sally's mind? I don't want to go."

"Believe me, if I thought there was chance I'd help you figure it out. It's hard to explain, but Sally seems like a different person since she had me set it up. It's been months since I've seen her so happy. Well, at least her way of being happy."

"I thought by staying out of the way everything would work out. I didn't see anything like this coming."

"I'm sorry, Carl. But when Sally makes up her mind it takes an act of God to change it."

"Maybe I should start praying," he said as he looked out the widow at the passing traffic. He noticed they were at the intersection where his mom and dad were killed. There was no sign of the crash and he knew the flowers he placed were long gone. It seemed like so long ago and not long ago at all. He had experienced so much that his sense of time was out of kilter. He did know the fear he had since the crash was justified.

The day before the party Carl gave it one last shot. There had to be a way to convince Sally not to send him to boarding school. He crept to her office and lightly tapped on the door. Sally looked up. "What are you doing here! You know the rules."

"I was hoping I could talk to you."

"What?"

"I have an idea. I know one of the reasons you want to send me to boarding school is because you don't like me staying here. So I was thinking maybe it would be a good idea for me to go to Boy's Town. That way you won't have to put up with me and I can still see my friends."

"Do you have any idea how that'd make me look? I would be making a fool of myself. Besides, it's the best thing for you. Now leave me alone."

With a complete sense of defeat Carl left.

Ruth was right about Sally being a happier Sally after deciding to send the boy to boarding school. Her armor was reinforced and none of the pesky emotions penetrated it after Sally called Ruth to make the plans. In fact there had not been one episode since. But as she watched Carl walk away she felt a pang in her heart. A brief moment of feeling sorry for the boy. It ended as fast as it started and she thought, "The sooner the better."

Carl walked into the kitchen as Matilda was putting away groceries. She asked, "How are you?"

"Not good."

"Carl, maybe you should look at it like an adventure, you might enjoy the journey."

"I've had more than enough adventures recently and I don't like where my journey is taking me. Why can't anyone understand that?"

"I understand! But when things are out of your control you have to figure out how to make the best of it."

"I've tried. It's not working. My life's being torn apart. I won't be able to see my friends or my dog. I have no idea what to expect. But I know I'm going to hate it and there's nothing I can do about it."

Matilda was disappointed she could not help the boy and her heart ached. She tried her old stand-by, "What can I make you for lunch? Anything you want!"

"Thanks Matilda, but I'm not hungry. I'm going to Joe's and say goodbye."

"Man, this is a bummer!" Joe said as he watched Mutt play with Carl. "I thought we'd be able to hang out the rest of the summer then conquer the new school."

"Me too. I'm going to miss you guys. I won't see you until Christmas."

"We can hang out tomorrow!"

"No we can't. I have to go to Sally's stupid party and leave the next day. So this is it until winter break."

Joe was surprised he was getting choked up. "I'm going to miss you."

They talked and played with Mutt, then Carl said his goodbyes to Joe's mom. He went to the backyard to say goodbye to Mutt again. He sat in a lawn chair and the scruffy dog jumped onto his lap. Carl hugged him. "I think I'm going to miss you the most."

Knowing this would be his last chance for a long time, Carl decided to ride his bike through the old neighborhood. He relived memories of times he and Joe played in the streets. He missed them and was afraid he would never have times like that again. As he rode by his old house he noticed a car in the driveway and a couple of younger kids playing in the yard. He stopped and watched, and then started to Sally's house. "I hope you guys have better luck there than me," he whispered.

The ride seemed to take a long time, and when he punched in the gate code and rode up the driveway his heart sank when he saw Sally's car. He was hoping she would be out so he did not have to hide in his room. When he walked into the kitchen he saw Sally barking orders at Matilda.

"Carl, I need you to be on your best behavior tomorrow. This is very important to me and I don't want any foul-ups like last time."

Carl remembered his outbursts at the reception after the funeral and what he thought was the soda fountain. "Don't worry; I'll stay out of everyone's way."

"I mean it Carl, I don't want any problems and I expect you to be well behaved and friendly. I'm doing this for you, you know."

He did not know. It was not for him at all. "Don't worry, I'll be good."

"What do you want for dinner?" Matilda called out after him.

"Not hungry," he yelled back.

When he got to his room he saw the reminders of his predicament. The new uniforms were neatly folded ready to be put into his suitcase and his school supplies were arranged so they could be placed into his backpack. He walked to his desk and looked at a letter he started to write to Kim. It was short; the only words were "Dear Kim." He had no idea what else to write.

He saw the suit hanging, waiting for him to put it on the next day for Sally's party and became more depressed. Carl walked into the bathroom and turned on the carwash to full blast and as hot as he could stand. He got in and let the water jets pepper his body for a long time hoping they would wash away all of the lousy things happening to him. It did not work.

"You sure you want to do this?" Matilda asked Sally.

"Do what?"

"Carl is a miserable boy. He's been through enough and I'm not convinced this boarding school idea is healthy. The boy needs stability."

"Well, so do I! " Sally scowled. "I'll take my dinner in my office."

"You're sure?"

"Yes, dinner in my office!"

"Not that. About the boy. He's your only family after all. That should count for something."

The rage ramped up at an alarming rate, even on the Sally standard. "Yes, I'm sure. And I'm also sure you'll be looking for a new job tomorrow if you don't mind your own business. Dinner in my office," Sally said as she left.

Matilda thought about Sally and Carl. "This is worse than I thought and I have no idea what to do about it."

Carl's going-away party with the social phonies was almost a carbon copy of the reception after his parent's funeral. The exceptions were his picture on the easel, he stayed away from the Champagne fountain and he tried a little harder to be nice to Sally's friends. She was much happier this time.

He was more miserable.

CHAPTER 17
FAREWELLS

Sally's trunk was filled with Carl's things and it was time for the long drive to the boarding school. It had been a hard morning. It was bad enough having to deal with the shock of Sally's decision. Now Carl had to say goodbye to Matilda. She made him a special breakfast.

"You all set?"

"I guess. I can't begin to tell you how much I hate this. If someone were to tell me I wouldn't want to leave, I would've thought they were nuts. Now I think I'm the one going crazy."

"Maybe you'll like it. You didn't want to go to summer camp and that worked out."

"I know. I thought about that too. It's different. A few days ago I was looking forward to the new school year. The only thing I had to worry about was avoiding Sally. Now I have no idea what to expect but I have a feeling it's not going to be good. Plus I'm losing a chunk of summer vacation. I think I'm a lost cause."

"Why do you say that?"

"I have a bad feeling. It seems so permanent. I'm going to lose my friends being gone so long."

"I'm sure you won't lose any friends. But like I told you, things usually turn out as well as you let them. I'm worried if you start with this attitude you're going to make it harder."

"I can't help it."

Matilda was frustrated. She had always been able to cheer up the people she cared for. "Let me think about it. When I come up with something I'll enclose a note in one of your care packages."

Carl raised his eyebrows, "You don't know?"

"Know what?"

"They go through the packages and throw out any food. They don't even encourage friends and family to write. They say it interferes with the adjustment process."

"Oh my."

"I think you're starting to see why I'm so upset. It's more than living someplace else and going to a new school. It's a different life."

She went to the refrigerator and pulled out a box. "I was going to put this in today's mail so you'd have a surprise right away. I guess you're going to have to enjoy it on the drive."

He opened the box, it was his favorite. Her homemade fudge. "Thanks Matilda. I'm going to miss your cooking."

"Well, now you have something to look forward to when you come back!"

"You think you'll still be here?"

"Yes I do."

That made him feel better and accomplished exactly what she wanted.

Ruth walked in and the three waited for Sally. Carl asked again if they could think of anything that could change Sally's mind and they had no idea. They did agree Sally had been in a much better mood the last few days. That was not to say that she was pleasant. Not at all. She just seemed to be happier with herself.

Sally walked in and said, "We need to go right now."

Carl looked at Matilda. "I guess this is it."

"For now," she said as she reached her arms around him.

Sally watched and became uneasy when the maid embraced the boy. "What the hell?" she thought. She was jealous. How could she be jealous? She was excited to be rid of the kid. But it was real and lasted long enough to make her uncomfortable. "We've got to go!"

she demanded, hoping to break the spell of the hug and her jealousy. It worked.

Sally was driving with Ruth sitting in front and Carl in back. Carl could tell Sally made Ruth come so she could go over the details of her upcoming trip.

"Make sure to call the florist and have her stop the deliveries in five days," Sally ordered.

One of Sally's indulgences was fresh cut flowers delivered to her house almost every day. Her love of flowers was an obsession and roses were her favorite. The house was always filled with huge arrangements with every variety imaginable.

For the first hour Carl listened to nonstop orders flow out of Sally. "Ruthy do this," and "Ruthy do that." He saw Ruth frantically taking notes. When Sally exhausted all of her demands Carl decided to take one last shot.

"Sally, I'm scared. There has to be something I can say to make you change your mind."

"You're being silly! Hundreds of boys will be there and there's nothing to be afraid of. It'll be good for you. Besides, we've already had your going away party. It would look bad if you didn't go. There's nothing to worry about."

"Then why am I so afraid?"

"You just need to grow up."

"I've been doing a lot of growing up over the last few months."

Sally looked in the rear view mirror and saw how upset he was and it bothered her. She thought, "Just a few more hours... hang in there. This will all be over soon and I can have my life back and never have to put up with this crap again."

As they pulled up to the boarding school they sat in silence. High walls surrounded the property and in the middle of one was a large sign that said Churchill's School for Boys. Next to it was a security gate and guardhouse. An older, worn-out looking man pushed a button to open the gate after Sally produced the papers showing Carl was a new student. As they drove through the gates Carl's heart sank. He thought the school would be like ones he had seen on television or in the movies with stately looking buildings with ivy covered walls surrounded by grass-covered, rolling mounds and walking paths. Churchill's was nothing like that. As far as Carl was concerned, Boy's Town was more inviting. Although well maintained, Churchill's looked like an old military base. There was little greenery and the buildings were gray. "You sure this isn't a military school?"

Sally was also surprised. She assumed with the high tuition it would look like a country club.

"Maybe it gets better on different parts of the campus," Ruth said. "The tour starts in a bit. I'm sure it will look better than this."

"I hope so," Carl whispered.

In the administration offices they were greeted by an older man in a ruffled suit. He explained he was the headmaster of Churchill's and had been for almost three decades. Ruth thought he must have started when he was fifty. They went into his office where the walls were covered with pictures of men, all graduates of the school. The headmaster pointed out each picture and explained the success of each. There were judges and big time bankers. "We take great pride that many of our alumni have accomplished every impressive feats," he said. He looked at Carl. "With hard work there is a very good chance your picture will be on this wall someday."

"So what," Carl thought.

The headmaster explained Carl would take placement tests right away and be assigned to the appropriate classes. He also bragged that the school had the highest college acceptance rate in the state. "We believe manhood starts the moment you walk through the gate. How seriously do you take your education?" he asked Carl.

"I never thought about it."

"You will from here on out. I can assure you the staff will as well."

After filling out paperwork the headmaster introduced them to a senior. "This is Mike, he's going to give you the tour. I'm sure he can answer your questions. He's one of our best and brightest."

The tour took an hour and with each passing moment Carl's spirits sank. There was no warmth to the campus and it felt old and foreboding. The dorms were dismal with twenty beds per room, ten along opposite walls. The bathrooms looked like they were from a movie set from the nineteen twenties. Ruth saw Carl becoming more upset and wanted to cheer him up. "I'm sure once you make some friends you'll feel better."

"It's a prison," he said. She could not disagree.

After the tour they returned to the headmaster's office where Ruth and Sally finished the paperwork, leaving Mike and Carl on their own.

"What's it like living here?" Carl asked.

"It took me a couple of years to get used to it. There's no free time with all the schoolwork. Even on weekends. From the minute you wake up until lights out they keep you busy. They give us an hour of free time at night, but most of us just hit the sack."

"Why?"

"A couple of reasons. One, you are so exhausted you just want to sleep. Two, there isn't anything else to do."

"What about TV?"

"No TV's here. They say it doesn't add to our growth."

"No offence, but this place gives me the creeps. Isn't there anything fun to do?"

"We try, but the staff is pretty strict. To be honest, I'm glad this is my last year."

In the headmaster's office Sally was seated in front of his desk. "I have to say, with the amount of tuition you charge I thought the living environment would be nicer. This place is very drab."

"Our focus is to turn these boys into successful men. We have the highest paid staff in the state and our results speak for themselves."

"It's not what I expected."

"I can assure that you will be happy with the results. We believe in strict control of our students and take their future seriously."

The discomfort Sally was experiencing was inexplicable. She was getting exactly what she wanted and paid for. She would be rid of the boy and still stay on the right side of the social circles. That was what she wanted, but part of her wished Churchill's was more inviting. The discomfort only served to reinforce her resolve to get back home and focus on her upcoming trip. Then her life would be back to normal.

As Carl unloaded his belongings from Sally's trunk she said, "This is a fine school. A lot of successful people have attended here. If you apply yourself you will find it isn't as bad as you think."

"I guess."

They took his bags to his dorm. Ruth felt like she was standing in a mental institution. Sally was thinking she should demand a discount. Carl felt like part of him was dying. As he looked around the dorm he realized the dread he had the last few days was justified. "Four years of this?" he thought as he pushed his hand into the bed. It felt like a floor mat.

"Sally, if you let me come back I promise there won't be any problems. I'll stay out you're way."

"This is best for you and we've already talked about it enough."

Her insides were twisted. She realized when she was not around the boy it was easy. The strange feelings never surfaced, for the most part. But when they were together she lost some control. She also now understood it had been that way for a long time. Although it was not his intention, he reached inside her and flipped a switch turning on the uncomfortable emotions, and the longer they were together the brighter they became. Having spent most of the day with him made her more than uncomfortable, it scared her.

She looked at Ruth. "We need to go. We have a long drive and Carl is all set here." She turned toward the door.

"Carl, make the best of it. I know you can. Like I told you, you're a very special person and I hope things go well," Ruth said as she gave him a hug.

Sally turned just in time to see Ruth hug the boy and was reminded of how uncomfortable she was when she saw Matilda do the same that morning. "Ruthy! Time to go."

Carl watched them leave and sat on his new bed. He went into a trance. Images of his mother and father, Mutt, and Kim played over and over mixed with thoughts of Matilda and Joe. It became hard to focus on the good memories and soon the fear of his future took over, making him as depressed as he had been since his parents' accident.

He did not know how long he sat there when an adult broke him out of his trance. "Time for supper. I'll show you where it is." Dinner was as dismal as the rest of the surroundings. He ate in a room full of strangers and could tell his schoolmates were as miserable as he was.

On the drive back Sally was quiet. Ruth did not miss the barking and constant demands, but seeing Sally like this made her uncomfortable. When they got to the house Sally went straight to her room and her only words to Ruth and Matilda were that she wanted to be left alone for the night.

Matilda looked at Ruth and asked, "What's going on?"

Ruth gave her a look of puzzlement and said, "I have absolutely no idea..."

CHAPTER 18

ADAPTING

The first days at Churchill's were a nightmare. Carl's first day, a Sunday, was spent taking placement tests. He started at eight in the morning and did not finish until six that evening. He thought about missing questions on purpose. "Maybe they'll kick me out if I flunk." But he thought better of it. He struggled through the different subjects and wondered if he really was going to flunk. But the teacher explained these tests were not for grades, only to make sure he was placed in classes suited for him. As he completed each he handed it to a teacher who graded and gave him results on the spot. Carl scored low seventies on all except for the last one.

As he handed the math test to the teacher Carl saw his look of surprise. "What?"

"There's no way you could have completed this so fast. It's impossible."

Then the teacher's jaw drooped. "Ninety nine percent?" Carl was relieved when he heard the score and thought he was done with the marathon pencil pushing. Instead he was rewarded by having to retake the test while the teacher stood over his shoulder. This time he did not miss a single question. "This has never happened..."

The next day was more intense. The instructors spent the first part of class explaining what was expected and then handed out homework. Carl sat in disbelief after dinner looking at the pile he had to complete before he went to bed. It was more than a week's worth at his old school and he thought, "Four years of this?"

The next day was the same with the exception of study hall after a lousy dinner to correct mistakes from the previous day's work and to start on the current assignments. He went to bed exhausted and unhappy.

It was no picnic for Sally either. The transition was a slow burn, not an explosion, and she was fighting it every step of the way. She knew Carl had somehow flipped the switch that destroyed her defenses and reopened parts of her she thought were dead. She felt the change begin on the drive back from Churchill's. By the time she arrived home she came to grips that she was not able to stop the flood of emotions. On the surface she was still the same. But as she looked inward she understood she was slipping and becoming what she might have become if it were not for the bad decisions, bad marriage and the way her life had turned out.

She devised a plan. Instead of fighting the ghosts she would let them run their course, endure the memories, confront her demons then regroup. She did not have the energy to fight back. She thought if she let her defenses down, if only for a little while, she could rebuild her armor.

Sally gave her staff strict instructions not to disturb her and stayed in her suite for two days. On the second day she had Ruth bring up a box filled with photos and papers that she had not looked at for years.

Sally stood over the box after Ruth placed it on her desk and left. She knew once she opened it she would go back to a place she wanted to forget. Her hands trembled as she pulled off the top.

A musky smell filled the room as she put the lid aside and looked at the contents which were thrown in without organization. She remembered filling it in a rush, hoping to put her pain away quickly. She took out the high school yearbook from her senior year. As Sally thumbed through the pages and read the notes she was surprised she was so popular.

Sally pulled out a handful of pictures of her with her family and others showing happy times. One that stuck out was of her and her little sister looking happy and vibrant at the beginning of high school. The two sisters were as close as sisters could be and were filled with excitement for the future.

Sally started to weep.

She looked at a picture from her wedding. She could not believe how young and good she looked. Even the SOB looked dapper in his tux and Sally smiled remembering how she felt that day. She was more than happy. She was optimistic and secure believing she was making the right choices.

She spent hours trolling through the contents allowing herself to relive the moments when she was a happy person. It was a lifetime ago. Now that Carl flipped her switch and destroyed her armor it seemed closer.

Sally was not sure her plan was working. She thought if she allowed herself to travel memory lane she would be reminded of why she liked the way things were now, of the pain of what she lost, and how important it was to preserve what she had become.

She returned the items to the box and had Ruth put it in storage. "Make sure you tape it up tight."

After Ruth left, Sally sat at her desk and reflected. "How does that boy do this to me?" she thought. She not dealt with these memories for ten years. They tried to sneak up from time to time, but she could always push them back. Allowing herself to go back and think about the way things were did not make her feel better. In fact, she felt worse than before she opened the box.

Matilda saw Ruth walk into the room and asked, "Is she alright."

"I'm not sure. I've never seen her like this. Normally with a trip being so close she'd have me run around with last minute details. She seems to be in a different world right now."

"It has to be something to do with Carl."

"I don't know. Sally was resolved when we dropped him off at Churchill's. But when we drove back she was different."

"Different how?"

"I've never seen her so withdrawn. It makes me nervous."

"Me too."

Sally woke up the next morning feeling better. She was changing back into the woman she was the day before she dropped Carl off at Churchill's. All the misgivings and doubts were fading and she became excited about her trip again. Her plan worked. She let herself go back and remember things that she wanted to forget, and now remembered why she wanted to forget them in the first place. Sally was comfortable in her own skin again and all of the baggage from the past did not matter anymore. "I'm back!" she thought as she picked the phone and screamed, "Ruthie, get over here right now. We have a lot to do!"

Sally knew she had to focus on strengthening her resolve to fortify her shell. It had been a close call. There were actually a few moments she was afraid she could not do it. She was drowning in old memories and had forgotten how to swim. Now she was getting back to normal and wanted to hold on to the selfish anger that protected her and avoid the uncomfortable memories. "Uncomfortable? Hell, they are lethal!" she thought.

She drove Ruth crazy with unreasonable demands and worked Matilda to the bone getting her things ready. It was very long day for Sally's staff.

During one of the few breaks from Sally's onslaught Ruth and Matilda stole a moment. They decided they earned a shot of Sally's expensive brandy. Sitting at the kitchen table they were exhausted. "Well, I guess Sally is back as strong as ever," Ruth said.

"I wish she would drink the whole bottle of this stuff and pass out. I need the break."

Sally spent hours on the phone with her friend from the city planning the month-long trip. She did not think about the boy once. But when she was getting ready for bed that night and there was nothing to occupy her mind she slipped. She had an urge to look at the boy's room. When she walked in and turned on the lights she looked around. All traces of the boy were gone, but she could still feel his pull. She went into the bathroom and looked into the mirror at herself but instead saw the boy shaving for the first time. She remembered the smile they shared and the way they connected. It should have been a pleasant memory, but it terrified her.

As she went to her suite she made a promise never to go in that room again. It was too dangerous.

Carl looked at the calendar and realized this was the day Sally was going to Paris. "I wish I could get far away from this place," he thought as he worked on the mound of schoolwork. The only thing he could be thankful for was his time was filled with so much he could not think about how miserable he was. Almost.

At mail call he was reminded of Camp Big Lake when the students gathered for it twice a week. The only similarity was that everyone was gathered together at the same time; everything else was different. The summer camp's daily mail call lasted almost fifteen minutes because so many names were called. At the boarding school it lasted ninety seconds because only half a dozen students received mail. Carl was surprised when he heard his name and received a letter. It was from Matilda.

As he walked to his dorm he opened the letter and found a touching card of encouragement and a thin plastic baggy. He opened it and saw a note, "This is my homemade rice candy. I'm thinking we might be able to pull this off! It's flat!!" It looked like a shiny piece of paper and at first he was nervous to try it. But he remembered it was from Matilda so he looked around to make sure no one was looking and ate it. He could not believe how good it tasted and hoped she would be sending lots of cards.

Matilda was loading Sally's bags into Ruth's trunk as Sally barked from behind, "Don't you think just because I'll not be here that I don't expect you to keep this place immaculate. I'm the one on vacation, not you."

Matilda nodded her head with a smile but thought, "Stay as long as you like…"

"I mean it! I'm going to have Ruthy check on you!"

"Not to worry, the house will be pristine, I assure you," she said knowing that Ruth was looking forward to the break as much as she was.

On the drive to the airport Ruth noticed Sally was more agitated than usual. "Sally, are you looking forward to the trip? You seem worked up."

"YES! Now leave me alone and drive."

Ruth was used to Sally repeating instructions for things to be done while she was gone. But this time Sally was silent, like the ride back from Churchill's.

When they pulled to the curb Sally saw her friend waiting with a bellhop. Ruth noticed Sally had calmed down and said, "Have a pleasant trip and don't worry about anything here. I'll handle every-thing to your satisfaction."

"I know," Sally barked. Once the trunk was unloaded and shut, Ruth pulled away hoping Sally could not see her shaking her head.

They had an hour to kill before the flight so Sally and her friend decided to have a mimosa in the first class club. Sally felt unsteady. Her resolve worked for the most part. Still, there was something nagging at her. It was like a bug bite, irritating but still manageable.

The women were going over their plans when Sally's friend noticed she was acting odd. "Are you alright?"

"Yes, yes. I didn't get much sleep last night. You know, being so excited for the trip and all," Sally half lied. She told the truth that she did not sleep much. But it had nothing to do with the trip.

"Well maybe you can take a nap on the plane. I hear they improved first class seating and it's more comfortable than ever!"

"As long as they keep the Champagne flowing I'll be fine!"

On the outside Sally was holding herself together. On the inside the bug bite now felt like snakebite. Her mind was spinning. She was excited about the trip and knew once she was airborne traveling at six hundred miles an hour away from her problems, everything would be better.

It was early for boarding but Sally looked at her friend, "Let's go to the gate and get on the plane as soon as we can. I want to get settled in for the flight."

Her friend was puzzled looking at the clock. "Don't you think we'll be more comfortable here instead of the waiting area? Those seats are atrocious and there's no Champagne!"

Sally needed to move to stop her mind from spinning. "I think it'd be a good idea to stretch our legs. It's going to be a long flight."

Her friend agreed and they went to the departure gate. Sally was walking fast and her friend struggled to keep up. "Hey, slow down. We have plenty of time!"

Sally walked faster. Something inside her told her the sooner she was on the plane the sooner she would be back in control.

Sally's friend was right. They had to wait before they could board the plane and she sensed Sally was more upset. "Is everything alright?"

Sally became angry her friend could tell something was wrong. "Yes I'm fine. It's just a combination of being tired and excited. Let's have a seat and you can catch me up on the latest news from the city!" she said trying to be perky but sounding shaky.

Her friend was not sure what to think, but thought hearing the latest juicy gossip might give Sally a distraction. So she started to dish out all the best stuff.

Sally did not hear a word of it. She nodded her head every few moments pretending to be enthralled. But the energy it took to put up the act was no match for the turmoil boiling inside her. "I can do this. Just get on the plane, have a few drinks and before you know it I will be in Paris," she thought.

It felt like hours, but it was only ten minutes when the announcement was made that first class was ready to board. Her friend was in mid-sentence as Sally jumped up, grabbed her purse and pushed an older man out of the way so she could be the first to board. She put her purse in the overhead storage bin and fell into her seat.

She started to calm down. Not out of control, but not in command of her thoughts either. Her friend was a minute behind her. "Wow! You are excited, aren't you? You left me back there."

"You have no idea how much I need this trip."

They were served drinks while passengers boarded. Sally was trying to settle in for the long flight. But it was not working. She was losing control as the snake bite started to feel like her insides were being mauled by a bear. Her heart was pounding and she was afraid it might explode out of her chest. The announcement came over the intercom that the cabin doors were closing and everyone had to put on their seat belts.

Sally snapped. The sledge hammer that cracked her armor before had turn into a jack hammer and instead of cracking it, the armor shattered. She jumped out of her seat and said to her friend, "I'm sorry about this." She grabbed her purse and rushed to the front of the plane where the attendant was closing the door. "WAIT!"

The stewardess was shaken seeing Sally rush towards her. "Ma'am, you need to take your seat. We're getting ready for departure."

"I'm not going."

"What?"

"I said I'm not going. Now open that door, get out of my way and let me off this plane! NOW!"

Her friend sat in shock as she watched Sally run out the door and off the plane.

CHAPTER 19
ADJUSTMENTS

In the woodshop Carl made the last cut. He looked at the boards of Santos Mahogany picturing how they would come together and become the finished piece. Although no parts of the project were simple, the next step would require more diligence. Sanding to assure the perfect joining of the pieces had to be exact. With the cutting he manipulated the wood within a fraction of an inch, but now the measurements had to be more precise.

"They should call this prisoner school," Carl thought as he woke up. He had been at Churchill's less than a week, but knew he would hate every minute of it. No "making the best of it" like Matilda suggested. He was not the only one who felt that way. Every other freshman he talked to agreed. Misery loves company and it looked like Carl was going to have a lot of company over the next four years.

At breakfast he felt strange being in a room full of people his age and so quiet. At his old school there was always a hum in the air. Here no one spoke and the atmosphere compounded his hopelessness.

In the first class after lunch the teacher's lecture was interrupted by a school secretary who handed him a paper. Carl could tell the instructor was irritated. The teacher looked at Carl and asked him to come to the front of the room. "This says you're to report to the headmaster's office right away."

Carl did not think it was possible as his heart sank deeper. He remembered when he was required to go to Yoda's office and to see the head of staff at the summer camp. "Now what?" he thought.

"Hurry along now. You don't want to keep him waiting. He doesn't like that," the teacher warned.

It was a long walk to the headmaster's office. Carl was trying to figure out what this could be about. Half way there he gave up. Things could not be worse than they already were. Besides, even if he had done something wrong what could they do? Take away his freedom? "Maybe they have a dungeon where they lock up trouble-makers," he thought.

At the receptionist's desk outside of the headmaster's office he was told to take a seat. Carl heard muffled voices through the door and it sounded like there was a heated discussion.

A half hour later the door opened and the headmaster stuck his head out. "Come in, son."

Carl did not like being called son. It reminded him of the police officer who told him about his mom and dad's accident. The tone of the headmaster's voice did not help either. Carl slowly walked into the office and was shocked. "What in the world..." he thought.

Sally was standing in the office. "Hello Carl."

Carl did not know whether to be happy or afraid. As far as he knew Sally was on her vacation. At first he thought he had done something so bad it required her to come back. If that were the case there were would be hell to pay and it scared him to death. But what? "Sally, what are you doing here?" he said, visibly shaken.

"I've come to get you."

"What?"

"You heard me. I'm bringing you back with me."

"Back to where?"

"Back to my house. Now get your things so we can leave. Hurry. I don't want to be here any longer than I have to."

Carl was shocked into paralysis. He was trying to process what she said and the way she said it. Her voice was different. It was not mean. It was businesslike. He looked at the headmaster and saw he was agitated and would not return his look.

"Go on Carl. Get your things and I'll explain everything on the way back," Sally said softy trying to nudge him into action. She looked at the headmaster and demanded, "Now get my refund check?" sounding more like the Sally Carl knew.

Carl was at a loss. If someone told him he was leaving forty five minutes ago he would have been elated. But now he was not so sure. When Sally and Ruth dropped him off he could tell Sally was glad to be rid of him. Now she was waiting for him to get his stuff so she could take him back to her house, and telling him to hurry. As much as he wanted to be happy about leaving he was afraid of what the alternative might be.

It took him a few minutes to pack his things. As he left the dorm he turned around and gave the space a final look. "I'm not going to miss this place," he thought. "I hope…"

The door was open to the headmaster's office when Carl walked into the administration area and he heard Sally and the headmaster talking.

"This is highly unusual, I cannot remember one time in all of my years that something like this happened," headmaster said.

"I don't care, and remember, I can use the same strings to hurt your reputation I did to get him here in the first place," Carl heard Sally, sounding as bitchy as ever.

He was not sure if he should go into the office, but after a few minutes he stuck his head in and saw Sally putting a check into her purse. "You have everything?"

"It's all right here."

Sally smiled. "Good. Let's go home."

"Home?" Carl thought. It was the first time he heard her use that word. It was always "the house" or "my place." He never said or thought of it as "home" either. He said, "Okay." in a shaky voice.

Sally looked at the headmaster. "Now I'll considerer this matter closed, but I don't suggest you use me as a reference." She walked out of the office with Carl following. He saw the headmaster shaking his head and looking defeated.

Sally was walking fast. He wanted to ask what was going on, but he was afraid he would not like the answer. Was she going to put him in a different school? Maybe one that kept their students year around. Maybe someplace overseas. He was trying to wrap his head around all the possibilities when they got to her car.

"Sally, is everything alright?"

"I think so. Let's get on the road."

Over the last few months Carl learned one thing, how to adapt on short notice. But now he was on verge of losing his self-control as he tried to figure out what was happening. His heart raced as he loaded his things into Sally's trunk. As he opened the car door and climbed in beside Sally he looked at her, but could not think of anything to say. He was too scared.

Sally saw the boy in turmoil and wanted to calm him. "Relax, everything's fine."

Carl did not feel any better. Sally's "fine" was usually everyone else's misery. He let out his breath. He did not realize he been holding it in. "I have no idea what's going on here."

"I don't blame you. For what it is worth, I'm not sure what's going on here either."

Carl could see she was as uncomfortable as he was.

They sat in silence as Sally drove and Carl wondered. He relaxed knowing he was getting farther away from Churchill's but still did not understand why he was sitting in Sally's car.

"Sally, what's happening here?"

"Carl, I've never spent any time around kids with the exception of you. At least not since I was a kid myself. So, I'm not sure how to talk to you."

"Just talk."

She started to talk.

CHAPTER 20
WHAT A DAY

There was tension during the drive but it was different. Before they would have been angry and resentful. For Carl it was confusion. For Sally it was confusion mixed with a healthy dose of fear.

When she rushed off the plane, the plan had been to take a taxi to her house and get her car to pick up the boy right away. But she had second thoughts. She knew the gossip was going to be disastrous, so much so she had a sinking feeling her status would not only be damaged but destroyed. What surprised her was she was not sure she cared.

The emotional strain exhausted her and when the taxi dropped her off she went straight to her room. She got into bed, called Ruth and told her to have the airline return her luggage. She also gave instructions to have the contractor come by right away. Ruth reminded her that it was Friday, her day off. "Please Ruth; I really need you to do this for me."

Ruth was not sure what surprised her more, the fact Sally did not go on the trip, the tone of her voice, almost pleading, or she had not called her "Ruthy." She was so shocked she dropped the phone. After she recovered she picked it up and asked, "Do you need me to come over?"

"I don't know. I think if you just make the calls I can have Matilda take care of everything else. I don't want to be a bother on your day off."

This time Ruth had to sit down as the blood rushed from her head. Could this be the same woman who was barking orders and making unreasonable demands earlier and every day before that? "Sally, are you alright?"

"I don't know."

"That's it. I'll be there in twenty minutes."

As Ruth walked into the kitchen she saw Matilda and asked, "Do you have any idea what's going on with Sally?"

"What do you mean? I thought she'd be half way to Paris by now."

"You don't know?"

"Know what?"

Ruth became more frustrated. "She just called me and I think she's in her room!"

"I was cleaning the pool house awhile ago; she might've come in then. I wouldn't have seen her."

"I'm going to check."

For Sally to come in and go straight her room with out abusing someone was so out of character that Ruth started to wonder if this was a joke. As she walked through the door of Sally's suite she saw her on the bed with her hands covering her face. "Sally. I'm here. What can I do for you?" Ruth asked, her voice trembling with confusion. "Why aren't you on the plane?"

"I don't know…"

Sally sat up and padded the bed signaling Ruth to sit. Another surprise, Sally never acted like this. In the next hour Sally offered no explanation why she suddenly changed her mind about the trip and explained what she wanted Ruth to do. Ruth felt like she was in the room with a stranger. She was not sure what she thought was odder, the things Sally wanted or the way she asked. Sally was almost kind and was making requests more than dictating orders. When Sally told her she was going to pick up Carl Ruth became alarmed. She wondered if her boss had had a stroke.

"Sally, I think I should go with you. You don't seem well."

"That won't be necessary. I'm going to lie down for a bit and then leave this afternoon," Sally said as she stretched out on the bed. "Please tell Matilda not to disturb me. I want to take a nap."

Again Ruth had to sit down. "Please!" She never heard Sally say the word. She looked at Sally, "Will do. I'll get started on these things right away. Let me know if you need anything else."

"Thank you Ruth."

Ruth had to get out of there. "Thank you" were also words she never heard her boss say and it was unsettling.

Matilda saw Ruth was pale when she came into the kitchen so she gently held her by the arm, "My goodness. You look like you have seen a ghost!"

"I think I have."

Sally's nap lasted eighteen hours. Her energy had been sapped by the emotional overload. And her sleep was filled with dreams. Things she forced herself to forget and would have been night-mares before became comforting. When she awoke she felt like she had been cleansed from the inside out. She was also confused. She looked at the clock and did not know if it was eight AM or PM. She looked out the window to see the morning sun.

Sally got up and decided to shower before the drive to pick up the boy. As she got ready she realized most of her make-up was still in her luggage. Normally this would have been a disaster, but not today. She found a few pieces she did not pack and took less time to paint her face than she had since her college days.

Sally saw Ruth sitting at the kitchen table and Matilda standing at the stove when she walked in. Both did a double take. Ruth could not help it. "Sally, you look great!" she said seeing her boss for the first time without over-done face paint.

"It must've been the extra sleep. I had no idea I was so tired," she said as she sat across from Ruth. "Did you get the carpenter started?"

"Yes. He started yesterday and said it'll be done by noon. Everything else is all set too. Are you going to get Carl?"

"Yes. I'm going right away."

"Right after some coffee and breakfast," Matilda said as she set a cup and plate in front of Sally.

"Thank you. I am pretty hungry come to think of it."

Ruth and Matilda did not know how to react to the new Sally. They were also nervous the bitchy Sally would raise her ugly head at any moment, but it did not happen. They had a pleasant conversation as Sally enjoyed her breakfast then left to pick up Carl.

Sally felt the person she had chosen to become ten years ago trying to resurface. Thoughts nagged telling her she was crazy. You don't want that boy in your house. What're the girls going to say when they find out you abandoned your friend on the plane? What are you thinking? There is no way this can turn out good for you. She felt like she had a little devil sitting on her shoulder screaming into her ear trying to make her turn the car around and fix the mess she made. But another voice held control. It was not that it was louder, just the opposite, it felt better.

When she parked at Churchill's she sat in her car for a long time. Part of her was scared out of her wits but another part was getting comfortable with the decision. She knew it was not going to be easy. In fact it would most likely be very, very hard.

"I thought you said you wanted to talk," said Carl.

He was going nuts trying to figure out what was happening. Sally was not abrasive as usual but not friendly either. In the first hour of the drive it was all small talk. "How was the school?" "Did you make friends?" and the like. She did not explain why she picked him up. Carl wanted to calm down but in order for that to happen he needed some answers and those were not coming. It occurred to him when he did get the answers he might be worse off, if that were possible. Why else would she be so elusive?

Finally Sally found the words. "Look Carl, I know I've not made things easy for you. But you have to understand this isn't easy for me. I think we both have to make some huge adjustments and it might be hard."

"I'm sorry Sally, but I have no idea what you are talking about. What kind of adjustments? A couple of hours ago I was in class and now we're going to your house and I have no idea why or what is going to happen. Are you sending me someplace else?"

"No. I want to try to make it work at the house. I know you want to go to school with your friends and you didn't like the idea of boarding school. To be honest I don't blame you. It was a dump."

Carl had to smile. What she thought was a dump felt like a prison to him. But he relaxed. If he heard her right he was going to start his new high school with his friends and still have some summer vacation left. It was exactly what he wanted. But then he remembered the tension between him and Sally whenever they were together. What bothered him the most was that he was not sure whose fault it was, his or hers.

Even though it was the best he could have hoped for he still wondered if it could work. He hated the boarding school but living at Sally's was no picnic either. He stewed on it and said, "Sally, I can follow your rules and I promise to stay out of your hair. I hope that's enough."

"I don't think that's going to work."

His heart sank. He thought he said what she wanted to hear. "Well, what then?"

Sally turned and looked at him and then back at the road and explained. She did not go into detail about her past or why she had become the person she was. She was not even sure herself. But she did talk about how she felt uncomfortable when she dropped him off at Churchill's. She also explained she felt miserable around him because it reminded her of all the things she lost. Even before the accident ripped his parents away she found it impossible to be comfortable in his company. But it bothered her when she saw how miserable he was when she left him in the dorm.

"I don't know. Something snapped inside and it scared me."

"Why?"

"That's just it, I don't know why. All I know is the accident wasn't your fault and not mine either. But it changed our lives forever and so far we haven't handled it very well. At least I haven't. I can see that you've tried."

Carl could not believe they were having a real conversation. Before, it was always orders of what and what not to do. Now she was talking to him, not at him. "I'm getting confused."

When they were half an hour from the house the atmosphere in the car changed. Even though they had not talked much, they talked. It was a start and Carl was hopeful. All of his hopes had been dashed over the last few months and he became afraid to let himself go there. But this time it was different.

"Sally, thank you. I appreciate your getting me out of that school. Maybe we can make this work. At least I hope so."

"It's not going to be easy but I'll try. I think if we're patient with each other, more of you putting up with me than me with you," she said as she looked over at him and smiled, "we might be able to make this work."

Her smile cracked his defenses. The only other time he saw her smile like that was when he looked at her in the mirror after she taught him to shave. "I promise to do my best."

Carl was confused when Sally parked in front of the grand entrance instead of the garage. "What's going on?"

"If we are going to make this work we're going to have to make some changes. To be honest I'd rather you use the kitchen door, but I also don't want you to feel like you have to. I want you to feel like this is your home and not just my house."

Carl was floored. She wanted him to feel at home? It sounded good but he could not see himself ever feeling that way. Not at Sally's house at least.

"Thanks Sally, but that's okay. I'll use the kitchen door."

She turned off the car. "Not this time."

They walked up the steps to the over-sized double doors. Carl stood behind her as Sally unlocked the door, walked in and motioned him in. He started through the door when she screamed, "Carl!"

His heart was in his throat. What did he do? He was just walking through the door and now she was screaming at him. "What?"

"Wipe your feet, please," she said regretting her outburst. Some habits were hard to break.

They chuckled. "Good idea. I can promise you one thing, I'll never forget to wipe my feet before walking into a house again!"

As they walked to the kitchen Carl saw roses all over the place. He felt like he was in a flower shop and they were all he could smell until they got close to the kitchen. Then he smelled something that made him hungry. As they walked in Matilda was at the oven.

"Perfect timing! Dinner will be ready in about ten minutes."

Carl saw his favorite foods waiting. "You did all this?"

"I figured you'd be starved after that long drive," Matilda said as she put down the platter and hugged Carl. "Welcome back!"

Sally felt that pang of jealousy again watching her maid hug the boy, but said, "Smells great. Thank you Matilda."

Matilda was again unsettled with the way Sally was behaving but was thinking, "I can get used to this." She looked at Carl and said, "Go wash up for dinner."

"Wait!" Sally yelled. Carl and Matilda looked at her and Sally said to her maid, "Are you sure his bathroom is ready?"

Matilda looked at Sally with understanding, "Oh yes, I almost forgot. Carl, use the guest bathroom, I still have cleaning chemicals soaking in yours."

"Isn't that against the rules?"

"I'd prefer you to use yours. But let's call it a request and not a rule. Go ahead and use the guest bathroom this time," Sally said as Carl left the kitchen. She looked at Matilda and they shared the universal look of "That was a close call."

Carl could not believe his eyes. It was the biggest and fanciest bathroom he had ever seen. Next to the toilet was another thing that looked like a toilet but did not look like a toilet. He had no idea what it was for and knew he would be too embarrassed to ask. After he got cleaned up he went back to the kitchen to find it empty. "Hello."

"In here." He heard Matilda from the dining room.

He walked in and saw two place settings and Sally sitting at one at the large ornate table. "Sit down and enjoy, I'll take your things up," Matilda said.

Carl was uncomfortable. They never shared a meal alone together except at the steak house. He saw Sally was also tense.

"Sit down and eat. It's going to get cold."

All in all things went well. Although the tension never completely left the room they were still able to talk as they ate. Both were standoffish and there were a few times the silence became awkward but they made it through the meal.

As they were finishing Carl became more comfortable, let himself have eye contact and it hit him. In the car he was looking out the windshield most of the time and never got a good look at her. Now they were facing each other and he could really see her. "Wow," he whispered.

"What?"

"I can't believe how much you look like mom. I noticed it before, but now I can see you almost look like, or looked like, twins."

Sally smiled, "Is that okay?"

"Yea. I think it is. Strange, huh?"

"We have a lot of strange things to get through," she said and explained what happened with her make-up and why.

"You were already on the plane?"

"I didn't get off until they were closing the doors."

"What made you got off?"

"I'm still not sure…"

"Well, for what it is worth, I think you look better with less makeup," he said immediately regretting it. He thought he blew it.

"Really? Maybe I'll go to the beauty parlor tomorrow and experiment. Sometimes it's good to change things up," she said, not realizing the irony.

They talked as Matilda cleared the table and then brought out her homemade fudge. "I thought you'd like this tonight."

"You have no idea how much I was going to miss your cooking."

Everyone laughed and finished the fudge. Then Carl said, "I'm a little tired. They made us get up early at Churchill's. I want to go up to my room if that's okay."

"Sure," Sally said.

As Carl started towards his room he thought it strange that Sally was following him. He saw Matilda smiling as he walked out of the kitchen. "What?"

Matilda acted as if she had been caught doing something wrong. "Oh, nothing. It's just good to have you home."

That word again. Home. Carl wanted to be comfortable saying or thinking that. But this was not his home yet. Not in his mind.

He took the stairs with Sally still in tow. He stopped and looked at her. "Good night Sally and again thank you. I'll do everything I can to keep you happy and stay out of your way," he said thinking that would stop her from following him.

"We'll have to take it one day at a time. I want to make sure you're all situated up there," she said as she passed him.

He wondered why Sally insisted on going with him. It felt strange but he did not dare say anything. He thought their truce was too fragile. He followed her and could see everything looked the same as when he left with the only change being on the door that led out to the balcony. "What's that?"

"Let me show you," Sally said as she walked to the door and opened the new doggy door.

Mutt bolted in and jumped on Carl knocking him down. Between the dog's frantic licks and whimpers Carl yelled, "Mutt!"

As Carl sat up he looked at Sally. "Are you kidding me? You're going to let me keep Mutt here?" he asked as a tear rolled down his cheek.

"Yes. You can have the dog here. But there're a couple of rules with this one. He's only allowed in your room inside the house. Outside he has to be in his dog pen unless you have him on a leash."

"Dog pen?"

Sally took him to the balcony and Carl saw a large area of the yard had been fenced off at the bottom of the stairs. In the corner was a large dog house. He followed Sally to it and he looked inside. He thought he would rather live inside there than the dorm at Churchill's.

"I had the contractor build this. When you're at school your dog needs to have a place where he can be comfortable."

"Sally, I don't know what to say."

"I have to tell you, that's the ugliest dog I've ever seen."

"Everyone says that. But everyone loves him."

"I can see why. He's kind of cute in an ugly way. Now come on. Let's get the first part of the rule taken care of."

Mutt was still hyper when they went into the room and Sally went to the hallway door. "Go stand in the hall and leave the dog in here."

Mutt tried to follow Carl, but when he got to the door Sally stood in front of him and said, "No," in a very stern voice and used a hand gesture. The dog stopped and sat as he turned his head looking at Sally. She told Carl to call him again and she repeated the process. "No."

She did it a few more times then went into the hallway. Mutt stayed put. "Try to have him come to you."

"Come here, Boy! Come on!" When Mutt got to the threshold he would not pass it. Instead he sat and looked at Carl with sad eyes. "How'd you do that?"

"Long story," Sally said with a tremor in her voice.

They tested Mutt a few more times. "Wow, Sally. I've never seen anything like that before."

"He's a smart dog," she said as she petted Mutt. "Maybe later I will show you how to teach him a few tricks."

All tension between Sally and Carl vanished for a few minutes. But after the joy of the moment had lapsed they could feel its return, although not as strong. Sally struggled with what to say. "I had Ruth call your friend, Joe is it? Well, he can come over tomorrow. I thought you would like to see him."

Carl was floored. "He can come over?"

"Yes. But only in your room or in the yard by the pool. Not in the rest of the house. There're some very expensive things in there and I don't want them disturbed. Understand?"

"Sure. How about the kitchen?"

"I suppose that'll be fine, but that's it."

Carl felt like he was dreaming as she walked down the hallway. He could tell she was tense and did not want to push it but had to say it. "Hey, Sally." She stopped and looked at him. "Thank you."

She nodded her head and walked off without a word.

CHAPTER 21
RENEWED

It took awhile to figure out where he was when he woke up and he was surprised to feel Mutt licking at his ear. "So, it wasn't a dream," he thought. He was thankful not to be at Churchill's and felt sorry for the boys left behind. He looked around the room and realized it was about half the size of the room he shared with ten others. "This is much better…"

He got up and walked onto the balcony. In the daylight he saw the dog house and the part of the yard that was fenced off. "Looks like you have improved your living conditions too," he said to Mutt who twisted his head then went down the stairs to run around.

Carl reacquainted himself with the carwash with a long, hot, steamy shower. He could not believe how good it felt and did not miss having to share like at Churchill's. His mind drifted from his mom and dad and back to Sally. She seemed so different and yet the same. She was nicer and it was the first time they ever really talked. But he thought the old Sally was just beneath the surface waiting to get out. So he decided to keep his guard up. The one thing he learned over the last few months was that things could change in a big way in a millisecond.

Sally realized that what used to be her worst fears were coming true after hanging up the phone. Her friend filled her in on the recent events. It had been just a couple of days but the rumor mill was charging ahead with full force and she was the only subject. The friend she abandoned on the airplane wasted no time when she arrived at Paris. She called everyone and let them know what happened. Sally could not begin to imagine what they must have been saying but she knew it was not going to be good. In fact it was going to be a disaster. She thought about the scuttlebutt that would be bouncing off the walls at the club and wondered if she would ever have the courage to go there again. If this had happened a few days ago she would be scrambling to find a way to get the situation under control. Strategic phone calls rounding up her closest friends to hide behind until something else came up to distract the attention would have been first on the list. Now she was almost calm. She thought about the people she called friends and realized they were not friends at all. In fact she was trying to figure out what she liked about them in the first place. Then she looked at herself. "Is this what I've become?"

She struggled to think of a single sincere moment she shared with any of them over the last ten years and came up blank. All of the lunches and get-togethers had been nothing but posturing to improve image and status. Sally also realized she did not know her so-called friends; she only knew what they wanted her to see. She came to grips with the fact that they knew her in the same way. "Why is, or was, image so important?"

Understanding the real situation did not make her feel any better. The emptiness was uncomfortable as she struggled to come to terms with her new reality.

Carl could smell Matilda's cooking as he came downstairs.

"How's French toast sound?"

"Sounds great!" He walked to the table and saw Ruth working on some papers and punching a calculator. Sally was standing behind her and they looked frustrated. "What's up?"

They looked at him and smiled. It was unnerving to be so close to Sally but her smile dulled the chill. "We've been trying to figure this out for an hour. We can't get the checkbook to balance and can't find the mistake."

"I've gone through it a hundred times and I still can't make it right," Ruth said.

"Can I look at it?"

"Go ahead, but it's not going to do any good. I'm going to have to have the accountant fix it on Monday," Sally said.

He looked at the figures for a few minutes and wrote on a piece of paper. After a couple more minutes he showed his work to the women, "Does this look right?"

Ruth studied it and looked at Sally and then back at Carl over her reading glasses. "I've been working on this all morning and you find the mistake in a few minutes?"

"You put one of the figures in the wrong column on the first page. Easy mistake, easy fix," Carl said like it was no big deal as he started to eat his breakfast.

Ruth and Sally shook their heads.

Later that morning Carl and Joe were sitting by the pool catching up. "It's great to have you back. I was pretty bummed when you left."

"Nowhere as much as I was to leave."

"This place is incredible. I knew this was a nice house, but I had no idea it was this nice. I'd kill to have your room! It is a long bike ride, but whenever you want to hang out here, I'm all in."

"It's cool and being able to have Mutt here makes it all the better."

They spent the afternoon swimming and playing with Mutt in the backyard. Carl had been back for less than twenty four hours, but he already felt like Churchill's was a lifetime ago.

Sally was standing at her window watching the boys. She could hear the muffled laughter through the window and could not help but be reminded of a time in her childhood when she was happy like that. Before Carl moved in and on very rare occasions she would allow herself to think back on her teenage years and it was always with sadness. When the memories haunted her she would force the images from her mind. This time was different. She surprised herself as she smiled and remembered swimming with her sister. Just like the boys were doing now, they would laugh and play like they hadn't a care in the world. For the first time in a very long time Sally realized it was a time of innocence and joy. And she was thankful for the memories. But something was still tearing her up inside. Part of her wanted to fall back into the habit of resenting what she lost.

She went into the kitchen and saw Matilda carrying a tray with drinks and sandwiches. "Is that for Carl and his friend?"

"Yes, I figure they must be getting hungry burning up all that energy."

"I'll take it out to them."

Matilda stood frozen.

"Hungry?" Sally asked as she walked up to the pool.

Carl looked up and was amazed to see Sally with a tray in hand. Without the heavy make up she looked kinder. And she was dressed differently also. Everytime Carl had seen her before she wore clothes that were gaudy and enough jewelry to sink a small boat. Now she looked, well, normal. Like a real person. And like his mom.

He remembered before how it unsettled him when he saw the resemblance of the sisters. This time he smiled.

As the boys climbed out of the pool and dried off Joe asked, "What kind of sandwiches are those?"

"Tuna salad."

Joe made a funny face. "That's okay. Thank you but I hate tuna salad."

Carl said, "But this is Matilda's tuna salad. Go ahead and try it."

Joe slowly picked up a half and looked at it with a funny face. He held it to his nose and raised an eyebrow. "This sure doesn't smell like tuna salad." He took a little bite, then another. Then he ravaged the rest of the sandwich. "Okay, I guess I like tuna salad."

Carl and Sally smiled. Another victory for Matilda's cooking.

"Carl, I was thinking of going to the city on Monday and you might like to come along. We can get the things you'll need for school. I don't think you'll want to wear the uniforms from Churchill's."

"Just you and me?"

"Just you and me. We can make a day of it."

Carl almost panicked. All day with her alone? It had been okay the day before, but he did not have a choice. Now he tried to think of what to say as he was freaking out. Finally he said, "Okay," not wanting to upset her.

"Great! We'll leave at nine and be back in time for dinner," she said as she turned and carried the empty tray back to the kitchen. She was freaking out too. She had no idea why she told the boy she wanted to take him to the city; it just came out. Sally was starting to wonder if she was losing her mind.

Later that night Sally went into Carl's room and saw the boys sprawled on the floor. They where fast asleep and Mutt was on his back between them, snoring. Sally pulled a blanket from the bed and covered the dog and boys. She looked at Carl, again being reminded about the good days from her youth. She was still at odds. In a way she wanted to get herself back to being the careless social-ite. It was easier and she was in control. But watching the boys play and hearing their laughter made it impossible. She began to feel like she was living inside someone else's skin.

The rest of the weekend went the same. Carl and Joe playing games and swimming, and Sally trying to figure out just what the hell was going on with her.

CHAPTER 22

REMINDERS

Carl was still not used to the old-time alarm clock's loud clanging so when it went off he was shocked wide awake instantly. Mutt nearly jumped out of his fur, leaped off the bed, and ran through the doggy door to escape the noise with his tail between his legs. Carl laughed as he watched and remembered what was planned for the day. He became somber and if he had a tail it probably would be tucked between his legs, too.

Even though Sally was nicer she still carried an uncomfortable air about her. On the few times he was around her over the weekend he still sensed the tension but it was different. He did not feel anger or resentment, just awkwardness. He could tell she felt the same. Now he was going to spend the day with her? "What was I thinking?"

Sally finally got a good night's sleep. It was not because she was feeling better, it was because she was exhausted from trying to adapt. As she was getting ready she wondered if it was a good idea to spend the day with the boy. At first she thought if she made the effort and tried to smooth things over she might be able to find relief from her emotional agony. But she had misgivings. Maybe she should have just taken him to lunch. Sally knew it was too late to make any changes. She was already unsettled internally and did not want to look like it on the outside. "I can do this…" she thought. Her biggest frustration was that this was a situation she could not buy or manipulate her way out of and it was going to take real personal effort.

Matilda and Ruth were drinking coffee and talking about their boss. They agreed the Sally who left for the airport days before was very different than the one who returned unexpectedly. But they found it difficult to understand the changes. Sally still had a commanding air about her, but now she also was softer.

"I think she's struggling with something, but I have no idea what," Ruth said.

"I know what you mean. I think she's trying to come to terms with things but she has no idea what the terms are. She's more pleasant, at least not as demanding, but watching her struggle like this is unsettling."

Carl walked in and said good morning. They could tell right away he was tense. "Hungry?" asked Matilda.

"I don't think I could eat right now."

Matilda looked at him with concern. It was the third time he turned down her cooking and her old stand-by of making him feel better failed. "It's just one day. Maybe you will enjoy it!"

"Maybe."

Ruth said, "I'm not sure, but I think this might be Sally's way of trying to make things between you two better. To be honest, I'm amazed she's making the effort."

"I'll try to make the best of it, but I'll be glad when its over and I'm back in my room."

Sally walked into the kitchen and looked Carl over, "No, no, no."

"What?"

"I had Ruth make reservations for lunch at a very nice restaurant. They're not going to let you in wearing that t-shirt. The jeans are fine but go put on a shirt with a collar."

As he went to his room Sally gave last minute instructions to her staff. Again, it was not the old demanding tone. But not kind or friendly either.

When Carl came back into the kitchen Sally said, "Ready to go?"

He nodded and they went to her car. As soon as the door closed behind them Ruth looked at Matilda and said, "I think they're in for a long day…"

The car was silent. Carl thought he should say something but when he opened his mouth no words come out. Sally felt the same. He was looking out the windshield and noticed where they were. "Sally, is it okay if we stop here? I want to show you something."

At first Sally wanted to say no, but she pulled into the parking lot and turned off the engine. "What did you want to show me?"

"Over here," he said as they got out and walked to the intersection. "This is where it happened. Where mom and dad died." He went into the details like the store clerk did months before. He pointed to where the cars were coming from and to the exact spot of the crash. There was no trace of the accident. He figured the rain washed away the blood stains. "If they'd been a second sooner or later they'd still be here."

"Carl, there is no way you can blame yourself. We've talked about that."

"I know. I just wish I didn't oversleep that day."

"You still think about them a lot?"

"All the time. But it's getting easier. I can't believe how much I miss them," he said as a tear formed in his eye.

Sally was speechless. She saw his struggle and wanted to say something to ease his pain. She gave him a hug, to her surprise. She held him tightly and he slowly started to hug her back. They stayed like that for a few moments and Carl started to sob uncontrollably. It lasted a long while and Sally could feel the stress leave his body. "Sometimes it's good to let the bad stuff out."

"I'm sorry."

"No sorry needed. It's completely understandable. Anytime you want to talk about it I'm here. We'll get you through this, okay?"

"Okay."

Back in the car they started to have a real, honest-to-God conversation and Carl could not believe it. He told her about Kim and how he was disappointed he lost her address in the move from Churchill's and hoped she would write to him soon.

"She sounds like a nice girl. Is Kim your first girlfriend?"

"Yea. The first girl I ever kissed…"

Sally glanced and saw his cheeks were flushed, so she made a point of looking out the windshield hoping it would make him less uncomfortable. "Sounds like you like her a lot."

He opened up about how he was dealing with his parents' death. "It's strange, but sometimes I feel like they're in the room with me. And I dream about them all the time. Sometimes I'm okay with it and others I'm a wreck."

"Some things take more time to get better," she said realizing she was giving herself advice too.

Carl told her about when he found out about the accident. "I don't think I've ever been more scared."

"I'm sorry I wasn't there to help you."

Carl's jaw dropped. He could not believe how sincere she sounded and how comfortable he was becoming with her. "Have you ever gone through any thing like that?"

Now it was Sally's turn to be surprised. For the first time in a very long time she opened up a little about her childhood and high school days. She shared stories about her and his mom that Carl never heard. In some ways it made him sadder for the loss but it also made him feel closer to his mom. "We were really close when we were growing up. I feel badly that I let us grow apart."

Carl was in pure shock. He never heard Sally admit she was wrong about anything. "Why do you think it turned out like that?"

He thought he blew it. Sally clammed up and Carl could tell his question hit a nerve. He became alarmed as he saw a tear run down her check. "Sally, I'm sorry. I didn't mean to…"

"It's alright. You didn't do anything wrong. I'll tell you, but not today. I guess you can say I'm still trying to figure things out myself."

"Believe me, I know what that's like."

Sally told him about her job working with animals and desire to go to college to become a vet. He wanted to ask something but was afraid to. She could sense his thoughts and asked, "What?"

Carl took a moment to gather his courage. "You told me you hated animals."

"Another long story I'll tell you some day. But I have to tell you, Mutt is really growing on me!"

The rest of the drive was pleasant. They let their guards down a little at a time and when they pulled up at the restaurant anyone who saw them would think they were close. A far cry from the way they were a few days before.

Carl's eyes grew wide as they were seated. He thought the place where he had the steak a few months before was amazing, but this place put it to shame. "I'm glad you made me change my shirt," he said as the waiter put a napkin on his lap and made him uncomfortable. He opened the menu, surprised he could not read it. "Sally, I have no idea what this says."

"Just tell the waiter what you like and he'll fix you up. Everything here is fantastic and French."

Sally ordered a soda and a Mimosa. When the waiter placed the order on the table Carl saw the little bottle of Champagne and glass of orange juice and his stomach tightened. "Are you alright?"

"I'm fine. I just remember that stuff from last time."

Sally remembered Carl's mistake at the reception and smiled. "Believe it or not you might like this when you're older."

"Don't count on it."

Everything was fine until Sally became clearly upset. Carl was getting ready to ask her what was wrong when three women approached the table and talked to Sally. The conversation had an edge to it.

They acted as if Carl was not there and grilled Sally about her sudden departure from the airplane. He could hear the "I can't believe you would do something like thats" and the "what were you thinkings." The women were more than rude. They were abusive and cruel in both their tones and words. Carl saw Sally was trying to defend herself, but the women were relentless. Carl had enough. "Hey look, we just sat down to have lunch. We don't need you here to ruin it."

One of the women looked down at him with a scowl on her face, "Why don't you mind your own business."

"Well, why don't you just leave as alone and go find someone else to chew out, lady."

"Look here young man, I'll not have you to talk to me in that tone. Do you have any idea who I am?"

"Nope and I don't give a crap. All I know is we were just sitting here and you showed up and chewed out my Aunt Sally. You're the ones who are wrong here."

It was clear the woman was getting ready to fire off another round of insults when Sally stood and said, "Come on Carl, this place doesn't feel as nice as it did. It has something to do with the clientele."

The women were in shock as Carl and Sally walked out leaving them looking awkward standing around an empty table.

Carl had to run to keep up with Sally, "Who were those women?"

"Friends of mine."

"Sure didn't look or sound friendly to me."

She stopped and turned. "You know what? You're right, it wasn't friendly at all. Thanks for sticking up for me. I don't remember anyone doing that before."

"I thought I had to. Sorry, but they were real bitches."

She reflected and smiled, "You're right! And you can call me Aunt Sally anytime you want."

They were still hungry and Sally said to Carl, "I don't want to go back in there, so you choose what we have for lunch."

He saw a hotdog cart on the corner. "How about a hotdog?"

Sally looked like she was going to be sick. "Hotdog? I don't eat hotdogs."

"Come on, everyone eats hotdogs!"

"I haven't had a hotdog since I was a kid and I have no intention of having one now."

"It's all about how you fix them up. You have to have the perfect balance of mustard, relish and all the other good stuff. My dad and I used to look forward to them. The ones from the cart are the best!"

"I don't know…"

Carl ordered two dogs. He took great care of putting just the right amount of fixings on them. "Try this. If you don't like it we can get something else."

Sally looked at it and held it away from her body like it was a snake. "I don't know. It doesn't look very good to me."

"Just take a bite."

She looked at it and thought, "What the hell." Carl watched her take a bite and saw she liked it.

"I told you! Sometimes a good old fashion dog hits the spot."

She did not want to admit it, but it did taste good. She also had to smile. Twenty minutes before she was sitting in a fancy French bistro ready to spend a couple of hundred dollars for lunch and now was standing on a crowed sidewalk enjoying a two-dollar hotdog.

The rest of the afternoon they spent shopping. The subject of his future came up. "The headmaster told me you're gifted in math. He couldn't believe your scores. I know you're only going to be a freshman, but we need to start thinking about your future."

"What do you mean?"

"Have you thought about what type of work you want to do when you are an adult?"

"Not really. I'm just trying to figure out how to get through high school. Math is easy, but the rest isn't."

"We can talk about it, but you should think about accounting. The money is good and you have a gift with numbers. You proved that the other day with Ruth and me."

"I guess." he said and changed the subject. "Why were those women so mean at the restaurant?"

"Again, long story and I'm not sure how to explain it," she said, wanting to avoid the subject.

Shopping complete, they began the long drive back. Carl fell asleep with his head bouncing against the passenger's window. When Sally looked over at him, he seemed at peace and she could not believe she enjoyed his company. She was also impressed with how he stood up for her when her so-called friends ambushed them. Sally was used to fending for herself and was not sure how to deal with someone else standing up for her.

It also reminded her of her predicament. After seeing how the women acted at the bistro she understood things were now very different. Spending days at the club catching up on the latest scoop might be over and be replaced with her being the subject of gossip. Sally spent the last few days worrying about the ramifications of jumping off the plane, but now she saw the results firsthand. Those women were, or at least she thought, some of her closet friends. Now they seemed like rabid dogs ready to attack. None asked why she left her friend on the plane. They rushed to judgment and could not wait to scold her.

As the road rushed beneath the car Sally was struggling to remember why she cared what they thought in the first place. It seemed important before. She thought if she could grasp the feelings from a few days before she could fill the void she was in now and get back to normal. But she realized that was not going to happen. The day she spent with the boy reminded her of how much she really did miss her old life. She was not yet ready to admit it to anyone or even herself, but she was starting to understand how shallow her life had become and what it was costing her. The armor was more than just broken now, the pieces were falling off leaving her exposed to her new reality and she was not sure she was ready to make the transition. She was also was not sure whether she had a choice.

"Carl, we're almost home."

"Sorry, I didn't mean to sleep the whole way back."

Sally smiled and said, "That's okay, I had plenty to think about."

They pulled through the gates and into her parking spot. As they were taking the shopping bags out of the trunk Matilda came out to help. Once everything was unloaded, Carl sat at the kitchen table. Matilda looked in disbelief as she watched Sally carrying shopping bags to her suite saying, "I'll be down in a minute. I want to hang these up."

"Wow," she said to herself and then looked at Carl and asked, "How did it go?"

"Great. Some of it was strange, but overall it was a nice day." He told her about the stop at the intersection, the confrontation at the restaurant and about the rest of the day. "It's hard to believe, but I had a good time."

Matilda smiled and saw Sally walking into the kitchen. "How about some hot cocoa and cookies? A perfect way to end a long day of shopping."

They nodded their heads and Sally joined Carl at the table.

The atmosphere was one of warmth and comfort and Matilda could not help but be surprised how well Carl and Sally were getting along. No tension, just them being them.

After awhile Carl said, "I'm going to go up to my room. I know I slept most of the way back but I'm still pretty tired."

They watched him walk out and then come back to the table. "Sally. I had a really good time today. Thank you."

Sally stood and said, "Me too and you're welcome."

Matilda watched them hug. Then Carl went to his room and Sally and Matilda talked. The maid could see her boss was more at peace with the boy, but she could also see she was dealing with the internal struggles that had bothered her before. "Sally, is there anything I can do for you?"

"I wish I knew the answer to that," Sally said as she left for her suite to endure a sleepless night.

CHAPTER 23
ROOKIES

The last weeks of summer vacation flew by. Carl hung out with Joe and played with Mutt at Sally's house. Although he was not ready to call it home he was becoming comfortable, feeling more like a visitor and less a stranger. Besides summer camp this was the longest he spent in one place since the accident.

His relationship with Sally improved but was nowhere near perfect. On several nights they had dinner together. For such a young man he was learning some pretty grown-up things. He was surprised when she opened up about her marriage and the mistake she made at the college orientation. As she told him her regrets he could tell it was uncomfortable for her. He wondered if she was trying to apologize for how she acted before. But their history was too full of conflict and turmoil for him to relax.

He opened up also. During one of their dinners he talked more about the passing of his mom and dad. He realized it was the first time he went into so many details. He had tried with Joe and Kim but always stopped himself from going into the ones that hurt most.

On many nights Matilda eavesdropped. She could tell the relationship was improving but saw the reluctance of trust. "Just give it time…they're still rookies," she thought.

One thing Sally never talked about was how much her life changed in a short time. Everything that was important before she got off the plane now was a burden. She used to love playing the games required to be high on the social ladder. It was fun to plan schemes and she took pride that she was good at it. She always knew what to say and the hints to drop to ensure her status. Now she did not have status and was trying to figure out why it had been important in the first place. She returned a few of the dozens of calls from her so-called friends and found the confrontation in the city had completely torched her already smoldering reputation.

Part of her wanted to care and the habit of damage control welled up inside. But when it was time to fix things she realized she did not have the energy to come up with a plan.

Sally was also coming to terms with her feelings for Carl. He always reminded her of what her life was like before she made the mistake in college. However, previously it brought pain. She was not sure when it began. At the funeral and reception? The night he said the accident was his fault? His dread when she dropped him off at Churchill's? She knew she would probably never know when he had gotten to her. But she did know she now had genuine concern for someone other than herself.

Sally went to the club a couple of times hoping to find a way to balance things. Maybe she could have the best of both worlds, a happy home and still be able to maintain her status at the club. But she soon understood it was impossible. The rumor mill had kept up its frantic pace and Sally only needed to hear a few words to understand she was the fuel of the gossip. Instead of being the respected queen she had become the jester providing the amusement.

On her last visit she had lunch with a couple friends, fending off question after question. They acted concerned for Sally but were on the hunt for more fuel for the gossip machine.

"Why on earth would you get off the plane like that?"

"And the way that boy of yours treated our friends in the city…,"

"That boy of *yours*?" Sally thought.

Her lunch companions grilled Sally about how she changed her make-up. They even expressed their disapproval of her new hair style, it was no longer flamboyant. Now it was natural.

"I have to tell you Sally, the girls and I are worried about you."

Normally Sally would have been maneuvering to regain the upper hand and manipulating. But as she looked at the women she felt an urge to strangle them. They sat with their painted faces, gaudy clothing and jewelry looking like complete idiots. They also had a look of judgment that drove Sally crazy. She was not sure if she should laugh or cry.

"Excuse me ladies," Sally said as she left the table and headed to the restroom. She stood in front of the mirror and looked long and hard. She barely recognized the image. The flamboyance was gone. She noticed that her resemblance to Jackie Kennedy was stronger now. She was more attractive not hiding behind a painted face and fake persona. She thought about another similarity she and Jackie shared with totally different results. Tragic and sudden death changed both of their lives. Jackie lost her love and her life would forever hold the void. For Sally the situation was completely different, the tragic death in her life might return the ability to love someone other than herself back.

Sally needed to get out of the club. She would not find any answers there. She walked back to the table. "Goodbye."

"What? We haven't finished and we still have questions for you?" one said in alarm.

"Sorry, I've lost my appetite. I think it has something to do with the company I've been keeping," she said knowing the jab would sting and add fire to the rumor blaze.

Sally did not go straight to her car. She stopped at the office and cancelled her membership and demanded to be taken off all of the lists. "I'll not be coming back and don't want to be contacted by anyone from here."

On the drive back she was confused. She was afraid that she just destroyed any chance of getting her life back. Yet she was relieved.

When Sally returned home and walked into the kitchen she saw Ruth. "Good afternoon Ruth. Can you please come up to my office when you get a chance? There are some things I need to go over with you."

It was still unsettling for Ruth. Although it had been the norm for awhile she had trouble adjusting to how Sally was now treating her. No more demands, and she was almost kind. She also could not believe Sally had not called her "Ruthy" once since the night she got off the plane. "I'll be there right away," Ruth said maintaining the habit of following instructions in fear of reprisals.

Ruth was in shock as she sat across from her boss. Sally cancelled her membership at the country club? It had been a strange couple of weeks for Ruth, but this floored her. For as long as she had known Sally the club and all it represented was the center of her world. In fact it was the only thing that existed.

"Sally, are you sure?"

Ruth had no idea what to expect now that Sally would have nothing but free time on her hands. She was also selfish thinking about how it would affect her. Sally's time at the club was a welcome relief as it was the only time she did not have to worry about her boss' demands.

"I think I am, Ruth. I'm not comfortable there. To tell you the truth, I don't understand why I liked it, or the people, in the first place."

"What are you going to do with your time?"

"I haven't gotten that far yet. I'll think of something," Sally said as she looked in the distance. "Have the florist bring extra roses next time. With all the money I'll be saving in club dues I can really afford it now!"

Ruth tried to be comfortable with her boss' new persona. Smiling and joking around? She had never seen anyone change so much in such a short amount of time. "Will do."

A few days before the start of school Carl was dealing with a growing sense of dread. He talked to Joe about it, asking him if he was having the same fears but Joe said he was just excited. When Carl had returned from Churchill's he was happy he was going to the new high school and to be able to see his friends. But as it approached he became uneasy. Now with the start of class right around the corner the fear was consuming him.

He walked into the kitchen to see what Matilda was making for dinner. He got a whiff and did not care. Matilda saw him walk in and smiled. She could tell something had been bothering him during the last few days. At first she thought it was the end-of-summer jitters but could now see it was something more serious. "Carl, I've noticed you have something on your mind. Wanna talk?"

"I'd love to talk about it, but I don't know what it is."

"Well, let's try to figure it out."

Carl struggled with how to begin, and no matter how hard Matilda tried to coax it out, he could not. He was becoming frustrated when Sally walked into the kitchen. "Whatever you are cooking I hope it doesn't take much longer, it smells great!"

Although it was easier for her than for Ruth, Matilda was still having a difficult time getting used to Sally's new personality. "Very soon. Carl and I have been talking. It seems he's concerned about something."

Sally sat across from Carl. "Is there something I can help you with?"

"I wish I knew. I'm bugged by something and I think it might have something to do with the new school year."

"Everyone gets nervous starting high school. It's a big step!"

"At first I thought that was it but now I don't think so. I was really excited, still am. It has to be something else."

Sally saw that he was becoming uncomfortable and had an idea. "Matilda, how about we have dinner in here tonight?" she suggested as she went off to find Ruth to ask her to bring in her box of memories.

"Why don't you two join us for dinner and maybe we can figure out how to help Carl?"

Everyone in the room except Sally was speechless and started to wonder if maybe the woman had been switched out for a nice twin. Matilda set the table and Sally opened the box and pulled out her high school yearbook and loose pictures. As they ate, Sally filtered through them and shared a story with each picture. "Maybe by looking at these we can get down to the bottom of what's bothering you."

It was just before dessert and next to the last picture when it hit him. Sally showed him a picture of her and his mom a few days before her senior year. Carl held it. He could see both were holding shopping bags and Sally said, "That's they day mom took us school shopping."

Sally saw Carl's hand trembling slightly and his eyes go wide. "Carl, what is it?"

"I think I know what's bugging me."

"What?"

"I'm excited to start high school. I know that for sure. What I'm not looking forward to is…"

"That's alright. When you're ready tell me. Maybe getting it off your chest will help." Sally could see his eyes well up.

"Mom and dad died just a couple of days before school let out last year. I was only there for one more day, but I remember how everyone acted. It was awful. What if it's the same?"

Ruth and Matilda could see Sally wanted to be left alone with the boy. "How about I serve you dessert in the dining room and Ruth and I clean up?"

Sally and Carl sat and she was struggling with what to say. She could understand why he was bothered. The feelings she dealt with were not unlike his when she went to the club last time. She hated what people were saying about and to her. Over the years she loved being the center of attention, but it was for the right reasons. At least she thought so at the time. Now it was different and the attention was painful. Sally wanted to say the right things to help him, but how could she? She did not do well handling it herself.

She could only come up with one possible solution. She thought it was a long shot but had to try. So she opened up about what had been happening at the club since his return from Churchill's. She explained how she knew what it was like to be the center of attention for the wrong reasons.

Carl listened. After awhile he could not help himself and said, "Sally, I'm really sorry everything changed for you because of me."

"You have done absolutely nothing wrong. It's their fault they're the way they are. In fact I'm embarrassed I was acting like them before."

As the words came out a ton, of bricks were lifted off her shoulders. There were still plenty left, but by trying to help the boy with his problem she inadvertently helped herself come to terms with her turmoil.

Carl saw her mind was drifting and worried he had said something wrong, "Sally, I'm still sorry. But you shouldn't let those people get to you. Who cares what they think?"

And there it was. Sally saw an opportunity. But she had to be careful not to waste it. "What do you mean?"

"My dad told me that you can't control what people think. He said as long as you do your best to be a good person it doesn't matter. So if it doesn't matter, why let it bother you?" he said with confidence hoping it would help his aunt. He was also surprised how important it was to him to help her

Sally smiled, "So what you're telling me is if I have no control over what others think I shouldn't let it bother me.

"Not one little bit!" he said, pleased he was helping. He decided to push his luck. "It really makes a lot of sense if you think about it. Who cares what everyone thinks?"

Now Sally's confidence was growing. "You know Carl, you're right and I'm not going to be bothered by those people anymore. Like you said, it doesn't matter, does it?"

"Not at all!"

She had to be careful. It had to be his idea to be effective, "Thanks! That's really good advice. Now let's talk about what's bothering you. What was it again?"

"I'm worried how everyone is going to...." He said and drifted off into silence. Sally could see the gears turning. Then he smiled and blushed. "Okay, okay. I get it. Same thing for me, right?"

"It really does sound like good advice to me," she said with an all-knowing smile and a sense of relief. It had worked.

"Yes it does. Thanks Sally," he said and gave her a hug.

For the second time in a decade Sally enjoyed a real loving embrace and how good it felt. "No, thank you, Carl," she whispered.

Chapter 24

Freshmen

In his woodshop Carl looked at the project. He was closer to the end than the beginning and was completely satisfied. He figured a few more days and it would be finished.

He knew he was blessed. Many of his friends were successful but did not enjoy their work. He poured a second cup of coffee and thought about how he got here and how it began.

The bus was filled with excited teenagers sharing stories about their summer vacations. Carl and Joe were sitting in the back. They were officially high school freshmen. Carl heard about the differences between high school and junior high from his friend's older siblings and it sounded pretty cool. One of the things he was most excited about were the electives. Computers, police club, drafting and many others. One thing he was not looking forward to was homework. He heard there was a lot more and prayed it was nothing like Churchill's.

When they got off the bus Carl and Joe were overwhelmed by the number of students. Much more than at their last school and they felt lost in the crowd. They walked up to a board with the students' names listed telling them where their homerooms were.

"Shoot, I was hoping we would be in the same homeroom together," Joe said.

"Oh well, at least I don't have to worry about you embarrassing me *all* the time."

"See you at lunch, wise guy."

Carl got lost twice as he searched for his homeroom, realizing the campus was three times the size of his junior high. He made it just ahead of the bell signaling the start of the day. The teacher welcomed the new students and handed out the schedules. When Carl heard his name, he grabbed the sheet, excited to see what elective he had. He was disappointed. His last class of the day was woodshop. "Aw man," he said out loud.

Then he remembered. His mother was going to call the school and request the computer class. It was not something he wanted to be reminded of.

The rest of the day was exciting and frustrating. He got lost a few times and was late to a couple of his classes but the teachers gave him a break. He saw friends and there were only a few times the tragedy was mentioned. Carl felt dumb thinking about how worried he had been.

At lunch break Carl sat with Joe and talked about their class schedules. Joe got the computer class and, of course, rubbed Carl's nose in it when he found out he got woodshop.

"Woodshop! That sucks. That has to be the most boring elective there is besides home economics," he said laughing. "What are you going to do, build little birdie houses?"

"You really can be a jerk sometimes."

Joe bought the school lunch and looked at Carl pull out his sack lunch from his backpack. "You brought your lunch! Kids in high school don't bring their lunch, that's not cool."

Joe saw what Carl was pulling out of his bag and recognized the sandwich Matilda made him on his visits to Sally's. "Hey, Carl. Wanna trade?"

"Not a chance!"

Woodshop was the last class and Carl noticed it was the smallest. In others there were between twenty to thirty students, in this one there were fifteen with room for a lot more. He looked at all the tools without any idea what they were for. When the bell rang a large man walked to the front of the room. He had kind eyes and a billowing voice.

"Good afternoon and welcome to woodshop 101," he said. "My name is Mr. Pecker."

The class chuckled, trying not to.

"I know. An unfortunate name for this class. But you are hereby on notice that the first person to call me Woody Woodpecker will receive an automatic F." It was easy to see he was not joking but was having fun with it too. His demeanor was kind and Carl liked him right away. "I'm going to make this easy, just call me Peck."

Peck outlined the requirements. "And we're starting today. The first project is building a birdhouse."

Carl rolled his eyes, sunk in his chair and was glad Joe was not there.

Carl rode the bus and walked the rest of the way to Sally's. He noticed the iron gates were open and a large box truck parked by the front door. As he walked up he saw two delivery men unloading large flower arrangements. He followed one and saw Sally saying where she wanted them placed. Carl could not believe how many roses filled the space. Sally saw him. "How was the first day?"

"Not bad. Overall it went pretty good. I think I'm going to like it," he said as he looked around the room. "You really like flowers, don't you?!"

"I love flowers, but roses are my absolute favorite. You can never have too may roses," she said as she was fussing with one of the arrangements.

"I don't know about that…"

"There are a lot, aren't there?"

"You can say that, but if that's what you like…"

Sally saw Carl looking at the roses and could tell he was thinking about something else. "You look like you have something on your mind."

"Did my mom like roses?"

Sally felt a tug at her heart and smiled, "Daisies were her favorite."

He looked at her and she saw he was fighting back a tear. He nodded and went to his room.

He was going into the kitchen and stopped short when he heard Ruth and Matilda.

"I can't believe this. Sally had me pack up a bunch of her clothes and put them outside," he heard Matilda say.

"I know. She wants me to set up donating them. I tried to explain she could sell them at consignment stores but she doesn't want to take the time. She just wants to get rid of them."

"It's like a different person lives here now. I can't believe how much nicer she is. To tell you the truth I find it unsettling but I don't miss the way she was one bit," Matilda said.

"I know what you mean. I haven't heard an outburst for a couple of weeks."

"I wonder why the change."

"I have no idea. I do know ever since she came back from the airport she's been different. At first she was still worked up. But now she seems fine. I have no explanation."

"I'm happy she and Carl are getting along better."

"I've noticed that too. But once in a while they look like they're still uncomfortable with each other. I hope it keeps getting better."

"One can only hope."

Sensing they were near the end of their conversation Carl walked into the kitchen. "Hello."

Matilda asked, "How was the first day?"

"Pretty good. The only bummer is I got stuck in woodshop. We're going to build stupid birdhouses."

"I like birdhouses."

"Why?"

"Why not?"

He shook his head and said, "Joe wanted me to ask you for a favor."

"And what would that be?"

"He was hoping you'd make him lunch. He saw what you made me. There's no comparison. Besides, I don't want him begging me to trade everyday."

"Well, since you put it that way, okay."

"Thanks Matilda. You always come through for me."

During the next two weeks Carl settled into the routine. The only surprise was he enjoyed woodshop. Peck taught him how to draw plans for projects and then build them. They were simple and straightforward but Peck told him he was a natural. Carl could tell other students did not like it near as much as he did and Peck could see it too. So Carl got more of his attention. He spent a few afternoons after school doing extra work at the woodshop and taking the later bus back to Sally's.

Sally was becoming comfortable with her new life. The misgivings about her decision to cancel her membership at the club faded but she did have to come to terms with one fact; she did not have any real friends. She had surrounded herself with what she now called the phonies and had no desire to be around them anymore. There were a few calls but when Ruth handed her the messages Sally threw them in the trash. She used the extra time to be circumspect. She spent her afternoons reading and thinking about her past. It was refreshing that she could look back and not feel the pain she avoided for so long. She still hated her ex-husband and had no plans to talk to him again but she also had a sense of forgiveness. She understood that letting go of the hate gave room on the inside to feel good.

She was also becoming more comfortable having Carl in the house. But not completely. It was confusing because it was so new.

Caring for the boy replaced much of the negative energy she was carrying but she was still adapting.

She also reflected how she treated her staff over the years and had pangs of guilt. She could not do anything about the dozens of maids she had gone through but she could do something about Ruth and Matilda. As she thought about it she was somewhat depressed. The only people that were close to being her friends were her maid and her assistant. But she decided to make the relationships better.

She called them to her office pretending to be upset. As they walked in she said, "I've been thinking and have decided there're going to be some changes around here."

Matilda and Ruth could not hide the fear and were thinking, "It was nice while it lasted."

"We need to add a perk for you both."

"A perk?" Ruth asked.

"Ruth, I know I've put you through hell over the years. Matilda, you haven't been here long but I could've treated you better. And you both have been good for Carl. To show you how much I appreciate it and hopefully make up for my mistakes, I'm going to give you a new assignment."

They were dumfounded. In a nervous voice Ruth asked, "A new assignment?"

"Yes. Ruth, I want you to find us a nice day spa where we can relax. We can't use the one at the club. No relaxing there. Find us a place where we can get a manicure or a nice massage. It doesn't have to be fancy, just a place we can go and enjoy girl stuff."

Now they were speechless. Although they were getting used to Sally's new demeanor this was unexpected.

Sally saw their confusion and smiled. "Take your time. Maybe you can set us up for every second Thursday of the month," she said as she left the office leaving Ruth and Matilda stunned.

Carl and Sally were talking over dinner.

"They have an open house at school. They want the parents to be there so they can meet the teachers and counselors," Carl said.

"When is it?"

"Next Monday. I'll understand if you don't want to go."

"Of course I'll go. I'd like to see your school. We can make a night of it."

"They have it set up so we go from class to class every fifteen minutes. Then we meet with the counselors and talk about what classes I should take for what I want to do after high school."

"Have you thought about that?"

"Not really. It's confusing and far off."

"Like I told you before, you'd do very well in accounting."

"I don't know. Math is easy but I'm not sure I want to be punching a calculator forever."

"Can you think of anything else?"

"I really like woodshop."

"I don't see a future in that."

"Why not?"

"You have such a gift with numbers, and I'd hate to see you waste that. How about we do this? Let's get you on track for accounting. You can always change your mind down the road."

Carl thought about it. "Maybe you're right. Math has always been easy. It'd be cool to do something easy for a living."

"Then that's what we'll tell your counselor."

Sally and Carl went from class to class at the open house. At first it was awkward, but when he introduced her as "Aunt Sally" it became easier. His math teacher told Sally what a gifted young man he was and the other teachers said he needed to study harder. On the way to the last class Sally said, "Sounds like I might have to get you some help."

"I'll make a deal with you. Give me a couple of weeks to bring my grades up. If I don't you can do what ever you think best," he said hoping she would agree. He did not want to have to deal with tutors or any extra school work.

"I can live with that."

When they walked into the woodshop he showed her two tables covered with the students' work. One had bird houses and Sally saw the example of what they were supposed to look like surrounded by the students' work. There was no comparison. The example was beautiful and the students' looked haphazardly thrown together. On the other table were cutting boards with the same set up. The beautiful example surrounded by the students' poor attempts.

"Hello, my friends call me Peck," Sally heard from behind her. The voice was not loud but still startled her. She turned around to see a large man with his hand held out to shake.

"Oh, hello. My name is Sally. I'm Carl's aunt," she said, looking a little uneasy. "This guy is handsome!" she thought.

"I've been looking forward to meeting you! I think we have a master craftsman in Carl," he said with an ear-to-ear grin.

"Really?" she said, a little giddy and shy.

"Let me show you." He pointed to the tables displaying the students' work. "Can you pick out Carl's?"

"Uh, no. He hasn't showed me yet."

"Well allow me." He picked up the two pieces Sally thought were the examples. "This is Carl's work."

She looked at Peck and then at the two projects. She took the birdhouse and examined it. "I thought this was the example."

"Nope. I teach how to follow plans and see what they come up with."

Sally looked at Carl. "You made this?"

He nodded.

The last stop was the counselor's office. They waited as other students and parents had their meetings. Carl was nervous in the days leading up to the open house. He was not sure how Sally was going to act. Now they were at the end of it and it was turning out okay. He could tell she had genuine concern for his education and was surprised the teachers liked her. She asked the right questions and acted more like a parent than an aunt.

It was hard to understand the feelings he had for her now when a few weeks before he could not stand being in the same room with her. Most of the fear and confusion was replaced with a comfort he did not understand.

When their turn came to meet the counselor Sally expressed her desire to guide Carl into taking classes that would help him get into a good accounting school. Carl noticed that she was not demanding; she was caring.

After the meeting, walking to the parking lot, Carl said, "Sally, thank you. I know these things aren't much fun."

"It's important stuff. We have to make sure we do what's best for you. I wouldn't have missed it for the world. But you're right. They're not much fun."

Carl stopped in his tracks and looked at Sally. She became alarmed, "Carl, are you alright?"

"We're really doing this, aren't we?"

"Doing what?"

"Getting along."

"Yes. We're really doing this."

He looked at her with a smile, started to walk and said, "Let's go home."

CHAPTER 25

GIFTS

Near the end of the first semester Peck and Carl were in the woodshop after school. "Carl, I have to tell you, you're coming along well. I have a few students in my advance classes but you, by far, show the most talent. I hope you stick with it, you have a gift."

"I was bummed when I first got assigned this class. But now I like it."

"There's a district-wide competition coming up in a few weeks. You should enter it."

"What, who makes the best birdhouse?"

"It's not like that. The only rules are it has to be made of wood and be your own design. Also, every bit of the work has to be done by you. No help from me. There's some tough competition."

Carl was surprised he found the idea intriguing. Besides sports he never competed in anything. "When do I have to let you know?"

"Sooner the better."

"I'm not sure what to make."

"Give it some thought and let me know."

Carl spent days struggling to come up with ideas. He wanted it to be different but also something people could relate to.

He got lucky in his other classes. As always math was a breeze. When he had trouble with science homework Sally helped. She explained when she decided to be a vet counselors had her take a lot of science classes. Ruth became his tutor for English. She was good at it. And Matilda had a love of history and social studies. He had an arsenal of knowledge to help him through the rough spots with his homework. He was also thankful the load was manageable. One week's worth of homework was equal to a day's worth at Churchill's.

One night after his studies and dinner, he and Sally were talking.

"Peck told me about a competition for woodwork. I'm thinking about entering."

"I know, he told me."

"What do you mean he told you?"

Sally blushed. "We've been talking. He's single and so am I so…"

"I don't want to know…," he said with a smile.

"Have any ideas for the competition?"

"Not right now."

"Let me think about it and maybe you'll come up with something in the meantime," she said as she got up, thankful Carl didn't press her about Peck.

Carl thought about what he could build for the competition, then gave it a rest and started towards his room. He stopped at the bottom of the stairs, looked around and it hit him. He knew what he was going to do.

Carl told Peck the next day.

"That's a great idea but it'll be a challenge, and remember, I can't help you."

"I know but I think I can pull it off."

"Me too."

"Do me a favor, don't tell anyone. I want it to be a surprise."

"No problem."

"Not even Sally."

Now it was Peck's turn to blush.

During the next weeks Carl's free time was spent in the woodshop. He sorted through dozens of woods and cut, formed and sanded them. Peck was right, it was harder than Carl thought and took longer than he planned. But in the end it turned out exactly the way he wanted. He and Peck looked at the finished project. "I think we might have a winner here. Great job Carl."

"You really think it could win?"

"You never know but my money is on you."

That night Sally and Carl had dinner together. They were comfortable in the same room, they had become family.

"Sally, I have something for you."

"What do you mean?"

"Remember when I told you about the competition."

"Yes. But you haven't mentioned it so I thought you gave up."

"I didn't give up. I finished it today, I'll be right back."

He went to his room and grabbed a wooden box. "Here, I want you to have this."

"Carl, did you make this? It is absolutely beautiful! Thank you." Sally held the box that was eighteen inches long and four inches square.

"Well yes. I made the box but that's not it. Look inside."

She saw a small clip on one of the long sides and hinges on the other. She placed the box on the table and carefully opened it. When she looked inside her eyes grew wide. "Can I pick it up?"

"Sure! It's yours."

Sally gently removed it. Carl had taken several types of wood and joined them into a wooden sculpture of a rose. She was nervous to handle it at first because it looked as fragile as the ones that filled the house but after picking it up she could tell it was sturdy. The stem was made of the hardest wood Carl could find and he placed a few wooden leaves on it. The flower was amazing. Each petal was slightly different, like a real rose, and the contrast of the woods gave it a depth that was breathtaking.

"Carl, this is incredible. I've never seen anything like this. To tell you the truth, I think it's more beautiful than the ones in our living room."

"You really like it?"

"I love it! No one has every given me a wooden rose before."

"Roses."

She looked confused.

"That's just one. I made a bouquet for the competition. Once it's over I'm going to give them all to you. If you don't mind, I'd like to give one to Ruth and Matilda."

"How many did you make?"

"Fourteen. The one you're holding was an experiment, the others are better and I wanted you to have a dozen. Peck said that's how they usually come. I told him, "Not at my house," Carl smiled.

"I'm sure Matilda and Ruth would love to have one." She was surprised she was holding back a tear looking at her wooden rose. It took a lot of work and love to create. "When's the competition?"

"Next week."

"Well, you'd better win. If not the judges are idiots!"

They said goodnight and Sally went into her office. In the bright light the wooden rose looked more spectacular. The grains and shades of the wood danced and it looked alive. Even more than a real flower. She spent a lot of money on sculptures and knew a thing or two about art, but this was beyond compare. Although she believed Carl made it, she had to be sure. She picked up the phone and dialed. When she heard Peck's voice she asked, "Did Carl really make this rose?"

"Every stem, leaf and petal."

"This sucks," Carl thought. "No one told me I'd have to wear a suit."

He was getting ready for the competition after being sent back to his room by Sally to change. "This is not a blue-jeans and t-shirt event."

He walked into the living room wearing his suit and saw Ruth and Matilda dressed up. What surprised Carl was Peck was standing in the living room also. They looked at each other and blushed with understanding. "I thought we could all go together. Is that okay with you?"

"Fine by me."

Carl sat in the back of the car with Ruth and Matilda. Peck and Sally were in front with Peck behind the wheel. Carl could sense something was going on between his aunt and teacher but decided to forget about it and talked to Ruth and Matilda. "I'm nervous. I've never done anything like this before."

"It will be fun!" Matilda said, "Thanks for inviting me."

"Me too," said Ruth.

As they walked into the exhibit room Carl became concerned. He thought some of the other projects were lame, but there were a few that would be stiff competition. The one he was most worried about was a large replica of a riverboat. The details and presentation of the project impressed him and he thought, "Second place wouldn't be so bad…"

They went to the table with his wooden roses. It was the first time Ruth and Matilda saw his work and were amazed. It was also the first time Sally had seen the completed project. She did not think it would be possible to be more impressed than she was with the rose Carl had already given her, but these did not compare and were more captivating.

"Carl, I am blown away!" Ruth said, as she looked at the bouquet.

"Wow! I can't believe it. They're beautiful," Matilda said. Then she looked at the wooden vase and saw it was as impressive as the flowers. "Did you make that too?"

"Yea, that was the easy part."

After the guests and judges spent an hour looking over the projects the time came for the vote. Normally Peck would have been one of the judges, but he had a student in the competition and was excluded. However he was allowed to be in the room where the vote was to take place. "Excuse me."

Fifteen minutes later the judges re-entered the exhibit room with Peck in tow. Ruth, Sally, Matilda and Carl were trying to figure out the look on Peck's face.

"What?" Sally asked as he approached.

"This has never happened before."

"What's never happened before?"

"This is the first time there had to be…" Peck said but was interrupted by a judge's voices over a loudspeaker.

"We are pleased to announce the award for best in show goes to the wooden roses."

Carl and his group were beside themselves. The women gave Carl hugs and Peck briskly shook his hand, "Congratulations, Carl. You deserve it."

Carl was speechless as the judge announced the second and third place winners. After the applause died and the visitors milled around Carl looked at Peck. "You had me nervous. That look on your face didn't look like it was going to turn out like this."

"Like I was saying, this has never happened. Usually there's just one vote. Whoever gets the most wins, the second most gets second and so on."

"What was different this time?"

"You got all of the votes on the first round. They had to vote again for second and third place."

Carl stood there for a moment with no expression on his face and then said, "Cool."

The crowd was thinning but there were still a lot of people hovering around Carl's wooden roses. Carl and Sally were standing nearby and overheard people expressing all kinds of accolades.

As the evening grew near to a close one of the judges came up and asked, "Are you the young man who entered this piece?"

"Yes."

"I've been a judge for a long time and don't recall anything so captivating."

"Thanks."

"Unlike the other judges I'm not a teacher. I own an art studio and think your work would fetch a good price. Would you be interested in selling?"

"No, sorry. It's already spoken for."

The stranger was disappointed. "What about these two on the table?"

"They're not for sale either."

"You sure? I'd be willing to pay three hundred for the pair."

"Thanks but I already have plans for those too," Carl said as he picked them up handed one each to Ruth and Matilda. "These are for you."

Neither said a word. They were too choked up from watching the boy they had come to care for receive all of the attention and then the gift of the wooden rose. Matilda finally spoke, "You really are a very special young man…"

"I think you're both pretty cool too."

The stranger looked on with irritation as he realized there would be no profit for him to make on this project.

Chapter 26
Maturing

R uth was sitting in front of Sally's desk gathering the courage to say what she had on her mind. It was almost summer and just over nine months since her boss cut her ties with the country club. Without the work helping Sally keeping up with the social circles Ruth had too much time on her hands. At first she believed Sally would eventually slide back into her old habits and rejoin the club but now realized the change was here to stay.

She enjoyed her time at Sally's house. She and Matilda became close friends and she and Carl also formed a strong bond. Her relationship with Sally turned into more of a friendship than an employee-employer relationship, and she felt like she was taking advantage.

Sally looked at her and said, "Ruth, you look like you have something on your mind."

"I do"

"Well?"

Ruth steeled herself. Her memories of Sally when she heard something she did not like were still vivid even though it had been a long time since any outburst.

"Sally, I love being here and appreciate everything you've done. But…."

"But what?"

Ruth decided to blurt it out, "I don't think you need me anymore."

"Why?"

"You keep paying me but there isn't much for me to do. I struggle to find ways to be useful."

"Do you like working for me?"

She did like her job but that was just it, she did not think she *was* working. "I like working for you very much."

Sally smiled. "Sounds like someone might be getting bored."

"No, that's not it. I'm happy here. I enjoy helping Carl but he's pretty independent and there is only so much Matilda and I can do around here. To be honest I think I'm wasting your money."

"I understand. It's been dull. To tell you the truth I think I have too much time on my hands also. That's why I've been thinking…"

"Thinking what?"

"We need a project."

She could not help it. Ruth's guard went up. It was not that long ago when one of Sally's projects involved endless phone calls and manipulating. "What did you have in mind?"

"I saw in the paper the animal shelter is in shambles. They don't have the funding and they're having trouble finding volunteers. Why don't you make some calls and find out what the story is?"

Ruth grew excited. The thought of having something to do besides helping Carl with his English studies and Matilda with household duties would be a welcome relief. But when Sally told her about the shelter she smiled.

Sally noticed that Ruth was acting strange and asked, "What?"

"I think I might be the right person to help you with this."

"I know, that's why I asked you."

"No you don't understand. I'm very familiar with the problems at the shelter. I've been volunteering there for several years."

It dawned on Sally. "Fridays?"

"Yup."

"Why didn't you tell me?"

"Because I thought you hated animals!"

"Let's say I've wised up!"

"What are you expecting for me to find out?"

"Find out if the county would like to have someone take over the financial responsibilities and run the place."

Ruth looked at her boss and saw her resolve. She knew Sally already had a plan and needed her help to pull it off. "You sure you want to do this?"

"I've been acting like a kid. It's time to do something meaning-ful. But I'll need your help and with what you just told me, you're not the best choice, you're the only choice."

"I'll get right on it!"

With only a couple of days left in his freshman year Carl should have been a happy kid but he was not. He could not sleep so he decided to get out of bed early and took an extra long shower in the carwash. Mutt kept trying to get his master's attention while he got dressed wanting to be petted but Carl did not notice.

He walked around the house looking at how things changed. The morning sun blasted through windows and lit up the projects he built over the last six months. At first he thought Sally was being kind to display his work but after awhile he understood she really did like it. He had to admit the projects added warmth to the house. He walked into the foyer and looked at the piece on the large table. Sally had insisted the bouquet of wooden roses be the centerpiece of the house. The way the new sun illuminated it made it even more spectacular and he smiled with the memories of how Sally bragged about it on the few times she had company. "My nephew made this for me, isn't it beautiful?"

He walked through the silence into the den. When he first moved to Sally's the walls were filled with paintings. Now one was filled with family photos. There were pictures of him playing with Mutt and others of him and Sally posing for a professional photographer. There were a few of Ruth and Matilda. The one that had captured his attention was of him with his mom and dad taken on a camping trip during his last year of junior high. As he looked at it he was reminded of how happy everyone was that day and how much they were looking forward to going camping again.

A noise from the kitchen broke his trance. As he walked in he saw Matilda pulling out cookware and Ruth walking in the door. "Wow! You're up early!" Matilda said.

"Yea. I couldn't sleep," he looked at Ruth and asked, "Why are you here so early?"

"Sally and I have an appointment to sign the final papers for the animal shelter."

"Things happen fast around here!" Matilda said.

"I know, but the county jumped on it. The crazy part is if she plays her cards right Sally might make a profit."

Matilda looked at Carl and asked, "What am I going to make you for breakfast?"

"Thanks Matilda but I'm not that hungry."

They looked at Carl and became concerned. It was not just what he said, it was the way he said it.

"You have to eat something. I can't send you off to school on an empty stomach. I have an image to keep up you know."

"I'll have toast."

Sally walked in fifteen minutes later and sat next to Carl, "Good morning. Only a couple of days 'til summer vacation. You must be excited!"

"Kind of."

Sally was concerned. "What's wrong, Carl?"

"Nothing. I'm fine…"

"Are you sure there isn't anything you want to talk about?"

"It's been one year ago today."

"What was one…" Sally said stopping in mid-sentence. She now understood. "Carl honey, I'm sorry."

"I was fine last night but I started thinking about them. I miss them so much it hurts."

"I have an idea. How about we visit them after school? I'll pick you up and go straight to the cemetery." She looked at Ruth, "We should be done by then, right?"

"With plenty of time to spare."

"You want to?"

"I think I do."

Being around a lot of kids excited about the up-coming summer break was contagious and Carl felt better. He was sitting with his friends when one asked, "Have you made up your mind about summer camp?"

"Not yet."

Joe asked, "What's the big deal. Either go or stay here and hang around with us."

Carl thought about it. Part of him wanted to stay home and play with Mutt and goof off with his buddies. He talked to Peck about taking a summer class he taught at the community college. There was a big part of him that wanted to go too. And it was only for one reason: Kim. Although it had been a long time since he had sent or received a letter he still thought about her. He was hoping if he went to Camp Big Lake Kim might be there. But he thought, "What if she was and doesn't like me anymore…"

"I still have some time to decide."

The bell rang and Carl was seated in his homeroom when the teacher called him to the front of the classroom. He handed him a note saying to report to the principal's office during the lunch break.

It was too eerie for Carl to comprehend. It been exactly one year ago when he was called to the principal's office and that did not end well. In fact it was the start to his new life and although it had been turning out well now, he still remembered the pain. His classes before lunch dragged.

When he walked into the administration offices he saw a couple of other students from his class. "Were you told to report here too?"

"Yes, I got the note at homeroom this morning."

"Do you know why?"

"I don't have a clue."

Soon the door opened and the principal stepped out and shook the three kids' hands, "This won't take long."

When the students sat down he began. "The reason I've asked you here is to inform you we're starting a new program next year. We get transfer students every year and think it'd be a good idea to have some of our best students show them the ropes. We'd like the three of you to be in the program."

The kids were relieved they were not in trouble but still confused. One of them asked, "Why us?"

"I've talked to your teachers and they all agree you are among our best students. Not just grades, but how well you get along with everyone and the way you conduct yourselves. This is an honor."

He went into details and congratulated them. "I'll get you back to lunch but first I want to give you these." He handed them each a framed certificate.

Carl stuffed the certificate deep into his backpack as we walked back to the cafeteria. There was no way he was going to let Joe see it.

After the final bell Carl stopped by the woodshop and picked up a box he built then went to where Sally was waiting in her car.

"How was your day?"

"Strange."

"Why?"

He told her what happened at lunch and reached into his backpack to show Sally the certificate.

"Carl, this is great. You should be honored! I sure am proud of you."

It surprised him how good it felt to hear her say that. He could not help but remember what it was like less than a year ago, but here they were. And now they were going to visit the reason why they were here in the first place. "Thanks Aunt Sally." He didn't always call her Aunt Sally, usually just Sally. But he could tell she liked it when he did. "And thanks for taking me today."

Sally pulled her car into the cemetery and parked as close as she could to Carl's parents' graves. They were quiet as they walked. Sally was carrying flowers she bought for the occasion and Carl his box.

Sally broke the silence, "How are you?"

"Not sure."

"That's understandable."

As they stood at the graves both were shedding tears. "I know what you mean about it seeming like a long time and not so long," Sally said.

"Yea, a lot has happened but it still feels pretty fresh."

"Would you like some time alone?"

"Is that okay?"

"Sure, take as long as you like. I'll be waiting in the car, but there is no rush."

Carl thought, "What a difference a year makes," as he remembered the limo horn blasting last time he was standing here.

He looked at the tombstones and said, "I can't believe you have been gone a year. I think about you all the time and miss you so much."

"A lot has happened since your accident," he continued and went into the details. He told them about breaking into the house, his escape to the theater, Camp Big Lake and Churchill's.

"And you're not going to believe it, Sally and I get along!"

He told them how at first he hated being around her and how things changed. Now he was happy and could call her house home. At least as happy as he could be without his mom and dad.

He lost track of time but knew he been there for a long while. "I better go. I don't want to keep Sally waiting," he said out loud as he opened the box. He pulled out a fishing lure he carved and placed it on his dad's grave. "I miss our fishing trips."

Then he pulled out his mother's gift. A wooden daisy as stunning as the roses he made for Sally. "Sally told me this was your favorite. I hope you like it." He laid it on his mother's grave then started towards Sally's car.

"Sally, thank you for this."

She nodded with a smile. There was no way she could speak. Not at that moment.

"Happy Birthday!" Matilda almost yelled as Carl walked into the kitchen.

"Thanks."

"Can you believe it! Fifteen! Such a wonderful time of life!"

"Kind of hard to believe."

"Peck is in back getting things ready for the Bar-B-Q."

He went to the pool and saw Peck unloading a large bag. Carl never saw bigger steaks. "Good morning, birthday boy!"

"Thanks Peck. Looks like there's going to be a lot of food."

"Well, I hope so. There're going to be a lot of people."

"It looks good. What's that?" he asked pointing to a large jar.

"That my boy is my super special sauce. I guarantee you it's the absolute best you ever tasted!"

"Can't wait to try it."

"Carl, I'm glad we have a moment alone. I want to talk to you about something."

"Okay."

"I wanted to make sure you are okay with Sally and I seeing each other."

"Why would I have a problem with that?"

"We never talked and I wanted to know how you felt about it."

"It's fine by me. You both get along and Sally likes you. I know that. Do you think you guys will get married?"

"HELL NO!" Peck yelled before he had a chance to catch himself. He gave himself a moment to recover then said, "Sally told me about her marriage and I had a horrible experience with it too. I don't think we will be getting engaged anytime soon. But we do like each other and it is nice to have someone to enjoy dinners and shows with."

"I'm glad you're having fun. Don't worry about me. I'm cool with it."

"Thanks Carl. Now give me a hand with this stuff. The guests will be here soon."

Carl and Peck spent the next hour setting up for the party. Sally, Ruth and Matilda brought out salads and drinks and before long the pool and backyard were transformed into party central.

As guests arrived Peck fired up the grill and was getting ready to put the steaks on when Matilda handed him a jar. "I made this sauce last night. I thought you might like to use it."

"Thanks Matilda but I have that covered. I brought my own special sauce. You are going to love it."

She opened her jar and handed it to him. "Try mine."

He dipped a spoon and tasted it. He closed his eyes and smiled. "Okay, we will use yours."

It was perfect. All of Carl's friends were there and they spent the day swimming and eating. Sally, Peck, Ruth and Matilda sat in lawn chairs talking about the animal shelter and watching the kids have a blast. The shelter was taking up a lot more time than they first thought it would but they were enjoying themselves. Peck was helping by repairing the neglected building. Ruth was getting the books straightened out and ordering much needed supplies. Even Matilda chipped in by cleaning. "This is a disaster! It looks like this dump hasn't seen a broom or a mop in over a decade. But that's okay, I'll have it cleaned up in four or five days." She got it done in two.

After Carl blew out his candles and the guests were leaving Carl and Sally were sitting together. He said, "I can't thank you enough. This has been awesome. The party, the gifts, the food, all of it!"

"I'm glad you're happy. Besides, I wanted to make up for last year"

"Don't worry about last year, today more than made up for it."

She looked relieved. "Have you decided about summer camp?"

"If it's okay maybe I can go for a couple of weeks. If it works out I'll stay longer. If not I'd like to take Peck's summer class." The only reason he wanted to go, of course, was the chance to see Kim. If he did and it worked out, he would stay longer. If not he would come home.

"That's fine. It's going to be quiet around here. I think I might even miss you a bit."

"Really?"

"Really," she said with a warm smile.

Summer camp turned out like a lot of things in his life over the last year. Good and bad. He was relieved to find Max had been barred. Carl was not going to miss the harassment or snoring. He was happy to find the twins there and they picked up right where they left off. His disappointment was compounded. He learned not only was Kim not there, but she might never be again. He was embarrassed to ask but he had to know so he asked the head staffer.

"I heard her family is moving. That's why she didn't come this year."

"Do you know where she's moving to?"

The staffer smiled. He noticed Carl said "she" and not "they." "I'm sorry, I have no idea."

Carl let himself have fun. He did the summer camp things and enjoyed seeing friends he made the year before but as the second week came to a close he got antsy. He knew Kim was moving and when they said goodbye last summer it really was goodbye. He made a point to forget about her and had to laugh when he realized he had to forget every day.

He was surprised when he called Sally that she sounded happy that he wanted to come home. She made the arrangements, and Ruth picked him up.

On the drive back Ruth and Carl talked. "I am surprised that you wanted to come back so soon."

"It was fun. I just got to thinking I want to take Peck's class." He almost opened up about Kim, but then chickened out.

Carl had a great summer. He did not have a single moment of boredom because all of his time was filled. He played with Mutt and hung out with Joe. Sally brought him to the animal shelter to help and he enjoyed every minute of it. He took care of animals and loved it when he saw his favorites get adopted.

Matilda tried to teach Carl how to cook. It was a disaster. After a week and several burnt dishes Matilda made the decision. She watched him pull an unrecognizable casserole out of the oven and broke the news. "I'm sorry dear but I think you should stick to your woodwork."

"I think you're right. I don't see myself being any good at this cooking deal."

"That's okay. Some people can cook and some can't. It is nothing to be ashamed of."

He gave her a sheepish smile. "Thanks for trying."

"You too!"

"I wonder if Mutt will eat this."

"What did that poor dog do to deserve that?"

His favorite part of summer was woodshop at the community college. He could not believe it. At his high school the shop was well equipped, but here he was overwhelmed. There were tools he had never seen and could not figure out what were for. Peck's summer class was held mornings and there were many afternoons when they had the shop to themselves. Peck showed Carl how to use the equipment and taught him new techniques. By the end of the six-week class Carl's talent magnified tenfold and it showed in his work.

On the last day of the class Carl helped Peck close up shop.

"Carl, I think you can have a future with your woodwork. You're the best I've seen."

"I like it but I promised Sally I'm going into accounting. She thinks it'll be better for me."

"I can't argue with that. I've seen your grades, and with the skills you show in math I can't blame her. But this could be a great hobby for you."

"It already is."

Carl's sophomore year was two days away and he was getting out of the pool after a day of swimming with Joe.

"Tomorrow is our last day of freedom! What do you want to do?" Joe asked.

"Today is my last. I have to go to the school and do that stupid orientation for the newbies."

"That sucks. See what you get for being such a good citizen!"

"Have I ever told you that you really can be a jerk sometimes?"

"Let me count. One, two, three…" Joe said as Carl walked off.

Later that evening Sally walked into Carl's room carrying shopping bags. She saw Carl sitting on his bed reading a woodworking book Peck gave him. She noticed some changes had taken place over the last several months. She smiled when she saw the picture of her with Carl next to the one of him with his mom and dad. She noticed a new bookshelf. Along with his school texts it was jammed with books about woodworking.

"Hey," she said.

"Hey back."

"I bought you clothes. You've grown a lot this summer and I noticed some of yours look small."

"Thanks Aunt Sally. You're right, they're tighter."

"You're really getting into woodwork, aren't you?"

"I like it a lot."

"I'm glad but I want to make sure you focus on your other studies as well. Remember what we talked about with the accounting. It's important for you."

"I remember and promise I'll get the grades."

"Okay," she said relieved. "What time do you have to be at school tomorrow?"

"They told me to be there by ten."

"I'll take you. Let's be out of here by nine thirty to be safe."

As she was walking away Carl called out, "Thank you for the clothes!"

"You're welcome, but slow down on the growing. It's costing me a fortune," she laughed.

The empty campus felt strange. Every time he was there before, a bunch of kids were around. Now it was just him and the two others who had been selected for the new program to help the transferring students. "It feels a lot bigger."

"Yea, it's a little spooky," one of the other students said.

The group walked to the administration offices. A receptionist smiled. "Welcome back to school!"

"I got screwed out of my last day of vacation," Carl thought but said, "Thanks."

"You three are here to help our new sophomores, right?"

"That's us," said Carl.

"Good. This works out well. There is one of you for each sophomore transfer, so this should be easy."

"Where are they?"

"They're in the principal's office. He wanted to welcome them personally. They should be coming out shortly."

They waited for a few minutes and the office door opened. Three girls walked out with the principal following. Carl's gaze went straight to one. The young lady was the cutest girl he had ever seen and his heart raced. Even with the braces covering her teeth she looked great.

Everyone in the room noticed the look on Carl's face and the one on the girl he was looking at. She liked what she saw too.

Carl couldn't help it. He smiled ear-to-ear as he walked up to the new girl.

"Hi Kim."

CHAPTER 27

REKINDLING

As Carl and Kim walked the halls of the deserted school it was like they were together days ago instead of more than a year. He was supposed to be telling her about school but the conversation took on a life of its own and had nothing to do with what she should expect her sophomore year.

"It's nice to see you," he said.

"You too!"

"I lost your address. I hoped you'd send a letter so I could write back."

"Your last letter said you'd write after you got to the boarding school. I waited and figured you probably met a girl you liked better."

"That would've been pretty hard to do."

"Why?"

"It was a boys school!" he laughed, "Besides, I was only there a week. One of the longest of my life."

"I thought about you a lot, Carl."

"I'm glad to hear that. I thought you'd lost interest."

"Not at all…"

Carl talked about what happened since he last saw her. At first he was not sure he should tell her about Camp Big Lake but then thought, "Why not?"

"I went back hoping to see you. They told me you were moving and I figured I'd never see you again, so I left."

"You went back to camp just to see me?"

He became embarrassed and regretted telling her. "Well, I wondered why you stopped writing and wanted to see how you were." He tried to sound nonchalant but failed miserably.

"That's sweet, Carl! They were right, we did move - to here!"

He thought, "Maybe it's good I told her after all..."

He explained his relationship with Sally, and Kim was shocked.

"I remember you told me things between you weren't great. In fact I got the impression you didn't like her."

"I didn't. She was impossible. But ever since she picked me up at Churchill's she's been different."

"How?"

"I'm not sure. She morphed into a different person. It was still hard when I got back, but as we spent time together it got easier. To be honest I'm not sure why she changed but I care for her now."

"That's great. It must make it easier."

"For her too. She's happier and the people who work for her like her now."

The last stop of the tour was where the electives were taught. "What elective do you have?"

"Computers!"

"I should've guessed."

"How about you?"

"Let me show you." He walked with her to the woodshop. The door was open and they went in. Peck was on a stepstool putting up posters.

"Carl! What are you doing here? Class doesn't start 'til tomorrow."

"I told you I had to help the transfer students."

"Oh yea, you seemed bummed about it."

"Not anymore..."

Carl introduced Peck to Kim and explained they knew each other at Camp Big Lake. Peck smiled. It was easy to see they were crushing hard on each other. "Has Carl mentioned his woodwork to you?"

"He just said he was in your class."

"Well, let me show you some of the things this master has made."

Carl blushed from the attention.

One of the walls was filled with students' work and an entire shelf with Carl's. "This is all his."

Kim's eyes grew wide. She was no expert but she did not have to be. Anyone could see how special Carl's work was. One of the wooden roses caught her eye. "Can I hold that?"

Carl smiled as he handed it to her.

"This is beautiful!"

"You like it?"

"Very, very much,"

"Then keep it. It's yours."

She smiled and kissed him on the check. "Thank you."

Now Carl's blush was in full bloom as he saw Peck's smirk.

The time came for the students to go home. Carl walked Kim to the parking lot and saw her father.

"Hi Dad! Remember Carl, my friend from summer camp?"

He did and tried to act happy about the fact the boy that his daughter had a crush on was now in the same school. "Hi Carl, it is nice to see you again," he lied, not hiding his discomfort.

Her dad looked at the rose in her hand and asked, "What's that?"

"Carl gave this to me. He made it." She handed it to him.

He turned it in his hand to examine it. "You made this?"

"Yes sir."

"This is very good work."

Kim and Carl exchanged phone numbers and planned to meet before school the next day. Sally pulled up and as he got in the car she asked, "How did it go?"

"I am having a great day!"

Sally recalled how angry he was when she dropped him off that morning. She shrugged her shoulders and drove off.

CHAPTER 28
INERTIA

Kim's transition went smoother than other transfer students because of Carl. He introduced her to his friends and soon she fit right in.

Carl noticed his friends were growing up. Their interests were changing and priorities replaced. What had been important to pre-teens turned into teenager dreams and with that came a certain amount of maturity for everyone except Joe.

Although Carl still reminded Joe he could be a jerk sometimes, it went from a daily ritual to a few times a week that his best friend still found ways to get under his skin. It became apparent Kim and Carl were a couple. They were not ready to say they were boyfriend and girlfriend, but their friends knew it was just a matter of time, and it gave Joe some new ammunition to rattle Carl.

Instead of giving him a hard time about being the good citizen Joe now had a new mantra, "Carl's got a girlfriend, Carl's got a girlfriend..."

Carl looked at him and said, "You can really be..."

"I know, I know, I can really be a jerk sometimes," Joe interrupted then started back up, "Carl's got a girlfriend...."

The students and parents were attending the open house. Sally was happy Carl kept his promise by maintaining a good GPA. At the end of the night they were walking to her car when he saw Kim and her parents. "Sally, I want you to meet someone."

"Hi Kim, this is my Aunt Sally."

"It is nice to meet you."

Sally was caught off guard then remembered Carl mentioned her over a year ago. "It's nice to meet you too."

They talked awhile and Carl noticed Kim's dad looking him over. As the adults talked Kim and Carl stepped away, "I get the feeling your dad doesn't like me."

"He's fine. He's just being a dad."

"You sure?"

"I'm sure. He said nice things about you."

"If you say so…"

On the drive home Sally said, "Kim seems like a nice girl."

"Yea, she is."

"Is that the same girl you told me about from summer camp?"

"Well, it's kind of a long story."

"I like long stories."

Carl was not sure if he wanted to open up about Kim, but decide to go ahead and tell her everything. He explained again how they met at Camp Big Lake his first trip there and about the letters and how they stopped. Then he confessed, "The reason why I wanted to go to Camp Big Lake last summer was I was hoping she'd be there."

"Wow! Sounds like you really like this girl."

"So, I thought I'd never see her again. But then I saw her at the orientation. I was really surprised and happy."

"You're still young, but I can see why you two get along. You make a nice couple."

Carl felt uncomfortable. It was strange talking to his aunt about girls. "Can we change the subject."

"Why?"

"It feels funny talking to you about stuff like this."

"Who else are you going to talk to about it?"

Carl realized she was right. Sally was both mother and father to him. He could talk to Ruth, Matilda or Peck, but when it came down to it Sally was his only family. He thought about the time between the present and his parents' accident and how much his relationship with Sally changed. He also realized his feelings for her evolved. He could not say he loved her like his mom and dad, but it was close.

"We've come a long way, haven't we?"

"What do you mean?"

Carl struggled. He wanted to be careful but also felt it important to say what was in his heart. "Sally, it scares me to think what my life would be like if it weren't for you."

She understood. "It scares me to think what my life would be like if it weren't for *you*."

"Why?"

"I know we had a rough start and it was my fault, but you crawled into my heart and opened my eyes."

"How?"

"Let's just say I didn't realize how miserable I was and what a horrible person I became. It scares me to think I might still be that way if you hadn't come into the picture."

Now Carl understood. "I guess you can say that we helped each other."

"I think you might have saved me…"

Sally pulled through the iron gates and into the driveway but neither got out of the car.

"I want you to know I'm here for you, Carl. You can talk to me about anything. You are turning into a great young man but everyone needs someone to talk to. Especially at your age. It can be a confusing time of life and I want to help you with it. You can trust me."

"I couldn't say this before, but I do trust you."

"You have no idea how happy that makes me."

They sat there in their own thoughts and understood this was an important moment in their relationship. Any misgivings or pent up resentments were gone and this conversation served to let them know they understood that now.

Carl smiled as he thought about how their talk started - Kim. Now he was even happier she was part of his life because he was not sure he and Sally would have opened up if they had not been talking about Kim.

"I guess we really are family."

"Yes we are now, and it's good to talk and get things in the open."

"You're right. I'm glad we talked."

As they walked to the house Sally stopped and gave him a hug, "I love you Carl."

"I love you too, Aunt Sally."

She smiled, "Now tell me more about Kim!"

"Do I have too?" Some things take a little longer to get used to.

Sophomore and junior years passed quickly. The stakes were higher now that the students had to think about college and what they were going to do with their futures. Sally and Carl talked about what colleges they should apply to weekly. Even though his grades were good enough to get in, it was clear that he was not going to qualify for a scholarship. Sally had Ruth do some checking on the outside chance Carl's woodworking qualified for financial aid but after some digging it was apparent that was not an option.

"That's okay. I'll just pay for it," she said to Carl. They were in her office looking at papers from the different colleges.

"I feel guilty about that."

"This is far too important to let money get in the way."

"Maybe we can figure out a way for me to pay you back."

"Now you're being silly! Just make sure you do well on the placement test. I'll take care of the rest."

"It seems like I'm always thanking you for something."

"Maybe you can redo the kitchen cabinets."

"Again? I did that last year."

"Sometimes change is good!"

He walked out of her office thinking how grateful he was for all she was going to do for him. But he was also uneasy. It was just before his senior year and he knew the time had come for him to decide and accounting looked like the best fit. He knew Sally thought so, in fact she insisted. But he was having a hard time seeing himself sitting behind a desk crunching numbers for the rest of his life. "Oh well, I'll have to make it work, I guess…" he thought.

In his room Mutt was sprawled on his bed. The dog was getting older but still spunky. Carl petted him as he looked around. There had been a lot of changes over the last couple of years. There were more pictures. He looked at one of him and Sally standing in front of the animal shelter. It was a success and Sally and Ruth spent most of their days there taking care of the day-to-day details. Carl enjoyed his part-time work there during the summer vacations.

He looked at one of him and Kim. They were now full fledged boyfriend and girlfriend. The transaction could have gone smoother except that her father put up resistance to the idea. Sally helped with that too. She invited Kim's parents for dinner on several occasions and soon they saw in Carl what everyone else did. A really good guy with a heart of gold. Carl unexpectedly sealed the deal.

Kim's mother invited Carl for dinner and as she started to prepare the meal she discovered she was missing some ingredients.

"Come on Kim, come to the store with me."

Kim was nervous. She knew Carl was not going to enjoy one-on-one time with her dad. But she also knew that was the plan in the first place. Her mother tried to open one of the drawers but it was stuck. She looked at her husband and asked, "Are you ever going to fix theses things? None of them work and I've been asking for months!"

"Yes dear."

After they left Carl asked her dad if he had any tools. The trip to the store was an hour. In that time Carl fixed every drawer in the kitchen, and when they got back her mom opened one to put her keys in. It was smooth as silk. Surprised, she tried them all. "Thanks, honey!"

"No problem. I'm sorry it took so long." He gave Carl a look that said, "Can we keep this a secret?"

Carl nodded. They got along pretty well after that.

There was a picture of Carl standing next to Peck in front of a newer model truck. Carl smiled at the memory of Sally giving it to him on his sixteenth birthday. His smile turned into an ear-to-ear grin as he remembered Sally teaching him to drive. It did not go well. Sally still did not have the patience. After an hour of near misses she made Carl park the truck, went into the house and called Peck. "I need a favor. Can you teach Carl to drive? I'm afraid he's going to kill me…"

He looked at a picture of him standing between Ruth and Matilda. Although he now felt closest to Sally he understood if it were not for them the bond with his aunt may never have taken place. He still could not believe how Matilda was able to keep Sally in check when she would be impossible. The memories of how frustrated Sally became at Matilda's power over her made him laugh out loud.

The picture of him with his mom and dad was still in the center. He looked at it every day and could not help but wonder what his life would have been like if it were not for the accident. Although it was rare, he still caught himself wishing he had not over-slept that morning. Sally helped him realize the accident was not his fault but sometimes he still wondered.

He walked to his desk and looked at the stacks of applications for colleges. He knew in a year he would be in one and wished he could find a way to be excited about it. He did not dread it like Churchill's, but it was close.

He knew Matilda was in the kitchen getting things ready for the party Sally planned the next day to celebrate the end of summer. A last hurrah for the kids starting school and an excuse for the adults to have fun.

"Need any help?"

"Sure, you can take the ice coolers in the garage out to the pool. Just don't touch any food. I've learned my lesson with that." She joked, remembering trying to teach him to cook.

Sally's house was again transformed into party central. All of his friends were there along with just as many adults. Many were parents of students but there were also a lot of Sally's new friends. He remembered the guests at the reception and how they acted. This was a totally different crowd. These people were down to earth and were there to enjoy each other's company with no pretense. He remembered Sally's former so-called friends were mainly trying to look and act like they were better than everyone else. There was not one of them at this party and Carl did not miss them a bit.

He noticed the difference in Sally. When she talked to her friends there was no ulterior motive or maneuvering, just sincere friendship. And even though she was a few years older now, she looked younger. It was more than the change in makeup and clothes, it was the way she carried herself and a new softness of her facial expressions.

Sally noticed Carl was looking at her and called him over "It looks like everyone's having a good time."

"Looks like you are too."

"You know what? I am."

"I like these parties a lot better than the ones you used to have."

"Let's just forget about those, I like this one a lot better too…"

Joe and Kim stayed behind afterwards to help clean up. After everything was put away and the last of the trash stuffed into cans they sat. They saw Peck and Sally relaxing together.

"Do you think they'll ever get married?" Joe asked.

"No way. I mentioned it once to Peck and he spazzed out. When I asked Sally she laughed at me."

"You can tell they like each other," Kim said.

"They do and they like it just the way it is."

They talked about the upcoming school year. "This is it, our last year before we have to start acting like grown-ups," joked Joe.

Carl thought he had grown up a few years ahead of him. He let it slide and asked, "Have you decided what you are going to do after high school?"

"My mom is pushing college. Dad wants me to work at his business. I don't know what I want to do. What about you, still focused on the accounting deal?"

"That's the plan."

"Yours or Sally's?"

"Where did that come from?" Carl asked with irritation.

"I just see how much you enjoy woodworking. I thought you'd do something with that."

"Sally thinks accounting would be better. I'm good with numbers and there's a lot money in it."

Kim looked at the large house. Even though she spent a lot of time there she was still impressed and intimidated at the same time. "Well, it's hard to argue with that. She obviously knows what she's talking about."

"Yup."

They relived the good times they enjoyed with each other and then talked about their senior year again.

"I'll tell you something. I know this last year will be fun but it also makes me nervous," Joe said.

"Why?" Kim asked.

"After this year it'll be more real. I might miss being a kid."

Carl tried to picture his future, but could not focus on seeing himself sitting behind a desk pushing pencils. "We'll just have to see how it goes…"

They sat, lost in their own thoughts, feeling excited and nervous at the same time, understanding they were very close to becoming adults.

CHAPTER 29

APPLICATIONS

"Congratulations!" Sally beamed as Carl handed her the acceptance letter.

"I thought you'd be excited. Thanks for all the help. No way could I've pulled this off on my own."

"We need to make sure to thank Ruth. She worked hard on this."

"There's an orientation in August. I was hoping you would come with me."

Sally became lost in her thoughts with the question. She remembered her orientation and the results. Years of pain, despair and living a life she was ashamed of. Then she thought about the life she had today and was grateful.

"Sally?"

"Oh, sorry. I wouldn't miss it for the world."

Kim was excited for Carl also but he could tell she had something on her mind when he told her. "You okay?"

"I'm great. It's just I'm going miss you. It's pretty far."

"We'll talk all the time and I promise I'll come back every chance I get." He wanted to reassure her.

"What if you meet someone else? I'm sure there'll be a lot of pretty girls there."

"Not a chance! I thought I lost you once. That's never going to happen again."

"Promise?"

"I promise."

With only a couple of months left of senior year the class was buzzing with excitement. They were getting ready for the prom and looking forward to summer. Some also received their acceptance letters and were elated. Sadly others received letters apologizing for rejecting their applications leaving them unsure about their futures.

Carl still spent a few days a week in the woodshop after school. He had taken every woodworking class the school offered by the end of his second year but Peck let him polish his skills.

He saw Peck sitting at his desk, "Hey Peck."

"Carl! Congratulations! Sally told me last night."

"Thanks. It was good news," Carl said without enthusiasm.

"You're happy, right?"

"I am. I know I told you how I was feeling before. But I've thought about it and I think it's a good thing."

"Then I'm happy for you. I know Sally's proud of you."

"That makes it better. She put a lot of work into it. Thanks for not telling Sally about how I felt before." Carl had a moment of weakness a few months back and told Peck of his reluctance to becoming an accountant.

"No problem. It can be scary making such a big decision. I'm glad you're good with it."

"I figure I can still do the woodworking as a hobby. For now I'm going to have to focus on my studies."

"I wish I could convince you to help me teach the younger kids during your breaks. I got approval from the principal."

"I know, and sorry. I don't see myself teaching it. When I work on projects I'm in a different world. To be honest I'm not sure I could help you teach. I'm not sure how I do it myself."

"You phase out. When I watch you work it's like you *are* on a different planet. You will have your hands full at college, but I hope you still do this. I'd hate to see that talent go to waste."

"I might have to hold off, the workload is going to be pretty heavy. Maybe you can let me come back on the breaks."

"Deal!"

At his graduation ceremony Carl had to laugh at Sally. She was the most emotional family member in the crowd and drew almost as much attention as the graduates. As he thought about the last four years he felt grateful but also sad. It was not easy to see his friends taking pictures with their parents. He missed his mom and dad more than usual. He wished they were there to see him get his diploma. As Sally walked up she could tell what was on his mind. "They would've been very proud of you…"

"I know."

It was a week before the orientation when Sally came into the kitchen and saw suitcases next to the back door. She first thought Matilda was helping Carl and her get ready for the trip, but this early? She did not recognize the luggage. Carl walked in. "What are those for?"

"I don't know."

"Those would be mine," Matilda said from behind them.

Carl and Sally turned to see Matilda dressed in a way they had never seen before.

"What's going on?" asked Carl.

"It's time for me to be moving on."

"What do you mean?" Sally asked, surprised.

"My sister told me about a family a couple of towns over that could use my help. There's a man who has two young boys and they recently lost their mother."

"What about us?" Carl asked.

"You'll be fine. You'll be off to college before you know it," she said then looked at Sally, "I've already arranged for my replacement. I'm sure you'll like her. She's reliable and probably does a better job of cleaning than I do."

"Can she cook as good as you?" Carl asked.

"Can anyone?"

"Matilda, I really need you here!" Sally said, visibly shaken.

"Sally, you're going to be fine. She will be here any minute and I'm sure as soon as you meet her you'll feel better."

Sally and Carl sat at the breakfast nook trying to think of what to say. "But why now? Are you unhappy here?" Sally asked.

"No, not at all. I'm very happy here and I know I'm going to miss you both terribly. Ruth also."

"Then why?" Carl asked, feeling a pit growing in his stomach. He recalled many fond memories with Matilda. He also knew she played a big part in soothing his relationship with Sally. She had become more than a friend. She was family and the thought of her leaving, even though he was going to college soon, did not sit well.

Sally felt the same. She recalled how much she did not like Matilda at first. Sally then laughed as she remembered times Matilda would completely control the house and how it drove her crazy. But now she was going to miss her.

"That must be my replacement," Matilda said as the gate bell rang. She opened the gate remotely and walked out to meet the new arrival. She returned with a pleasant looking woman. "Let me take some time to show her around and explain how you like things. After that we can say goodbye."

As Matilda and the new maid left Carl and Sally looked at each other, dumfounded. "Can you believe this?" Carl asked.

Sally did not answer. She found it ironic Matilda still had that power to control, in a loving way, the household and everyone in it. She struggled to figure out a way to talk her into staying and realized it was pointless. Sally never had any control over Matilda, and why should that change now?

"I'll be right back," she said to Carl and went up to her office.

When she came back she had a piece of paper in her hand and sat next to Carl.

"You okay with this?" she asked.

"I don't know. It's so sudden." Sally could tell by the tone in Carl's voice he was not okay but also understood, just like she did, there was nothing that was going to change Matilda's mind.

Matilda and the new maid came back. They heard a car pull into the driveway. "Well, that's it then. I'm not one for long good-byes so I will be leaving now," Matilda said as she turned to pick up her bags.

"Matilda, wait! I want to give you this," Sally said as she handed her the paper.

Matilda looked at the check and her eyes grew wide when she saw the amount. "I'm not going to except this Sally."

"Why? I want you to have it."

"To be honest when I first came here I found you to be a bit of a challenge, but I can now say I have enjoyed being here. Thank you for the opportunity." She handed the check back to Sally.

"No Matilda, thank you."

Matilda saw Carl was upset. "And you! I knew from the very first moment I met you that you were special but you never stopped amazing me. Do me a favor. Never stop amazing me, okay?"

Carl could not speak. He knew if he did he would not be able to hold back the tears that were fighting to get out. He nodded his head and gave her a long hug.

"Don't worry. I know you'll be happy with my replacement and who knows, maybe I'll stop in and check in on you from time to time." She picked up her bags then stopped. "I almost forgot, could you please give this to Ruth for me?" She handed a note to Sally.

Then Matilda left, being able to control her own tears until she got into the waiting car that took her away.

A few hours later Ruth walked into Sally's office. "Who's that maid and where's Matilda?"

Sally handed Matilda's note to Ruth. As she read it she shared the same sense of loss.

The college was filled with beautiful buildings, some old, some new, and surrounded by green rolling hills that gave a park-like feeling.

As Carl and Sally attended the various receptions Sally became convinced she had chosen the right school for Carl.

"I think this is going to be a good fit for you."

"This place looks like it cost a fortune."

"It does, but I told you not to worry about that. You just focus on your studies and when you graduate I'll make sure you get with a good firm."

"I'll get the grades..." he said, intimidated by his new surroundings.

With less than a week to go before he would start his freshman year at college Carl made a point to spend as much time with Kim as he could. He could tell she was worried about their separation and he could not figure out to help her feel better. He also could not figure out how to make himself feel better. Part of him was excited but he knew he was going to really miss home.

He was not worried about the same things Kim was. He knew their relationship would survive. But he also knew he would miss her and every other part of his life at home. Joe decided to start working with his dad early in the summer so they did not get to hang out much. On the few times they did Carl could tell their lives were taking different paths.

He also had a new understanding about Matilda's sudden departure. He missed her and knew it would be the same, if not more, for Sally when he was gone. He wondered if it was another lesson Matilda was teaching him by leaving the way she did. He was not sure but made a point to spend as much time with his aunt as he could. It was important to him.

CHAPTER 30

THE SCHOLAR

Carl started college thinking it would not be much different than high school. He was wrong. The work load demanded ten times the effort and instead of being able to go home at the end of the day and play with Mutt and have dinner with Sally he was stuck in the dorm trying to finish his assignments on time. The intensity of the studies would have been bad enough but it did not compare to his homesickness.

True to his word, he and Kim spoke almost everyday. It was the part of the day he looked forward to the most. Hanging up was the part he hated most.

Sally kept him up to date with the animal shelter and assuring him Mutt was fine. She also repeatedly told him how proud she was of him. He filled her in with his progress getting used to college life. "It's getting a little easier," he lied.

When he first arrived he thought the homesickness was normal. The other freshmen were suffering also. But after three months his classmates where feeling better and Carl was worse. At first he was embarrassed, thinking he was still a kid and everyone else was grown up. He made a few friends and when he talked about what he was going through they would say, "Give it time, you'll feel better."

His friends were also feeling the same pressures he was but not as intensely. For the other students it was an obligation for their parents to do all they could for their offspring. It was not a matter of wanting to; it was expected. Carl knew Sally did not have the same motivation. If Sally did not want to help with college no one would have given it a second thought. She had already gone far beyond the call of duty by taking him in and providing a loving home after the tragic death of his parents. She was not obligated to provide Carl with a college education; she did it because she wanted to. Carl understood how grateful he should be for her selfless generosity and it put more pressure on him. "There's no way I can let her down," he thought and resolved to do whatever it took to do well. But he wished he could find a way to feel better about it.

After enduring the first semester and finishing his finals Carl believed he was the happiest person on the planet. Sally picked him up at the airport and surprised Carl by bringing Kim along, and they had a nice dinner together.

After they dropped off Kim, Sally said, "It's nice to have you home!"

"You have no idea how good it feels to be back."

"How do you like the college?"

Carl wished he could be honest and tell her how much he hated it and was dreading going back. But he could not do that to her. During dinner he could tell Sally took his college education much more seriously than he did. It became an obsession and he knew if he told the truth it would crush her. "It takes a little getting used to. But I think it's going to work out."

"I saw your grades. You're doing great! Keep that up and I'll get you in one of the top firms the minute you graduate."

"I'll do my best."

"Great! Now it's time for you to relax. What do you have planned for tomorrow?'

"I want to stop by the woodshop."

"Have you had a chance to do any woodworking at the college?"

"Not one bit."

Later as he sat on his bed with Mutt nudging at his hand to keep petting him every time he stopped, Carl relaxed. He and Sally had said their goodnights and went to their own parts of the house. Now he did not have to pretend. He realized how much he hated what his life had become and what his future was looking like.

Carl reacquainted himself with the carwash hoping the steamy retreat would wash away the stress. It helped but as Carl crawled into bed he was still thinking about his predicament.

When he went to visit Peck at the woodshop he was surprised to see his work still filled a shelf. "I would've thought you replaced those by now," he said to Peck's back.

"Carl! It's great to see you! Welcome home." He saw Carl looking at the shelf. "I tell my students they have to build something worthy of replacing your work. So far no winners."

"I'm sure your students are turning out good work."

"Nowhere near the quality of yours. How's college?"

With Carl now older and Peck's relationship with Sally being what it was, they had become friends, not just student-teacher. Carl remembered he could confide in Peck but knew he could not tell the truth now in fear it might get back to Sally. "It's going good."

Peck could hear the reservation in Carl's voice. "You sure? You don't sound very convincing."

"I'm just tired. Exams took a lot out of me and I think I need to rest."

"Okay, but if you want to talk…"

"I know. How about showing me the new power tools," Carl said, pointing to the unfamiliar equipment.

"Sure."

Halfway through winter break Carl's anxiety was growing. He was having a great vacation spending time with Kim, doing woodwork and having dinners with Sally. But as the time grew closer to return to college he found it harder to enjoy himself. Sally sensed his tension and asked, "Carl, is everything alright?"

He was surprised at the question. He was trying hard to hide his misgivings and thought he was pulling it off. "Everything's great."

"You seem wound up."

This was it. It was his first, and maybe only, chance to tell Sally the truth. But when he looked at her and saw the expression of concern he knew he would have to hide his unhappiness. "I'm just getting my head ready for next semester. I think the classes are going to be tougher."

"You should relax. No reason to worry about school now, there'll be plenty of time for that soon."

"That's for sure."

He was lying to everyone. He even told Kim he was happy to be going back to college.

"You sure don't act like it."

"I'm sorry. Too much on my mind."

"Like what?"

There it was again. A chance to open up. If he could not be honest with Kim then with whom? But as the truth reached his mouth he stopped himself. They only had a little time and he wanted to enjoy every second and not give her anything to worry about. "I just want to make sure I'll have everything I need when I go back"

"Okay," she said, not convinced.

The next semester was the same as the first. Hours and hours of studying for something he did not want to do mixed with phone calls lying about how great everything was. Carl was unhappy and trapped. He thought about opening up to Kim a few times and even thought about telling Sally once, but every time he got up the nerve to follow through he became flooded with guilt.

He and Sally had very rocky start, but once they got along his life became tolerable. Once they became close he was happy, or at least as happy as he could be with his parents gone. Now with five years since the accident Carl understood just how lucky he was. He could not believe he had wanted to go to Boy's Town and how angry he was that Sally prevented it. Now he could not imagine what his life would be like if he had ended up there. All the great memories of the last few years were only possible because of Sally.

What made it harder was he knew Sally's desire for him to be an accountant was because she wanted the best for him. He thought he had the answer before and reflected on what might have happened if he was allowed to follow his plan. Growing up in an orphanage? Was he crazy? Maybe this wasn't so different. Sally might be right again and he should listen. Besides, it was costing her a lot of money, and even though she had plenty of it, he was still obligated.

Halfway through the second semester Carl adjusted. He understood he did not have to like what he was doing to be comfortable. With a new resolve he began to play tricks with his mind to help him deal with the uneasiness and it worked, for the most part. Kim and Sally could tell the difference. Carl sounded more at peace during the phone calls and they both were relieved.

It was not until the beginning of summer when his new-found strength fell apart.

Carl's hard work and dedication paid off. He was in the top five percent of his class and his efforts earned him an honor. The college had a program where the top students finishing their freshman year could be interns at accounting firms in the area. Usually these programs were reserved for upperclassmen, but the school wanted to try something new. Carl was selected to work at one of the firms for two weeks after final exams. At first he wanted to decline. The thought of wasting any of his summer was out of the question. But after he told Sally about the offer she talked him into it. "Carl, not many opportunities like this come along. It would be a shame to waste it."

The firm was close to his college and the staff let him stay in the dorms. Sally decided to visit Carl. Some of her old habits were still strong; she used shopping as the excuse.

They spent the day shopping and were having dinner.

"Are you excited about tomorrow?" she asked.

"I am. I have no idea what to expect but I'm looking forward to it."

"I talked to your counselor and she told me you are doing very well."

"It's been a lot of work, but so far so good."

"I have noticed you're getting accustomed to things."

"What do you mean?"

"For awhile I had the feeling you weren't happy."

He was still miserable but said what she wanted to hear. "It was pretty hard at first, but I'm starting to get used to the idea of becoming an accountant."

"I thought that's what you wanted."

Opps! He thought. "It is. It just took longer than I expected to get used to it."

"Are you happy?"

"I am."

"You sure?" she pressed.

Carl could tell she was concerned and wanted to put her mind at ease. "I'm just tired from the exams, that's all."

"Okay."

Sally flew back the next day and Carl reported to the accounting firm. He looked around the office and became impressed and intimidated at the same time. His old woodworking self kicked in as he admired the cabinets and desks. "Not bad work," he thought. It was the air of the place that intimidated him. As employees started their day Carl was reminded of Sally's old friends, the ones from the country club. Although they were nowhere near as fake, they were also not as real as the people Sally befriended over the last few years.

With each passing day he understood more why he did not like the place. He watched people interact and work, and none of them enjoyed what they were doing. No one ever came in early and the office was a wasteland thirty seconds past five.

On his last day he asked one of the accountants if he enjoyed his work.

"Not really. It's pretty boring but the pay is good. I have my fun on the weekends."

The plane ride home seemed to take twice as long as it did. All Carl wanted to do was to hug Kim, play with Mutt and see Sally. But spending time with Sally scared him. What was he going to say? Everything that was bothering him before was screaming through his head, and what control he had playing the mind games was gone. He sat back in his seat and closed his eyes. He was afraid his head was going to explode and asked himself, "What am I going to do?"

He had been home two weeks and could not take it anymore. His insides were ready to explode with the stress and he had to tell someone the truth. So far he pulled it off. Everyone thought he was happy with the path his career was on.

Carl and Kim were sitting by the pool. Sally had invited Kim's family and Peck for dinner. Afterwards Peck and Kim's parents left and Sally went to her suite.

"I need to talk to you about something," Carl started.

"What?"

He rehearsed what he was going to say a hundred times, but now that the time had come Carl was scared to death. "I haven't been completely honest with you, or with anyone else for that matter."

Kim instantly became alarmed. She had no idea what he was going to say and feared the worst. At least what she thought was the worst. "Have you met someone else?"

"What?"

"Have you met another girl at college?"

"No!" You're the only girl for me."

He saw relief that quickly turned into confusion. "What is it then?"

"I'm miserable," he said in almost a whisper.

"Why?"

"This is going to be really hard, but I have to tell Sally I don't want to be an accountant."

Carl watched Kim, trying to see if he could read what she was thinking. He was surprised to see her smile.

"You're smiling! Why are you smiling? Can't you see how hard this is going to be?"

"Carl, I could tell you were bugged by something and was pretty sure why."

"Why didn't you say something?"

"Why didn't you?"

"Well... I am now."

"It's about time."

"So are you okay with me not doing this?"

"Why wouldn't I be?"

"It's our future, I thought you wanted me to do the accounting deal too."

Although they never said the words, it was assumed they would always be together. It was a slow and simple transition over the years from you or me to us and our. So when Carl said *our future* Kim was just as comfortable hearing it as Carl was saying it.

"Do you think I want to be stuck with you being unhappy all the time?"

"It's just that I thought you liked the idea."

"You should have asked me."

Carl sat back and realized she was right. He never asked. He blushed as he said, "I'm feeling pretty foolish right now. I should have told you before."

"I understand. Sometimes we get wrapped up in things and it is hard to decide what to do. I want you to know I want to be with you no matter what," she said as she reached for his hand.

"I want that too," he said squeezing her hand. What he thought was going to be stressful turned into a special moment as he looked at her and realized what he had already known for a long time, she was the one.

But then he thought and asked, "What about Sally?"

"You need to talk to her. That's all."

"She's going to freak out. She put so much time and effort into this. Now I'm going to tell her 'Thanks for all the hard work and spending all that money, I'm dropping out.'"

"She cares for you. I've gotten to know her well working at the shelter and I know she wants you to be happy. She might surprise you."

"I get the feeling she really wants me to be an accountant. I'm afraid she will be disappointed if I tell her the truth."

"Carl, you have to."

And there it was; the real truth. It was not a matter of if he wanted to, it was a matter that he had to tell Sally and deal with the fallout. "When did you get so smart?"

"When you started to listen to me," she said with a smile. "When are you going to tell to her?"

"I want to get this over as soon as I can. You don't know how much I don't want to do this, but you're right, I have to."

Kim stood up and gave him a kiss. "It's still early. You should go talk to her right now before you chicken out."

"You're calling me chicken?"

"Aren't you?"

"Yea, I guess I am."

"Go get it over with and call me later and let me know how it went," she said as she kissed him and left. "Good luck!"

"I'm going to need it…" he said under his breath.

Carl thought about what he had to say to Sally while trying to muster up the courage to do it. Finally he went into the house and as he walked through it he looked around at what was now his home. His mind flooded with memories, both good and bad, but mostly good. Sally had become one of the most important people in his life and he loved her. The thought of hurting her brought waves of pain.

He stopped at the bottom of the stairs and stood knowing that he was going to have to endure the most difficult discussion of his life. As he walked down the hall towards Sally's office he could see the light shining through the door. He poked his head in and saw Sally sitting behind her desk. She looked up at him and smiled, "Carl!"

He stood frozen like a statue.

Sally saw he was tense, "What is it, honey?"

"Aunt Sally, I need to talk to you…"

Chapter 31

Decisions

It was Sally's turn to be consumed by guilt. She knew by looking at the boy when he stuck his head in that something was bothering him. She was blindsided when she found out what.

"Come in Carl."

He slowly walked in and plopped in a seat.

"If you have something you want to say just say it," she said encouraging him to open up.

"Aunt Sally, this is hard…" he stammered.

"Carl, tell me what's on your mind. Whatever it is I'm sure we can figure something out."

He looked at her with a deep-seated fear in his heart. Would she be angry? Disappointed? Would she kick him out? He did not know but knew he had to tell her. "I don't think this accounting deal is for me," he said, as the relief washed over him having the truth out in the open.

"I thought that's what you wanted."

"When we first starting talking about it I thought it was a good idea. Now I know I can't do it. I hate it, and the thought of doing it for the rest of my life scares me."

Sally thought about how they got Carl on track to be an accountant. She remembered when he helped balance the checkbook when she and Ruth got stuck. She thought about how his teachers said he would be a natural. The one thing she could not remember was asking him if it was what *he* wanted to do. She felt uneasy and asked, "How long have you been feeling like this?"

"Pretty much from the beginning of college. I never liked the idea, but you were so excited and I thought I should listen to you."

"Why didn't you say anything before?"

"I didn't want to disappoint you."

"Aw Carl, you should've said something."

"I wanted to, I really did. And I thought the idea might grow on me but it didn't. The more I studied the more I hated it."

"So you've been unhappy?"

"That's an understatement."

She was excited for him to become an accountant but it had nothing to do with what she wanted. She assumed it was what he wanted, and now she understood the truth and her mistake. "Carl, I'm so sorry. You're so good with math. I just assumed…"

"I know I should've said something. You worked so hard and you've spent a lot of money. I feel bad, but I can't do it."

"It's okay but you should have told me."

"I wanted to. I was afraid of hurting you."

Now Sally was feeling really bad. It was easy to see where he was coming from and how he would have thought it would hurt her if he told her the truth. She tried to smile, "Carl, this is my fault. We should've talked about it more. I have a habit of assuming things. I'm sorry."

Now Carl was taken aback. He expected her to be angry and talk him into sticking with it. But she was apologizing. It surprised him and he was not sure what to say. He thought he would have had to pull hard to get her to see his point but it only took a little tug. "You're not mad at me?"

"Why on earth would I be mad at you?"

"I thought this was what you wanted me to do."

"Because I thought it was what you wanted to do."

They sat there for a while, neither sure of what to say next. Finally Sally broke the silence. "Okay, we have a new rule as of right now."

Carl remembered the rules from before and his guard went up still thinking Sally might be upset.

"We talk."

"What do you mean?"

"I made the mistake thinking you wanted a career in accounting. You made a mistake not being honest with me. I understand why you thought I'd be upset, but you still should've told me. So from here on out we be completely open and honest with each other. Okay?"

"You're sure you're not mad?"

"I promise I'm not mad at all. In fact I'm sorry I pressured you. Like I said, as long as we are honest with each other this won't happen again."

Carl could not believe what he was hearing. He also could not believe all of the suffering he put himself through. He did not want to hurt her so ended up hurting himself and it was all for nothing.

"I feel silly."

"Why?"

"I just do."

"I want what's best for you and being happy is by far most important."

"Thank you for understanding."

"Thanks for being honest. Go get some rest and we can talk about your future tomorrow. Do you have any ideas?"

"I do…"

"I see a lot of woodwork in your future."

"I think you're right about that," he smiled as he got up and went to his room.

As Sally got ready for bed she looked in the mirror and thought about the last five years. If Carl talked to her the way he did on this night when he first moved in she would have been furious. She had no tolerance for anyone who disagreed with her, let alone a boy who was thrown into her life. Now she had become comfortable caring for someone else, something she could not stand before.

She also understood some of the bad habits from her country club days were still part of her. The guilt from forcing Carl, even though unintentionally, into becoming an accountant turned into a wake-up call. She had to pay more attention.

As she got into bed she wondered if she had experienced what others would call a full circle moment. She was more like the Sally of her youth; happy and optimistic. She was not concerned about what others thought and could admit when she was wrong. But, after what happened with Carl tonight she realized she still had some growing to do. As she closed her eyes she thought, "This parenting deal is harder than I thought. But that's okay."

"I can't believe it, she didn't freak out. In fact she apologized! Can you believe it?" Carl said into the phone.

Kim was relieved her boyfriend sounded happier. "I'm glad it worked out. You can relax now."

"I already am. I can't believe how much better I feel."

"What did she apologize for?"

"That's the weird part, she thought I wanted to do the accounting and I thought that's what she wanted me to do, we were both wrong. If I'd been honest a long time ago I could've saved her a lot of work and money and I could've saved myself a lot of grief."

"What's the plan now?"

"What do you think?"

"I think you're going to smell like sawdust. That's okay, I like that smell."

"When did you get so smart?"

"You don't get the listening thing, do you?"

After they hung-up Carl went to bed. It was the first time in a long time he was optimistic about his future.

The next morning Carl sat across from Sally at her desk. "Aunt Sally, thanks for understanding."

"I'm just sorry you didn't say anything before, but that's water under the bridge."

"Now I have to figure out what I'm going to do."

"My guess is you want to pursue a career in woodwork, right?'

"That's where my heart is."

Sally looked at him over her reading glasses and said, "You're absolutely sure. I don't want to make the same mistake."

"I know it sounds crazy but ever since I took Peck's class I knew I'd be happy doing it. At first I thought I'd hate it. I was bummed I didn't get into the computer class. Now I'm glad I didn't."

"Okay. I talked to Peck and he's coming over after school. We can put our heads together and figure out the best way to get you started."

"Sounds good to me."

"In the meantime I'm giving you your first job."

"Really?"

"Really. Things at the shelter are going well and I need more storage space. You interested?"

"Sure, when do I start?"

"In about an hour…"

As they pulled into the parking lot he saw Kim's car . "Wow, is she always this early?"

"Always."

When Kim started working for Sally it was going to be temporary and parttime, but with the success of the business and the impression Kim made on Sally, she soon became a vital part of the business. Ruth handled the bookwork and ordering, Kim managed the day-to-day affairs. Sally was so happy with Kim's work she sent her to the local community college and paid for her business classes.

Part of the business contracted to handle the strays for the county. Sally soon included a private veterinarian, boarding and a large pet supply store. Carl was impressed. "This place looks a lot different!"

"I know! When we started I wasn't sure what I was getting myself into but with Ruth and Kim's help it's turned out to be fascinating. The fact that it's making a nice profit doesn't hurt."

Carl could hear the pride in her voice. "You enjoy it, don't you?"

"I do. I guess this place is to me is what woodworking is to you."

He understood and, again, the relief washed over him as he remembered his accounting days were over. "I'm happy for you."

"Thanks. We're thinking of expanding. I want facilities to take care of large animals. We have a few places lined up."

"Can't do it here?"

"It's not big enough and the zoning is impossible. We're looking just outside of town."

They walked inside and saw Kim arranging boxes behind a large counter. She looked up and said, "Good morning!" She walked up to Carl and kissed him on the cheek. "You look a lot happier than last time I saw you."

"You have no idea…"

"Kind of funny how good things feel if you're honest with the ones who care for you," she said.

"I'm sorry. I've learned my lesson. No more hiding things. Especially from you."

"Good. Sounds like you can listen after all."

After Sally showed Carl the work she wanted done he made a list of the materials and tools he would need. When he added up the cost he shuttered at the amount, most of which was for tools. He slowly handed it to Sally, stealing himself for her response.

"Wow! This is a lot cheaper than college!"

Kim looked on from a distance and wondered what Sally and Carl were laughing at.

Peck introduced Carl to his friends in the construction industry and before long he had so much work he had to turn down many requests. All of the misgivings and fears he had at college became distant memories. He was beginning the rest of his life, and it was looking really, really good.

CHAPTER 32

SOWING

Carl's twenty-third birthday was not anything like his teenage ones. Instead of dozens of kids splashing in the pool and downing gallons of soda-pop it was a few friends from the woodworking industry sitting around patio tables and a cooler full of beer. Peck and Sally were there along with Ruth, and Kim had taken on the chores of putting the party together.

Carl enjoyed the day remembering the last few years and understanding he was a lucky man. His reputation grew quickly and instead of just in town, everyone in the county came to know him as a master woodworker. He was the go-to guy for the tough projects. He lost count of times clients called him saying other woodworkers said their requests were impossible. More times than not Carl found a way and commanded a high price for his work.

Even Peck called him for advice. The student's skills had surpassed the teacher's by far. The only frustration for Peck was Carl's refusal to teach. Every few months he would ask, "Hey Carl, how about you help me teach my advanced class?"

"No," was always Carl's answer.

Carl and Sally were closer than ever and her business was thriving. He remembered a day not long after he started his chosen career when he, Sally, Kim and Ruth rode together in Sally's crew cab truck. He was surprised when she pulled up in her new ride. "If someone were to tell me you'd be driving something like this I would've called them nuts."

"I know! I can't believe what I've been missing, I love this thing!"

The day was filled looking at properties for the expansion of Sally's business so she could care for large animals. All of the prospects were on the edge of town and most were dismal. One, however, stood out.

As Sally parked her new toy on the five-acre property they were amazed. "Wow, this is beautiful," Sally said.

"I can't believe all these trees and look at that view of the mountains!" Kim said.

"I'm going to check it out," Carl said as he walked the property. There was a small stream running from a hill. When he stood on top of it he soaked in the view.

"Isn't this spectacular?" Kim asked as she walked up behind him.

"It is. I can't believe it's so close to town yet feels like we're miles away."

They held hands and walked back to the truck. They saw Ruth talking on her new cell phone with Sally standing next to her listening. Ruth was asking questions about the property. She ended the call and looked discouraged.

"The good news is the owner wants to sell and it's a great deal. The bad news is the county is never going to grant you the zoning you'll need, Sally."

"Shoot! This would've been perfect."

"That's too bad. This is a beautiful spot," Carl said.

They got back in the truck and spent the rest of the day looking at other properties. Within a few weeks a deal was made for a second choice and building began. Months later there was a grand opening celebration for Sally's latest addition to her business which could now care for horses and other large animals. It was an instant success but they still talked about the first property and wished the business could have been located there instead.

The birthday party was coming to an end and the last of the guests left and Kim was on her way out. "I have to be at the shelter early tomorrow so I'm calling it a night. Happy Birthday Carl!"

"I'll walk you to your car," he said as he stood, then looked at Sally, I'll be right back."

When he returned Sally had gotten a small bottle of Champagne and two glasses of orange juice. "I thought we'd have a toast to your birthday."

He looked at the bottle and two glasses and reached for a beer. "We can have the toast, but I'm sticking with beer."

"Not even a sip?"

"No chance."

They laughed remembering his ordeal with Mimosas years before.

"Sally, I want to talk to you about something."

"What's on your mind?"

"I love living here, but I've been thinking…" he said trying to find the right words.

"Let me guess, Kim!"

Carl's blush was instantaneous. "How do you always know what I'm going to say?"

"Are you kidding me? I know you and I've been waiting for this day forever! Have you asked her yet?"

"I didn't say I was going to ask her anything." he said with a wry smile.

"Oh come on now. You two are meant for each other. You have to get married!"

"I think so too, but I'm not sure when to ask her or how…"

Sally put down her drink and took Carl's hand. "Come with me, I have something I want to show you."

In her office Sally pulled a small box from her wall-safe and handed it to Carl.

"What's this?"

"Open it."

He took the lid off and saw an engagement ring and wedding bands. He carefully placed them on Sally's desk.

"Those were your mom and dad's."

He picked up his father's ring and looked closely. He noticed it was scratched. "This must have been from the accident."

"Oh no, I'm so sorry. I didn't notice or I would've had it fixed."

"No, it's okay. This is very special and I'm touched."

"You sure you don't want me to have it repaired?"

"No, I don't think so. I can't explain why but I want to keep it the way it is." He put his dad's ring down and examined his mother's rings. They were flawless and beautiful. "Do you think Kim will like these?"

"I'm sure she will. When do you plan to ask?"

"We're going to dinner tomorrow. I was thinking then."

Sally jumped out of her chair like a hyper youngster. "I'm so excited for you!" she said in a squeal as she threw her arms around him.

Even though no one was around to see her outburst Carl was still embarrassed but decided to let her enjoy the moment. When she let go and stood back he could see the tears. "Are you okay?"

"I'm great!"

"What if she says 'No?'"

"Fat chance of that happening."

They talked awhile longer, Sally's excitement using all the oxygen in the room. After she calmed down they said goodnight and Carl went to his room.

It was not a teenager's room anymore. Now it was a young man's studio apartment. He walked to the wall where pictures were hanging. Many were of his favorite projects he built over the years. Others were of him with Kim, Sally, Peck and Ruth celebrating different milestones. There were also older photos of Matilda and Mutt. Carl looked at the picture of his dog and said, "I miss you, boy. You helped me get through some pretty rough times."

He sat at his drafting table and pulled out the rings. He fixated on his dad's and the scratch. It seemed so long ago when Yoda told him about the accident. He wondered why he did not want to have the damage repaired. He was not sure if he should, but he put it on. It fit perfectly. As he moved his fingers and made a fist he noticed the scratch. It was not irritating, he could just feel it. Part of him was sad remembering why the scratch was there, but another part was grateful for the life he now had and somehow the scratch reminded him. He held up his hand and looked long and hard at the ring before putting it back into the box and thought, "Thanks Dad."

Carl came downstairs in his usual attire, blue jeans, flannel shirt and work boots. Sally saw him and said, "You're not going to dinner dressed like that!"

"Like what?"

"Like that!"

"Why not? I always dress like this and you've never said anything before."

"Do you think I'm going to allow you to propose to Kim in that get-up? Not a chance!"

She looked at him and turned her head. "Where're you taking her?"

"The rib joint."

"What? Are you out of your mind? Go put something nice on right now. I'll handle this. I'll make reservations at that steak house you like. Then I'm calling Kim to tell her Peck and I were planning on going but had a change of plans, so you two can go in our place. Now you can propose over a *nice* dinner."

Carl knew that it was no use to argue so he gave up and changed.

"Sally was right, again," Carl thought as they walked into the prestigious restaurant. It had been a long time since he had been there and he forgot how much he liked it. This was a better setting to ask the big question. He had been thinking about it for several weeks and was calm. Today was a different story.

When he awoke to the old-time alarm that morning he felt the jitters right away. It was not because of the loud clang of the bells; it was because he knew his life was going to change today, forever. If she said "yes" he would be the happiest person on the planet. But what if she said "no?" The thought made him shiver.

Although they had been together for a long time there were only a few occasions when they talked about the future, and they were never specific. It was the gradual growth of their relationship that led Carl to assume they would always be together and he was confident Kim felt the same way. But today he was going to find out for sure. What if she was not ready or did not want to get married? Fear consumed him the entire day and by the time he was getting ready for the date he had spun himself into a nervous wreck.

Earlier in the afternoon he tried to talk to Sally about his concerns. She laughed at him. "Are you out of your mind?" It did not help at all.

On the drive to Kim's he kept telling himself over and over, "I can do this. I can do this." By the time he pulled his truck into her driveway he was almost convinced. When he saw her standing at the door his mantra changed to, "I have to do this…"

With Carl in woodworking and Kim working at the animal shelter it was rare that they dressed up. They were a blue jeans couple and that suited him fine. Now she was dressed to the nines and wore a little makeup. Her dress clung in all the right places and she looked spectacular.

"You clean up pretty good," she said after giving him a kiss. "Let me get a good look at you." She looked him over and gave an approving nod then asked, "What do you think?" as she did a slow spin to show off her dress.

The sight of her took his breath away. "Wow, you look absolutely beautiful…" he said, almost stammering.

Carl recovered by the time they were seated in a secluded booth at the steak house. They were surprised when the waiter brought a bottle of wine. "This is a gift from Sally and she wanted me to convey a message, 'Have a wonderful evening.'" He poured the wine and left.

Carl looked at the wine list and found the one Sally gave them. It cost more than ten cases of his favorite beer. "Wow."

"This is nice. It was a total surprise when Sally called me. I've never been here before. Have you?"

"A few times. I like it here and the steaks are incredible."

"I'm glad I found something to wear for a place like this."

He looked at her and smiled, "Me too…"

Carl was trying to keep his voice in check and not show Kim how nervous he was. He was also trying to decide when to ask the big question. Before dinner, during or after? Kim helped him make his choice.

"Why are you acting so funny?"

"What do you mean?"

"Ever since you picked me up you've been nervous as a cat. What's going on?"

He knew she was right. He had shoved his hands in his pockets a couple of times to hide the fact they were shaking. When the night began he thought the best time to pop the question would be over dessert but now knew that was a bad idea. There was no way he was going to be able to hold himself together through the courses of the meal. "Well, here it goes…" he thought as he reached into his pocket and pulled out the box.

He wanted it to be the perfect moment and tried to be smooth but his hand started to tremble again and he dropped the box. "Great."

"What's that?"

Carl concentrated on keeping his hand steady as he picked it up and handed it to her. "I have something for you…"

She took it and looked puzzled. "What's this?"

"You'll see when you open it."

She froze the moment she looked inside. It felt like an hour and he started to wonder if she was trying to find a nice way to say "no." Then he thought maybe he should have waited until dinner, or dessert or next year… His mind was racing in so many directions he felt dizzy and he knew her silence was not a good sign. Not good at all. He was struggling to think of something to say when Kim looked up at him with watery eyes.

"Is this what I think it is?"

He still found it hard to speak. "It was my mother's. Now I would like it to be yours."

She slid close, put her arms around him and kissed him. As she pulled back Carl saw a couple of tears running down her cheek but noticed she was not saying anything. Were those happy tears? Was she mad? Or was it something else? He had to know and he had to know right now. "Well, are you going to marry me?"

Kim nodded her head and kissed him again. "About time."

CHAPTER 33
BEGINNINGS

A freight train could have blasted through the restaurant and Kim and Carl would not have noticed. They were in their own world, happier than they had ever been. It did not matter what was served or who was around, this was an incredible moment and nothing could take away from it

"You've made me a very happy guy."

"I've been waiting for this. I was worried you were never going to ask." Kim was looking at her ring.

"Why didn't you say something?"

"I almost did a couple of times but I was afraid."

"I know that feeling."

"I can't wait to show this to my mom; she's going to be excited."

"What about your dad?"

"He's going to be happy too, he likes you."

They enjoyed dinner and talked about their future. Kim planned to keep working at the shelter and Carl knew he could provide for them with his woodworking. They were complete and secure in each other's love.

After the dessert plates were removed, Carl asked for the check.

"Your dinner has been paid for," the server said. "In fact, you are requested in the lounge."

"What's that about?" Kim asked.

"I don't have a clue."

They got up and went to the lounge. Sally, Peck and Kim's parents were sitting around a large table. Kim ran to her mother and showed her the ring. Sally jumped up and hugged Carl.

"How did it go?"

"You were right."

"Congratulations!" Peck said as he gave him a bear hug, embarrassing Carl to no end. Then Kim's father held his hand out to shake.

"I guess I should've asked you first," Carl said.

"Are you kidding me, my wife and I have been waiting for this. I can't begin to tell you how happy we are."

Carl turned to Sally, "Am I the only one who wasn't sure she was going to say 'Yes?'"

"Yup."

"What are you guys doing here?"

"I couldn't stand it. I called Kim's parents and we decided to surprise you. I hope that's okay."

"It's fine. But what if she'd said 'No?'"

"Then we would be ordering much stronger drinks..."

The women sat on one side of the table making plans and laughing like a bunch of schoolgirls. The men sat across from them, sipping their beers and knowing they were going to be out of the loop for awhile. There was no way to compete for the women's attention; there was a wedding to plan.

A few days before the wedding Sally invited Kim to have dinner with her and Carl. After the table was cleared Sally said, "I'll be right back."

She returned with two large, official-looking envelopes. "I know it's a little early but I wanted to give you these."

"What's this?" Carl asked as he took an envelope from her.

"That one is from me. Do you remember that property we looked at when we wanted to expand the shelter?"

"The one with the stream and the hill?" Kim asked.

"That's the one. When I saw the looks on your faces I knew I had to get it for you. That's the deed in both of your names."

Kim and Carl were shocked. "Sally, this is too much. You have to let me pay for this."

"I have to agree with Carl," Kim said.

"First of all you couldn't afford it. But I want you to have it. It's already yours, and after all you have become to me, I insist."

They saw Sally was not going to take no for an answer. "Sally, I can't thank you enough for this. It' is a great surprise and so kind," Kim said, with disbelief.

"All I ask is you have me over all the time to play with your kids!"

Carl was speechless. He loved his aunt and knew that she loved him, but he was struggling to be comfortable with the enormity of the gift. He wanted to find a way to refuse but he knew it was pointless. When Aunt Sally made up her mind that was that.

He looked at the other envelope. "I'm scared to ask, but what's that?"

"This one is from your mom and dad."

He saw it was the title to house he lived in with his parents. "I thought you sold that."

"I tried but the market was down and your dad borrowed pretty heavily against it. So, with Ruth's help, we leased it out. There's still a loan against it, but being paid down over the years and the market doing so well now, there's quite a bit of equity. You can live there or sell it and use the profits to build on the land."

Carl was silent. Sally saw he was uncomfortable. "Carl, honey, it's yours. It's what they would have wanted."

"This is a lot to digest."

"The renters moved out last week. Why don't we go check it out tomorrow and you can figure out what you want to do."

He had not been here for nine years but it was still familiar. He also felt like an intruder. Sally and Kim were there but he might as well have been alone. His thoughts drifted between the present and years ago. In the kitchen he looked where Mutt's food and water bowl would have been. Then he looked at the window in the backdoor and remembered smashing the glass to break in. He looked at his arm and saw the scar, almost completely faded, and no one would have noticed it unless it was pointed out. When he looked at the empty breakfast nook his mind's eye saw half empty coffee cups.

He was surprised how small his old room was. Carl saw the spot on the wall where he threw the clock. It had been repaired, but like the scar on his arm, there was still a trace of the damage.

The hardest part was his parents' room. It was empty but Carl could see, in his mind, the disarray that was there last time he was there. "How could I ever sleep in here?" he asked himself out loud.

Kim was standing behind him and growing concerned. "So this is where you grew up?"

"Until I was almost fourteen..."

"Are you alright?"

"I don't know."

"I think we can be happy here."

Although Carl told Kim almost everything, he did not tell her about the first couple of nights when we was an intruder after the accident. He opened up hoping that letting out the memories would help him feel better. It didn't.

He walked through the house a second time, this time with Kim and Sally by his side and he told them everything. The more he talked about it the more vivid the memories became and by the time they reentered his parents' room he was afraid he was going to lose control. "I have to get out of here..." He turned and ran out the front door.

Kim and Sally followed and found him staring at an empty spot on the porch. "That's where the cop was sitting."

They were speechless as he walked to Sally's truck.

"There's no way I could ever live there again," Carl said as they were driving away.

"Carl, I'm sorry. I didn't think about how that might affect you," Sally said.

"Don't be. You had no way to know. It surprised me too."

"I can have Ruth put it on the market right away. You and Kim can live at the house in the meantime while you build on the property."

"What do you think?" Carl asked Kim.

"After seeing what you just went through I think that's a great idea."

"I have an idea," Sally said as she drove.

"What?"

"You'll see."

A half hour later they were standing on the property. His nerves calmed immediately as he shared his ideas on how to build on it. It was more beautiful than they remembered.

"I have only one request. No pool. I want you to bring your kids to my house to swim."

"Kids! Who said anything about kids? We might wait a long time for that."

"Wanna bet?" Sally said with a grin.

The wedding was perfect. The newlyweds insisted it not be fancy. In fact the invitations said to bring swimming suits and anyone wearing a tie would have it cut off at the door. The reception at Sally's turned into a pool party.

Carl looked at the growing pile of gifts. Then he was glad to see what he was looking forward to most. "Hi Matilda!"

"Look at you! You kept your promise by never stopping to amaze me…" she said and turned to Kim, "And you make the most beautiful bride I have ever laid eyes on."

"I'm so glad you're here."

"I wouldn't have missed it for the world." Matilda handed a gift-wrapped box to her. "Open it."

Kim pulled out a weathered book. "What's this?"

"That was my mother's cookbook. You will be doing the cooking, right?"

"I will."

"Good. If you left the cooking to him you would have some pretty skinny kids."

Carl rolled his eyes and said, "Very funny."

After Carl said goodbye to the last of the guests he walked to a table where Sally and Kim were talking. "How are my girls doing?"

"We're talking about you," Kim said.

Sally said, "I know he can get a little testy sometimes. If he does let me know and I'll whip him back into shape."

"I'm standing right here, you know…"

"Yes, I can see that. Run along now. Kim and I still have some girl talk to finish."

Carl shook his head and found Peck. "I think they're ganging up on me."

Carl and Kim began their lives as husband and wife. The quick sale of the old house gave them the funds to start building on the property. They spent every second of free time working on it, and in a year invited Sally, Peck and Kim's parents for the first dinner in their new home.

"This is a lot harder than I thought," Sally said as Carl was giving her the tour.

"What?"

"I was used to having you around. I'm realizing how much I'm going to miss you."

"Come over whenever you want and I'm sure we'll be at your place all the time."

"I'm happy for you, I just liked it better when you called it our place."

He gave her a hug. "Come on, there's one more room Kim and I want to show you."

The newlyweds planed in advance how to tell Sally. Kim opened the door and they walked into the last room of the tour. Sally became elated. "Are you kidding me? A nursery!"

"You were right. We just found out you are going to be a grand-aunt. But we like the sound of grandma better."

"I can live with that!"

Kim told her parents the day before and they agreed not to spoil the surprise for Sally, but now the news was out in the open the girls went back to the habit that drove Carl nuts. Sally, Kim and her mother huddled to talk about the baby.

"Come on guys. I'll show you the shop. I don't think we're going to be missed here."

When he slid the woodshop door open, Peck and Kim's father were more than impressed.

"I can't believe all of the tools you have. You're better equipped than the community college!" Peck said.

"I thought you'd get a kick out of it." Carl retrieved three beers and handed them out. "Let me show you around. I have a feeling we'll have plenty of time with the women having so much to talk about."

The women would have a lot more to talk about. By their fifth anniversary Kim and Carl had three children. And they loved every minute of it.

CHAPTER 34
REQUESTS

Days after their eighteenth anniversary Carl and Kim had Sally over for dinner. Sally and Peck visited once a week and Sally much more often. Carl kept his promise of not building a pool so the children spent a lot of time at Sally's.

The kids loved Sally, bragging how much fun she was and that they could talk to her about anything. And Sally loved them. It worked out well because their parents had a babysitter on call 24/7. If they wanted to get away they called and Sally picked up the kids within an hour. She converted part of her house into what they all called "The Kid's Zone" and the children enjoyed it so much they often said, "Hey Mom and Dad, shouldn't you go on a trip?"

Sally's visits were always filled with love and laughter. This one was different. The home was still filled with joy, but Carl noticed Sally was nostalgic.

They talked about the animal shelter and how Ruth had taken over. It was successful and Sally told them about her plans to give it to Ruth.

They relived special moments with the kids. Sporting events and plays, some had great outcomes, some did not, but all were memorable.

They also talked about sad times. It had been five years but Carl remembered it like it was yesterday.

Sally had called asking him to come over right away. He heard in her voice something was wrong and as he walked into her office saw by the redness of her eyes she been crying.

"Sally! What's wrong?"

She did not say a word and handed him a letter. After he read it he wept also. It informed him Matilda had died and of the funeral arrangements. It had been a long time since he dealt with the death of someone he cared for.

"I can't believe this. I talked to her a few weeks ago and she was fine." His hand trembled holding the letter.

"I know. It's a shock."

"We'll go to the funeral together."

She slowly nodded her head.

At the reception after the funeral, Sally, Ruth, Kim and Carl talked to several people Matilda had worked for over the years. It struck Carl and Sally how the memories of Matilda were so much like their own. She came into families' lives soon after a tragedy that resulted in a dysfunctional home life. Matilda showed up and was more than a maid or cook, although they all remembered the wonderful meals. What they could not explain was how she helped them heal. Was it what she said, the atmosphere she created or Matilda just being Matilda? None could put their finger on it. But all agreed if Matilda had not arrived when she did to become part of their families there might not have been a family to keep together much longer.

As they listened to strangers tell stories that might as well have been their own, Carl and Sally shared a deep sense of loss but were also grateful for Matilda.

On the drive home Sally asked Carl, "How do you think she did that?"

"I have no idea."

"You know, there were times I wanted to strangle her."

"I think the feeling was mutual."

She looked at him as he was driving. "I wasn't a very pleasant person back then, was I?"

"I'm taking the fifth on that one…"

They moved the conversation to the den after dinner. At the bar Carl mixed Kim and Sally a Mimosa. As he handed one to Sally she looked at the drink. "Now that's a memory for you!"

"You have no idea." He shivered at the smell. He counted three ice cubes and poured three fingers of his favorite bourbon. He swirled the glass enjoying the sound.

He sat next to Kim and saw Sally looking at the family pictures on the wall. "I can't begin to tell you how proud I am of you, Carl. You too, Kim. The kids, the business, this wonderful house. You have no idea how much joy it brings me seeing how happy you all are."

"We had a lot of help. Mainly you!"

"I might've helped here and there, but you both deserve the credit."

"I don't know about that. You've done a lot for me, Sally. For us."

"Remember when you first came to live with me?"

"Kind of hard to forget."

"I bet you never thought we'd be enjoying these memories together."

"That would be a very safe bet." He smiled. "But here we are!"

"Yes, here we are."

Sally was still her joyful self, but also acted like something was on her mind. He thought about asking if anything was wrong but Sally started to talk.

"I have something I need to tell you."

"Go ahead."

"I want to apologize, Carl. I'm not sure I ever did."

Carl was confused. "What for?"

"I treated you horribly after your mom and dad's accident. It was a time you needed someone most and I pushed you away. I feel terrible about it."

Now he was shocked. They had been talking about good memories and sharing family stories and now this? "What's going on here?" he thought.

"Sally, why are you talking like this?"

"I've been thinking. I look back at the person I was before. Now I realize how happy I am. Then I think about how I almost pushed away one of my biggest blessings."

"What's that?"

"You."

Carl smiled and said, "Sally, you're one of my biggest blessings."

"But I still feel guilty. That awful boarding school. My stupid list of rules. How I treated you. You must have hated me."

"We had a rough start but look at us now!"

"I know. You're right. But I messed up with everything except Camp Big Lake. I think that worked out pretty well," she said looking at Kim.

"You got that right!" Kim smiled.

Carl was hoping to find the right words. It had been a long time. He still thought about his parents often and wished they lived to see their grandchildren. Less often he thought about the accident but he never thought about how his relationship with Sally began. So many good things happened for and between them that any misgivings evaporated decades ago. He looked at Kim hoping she could bail him out of the conversation but she looked as confused as he was.

"Sally, listen to me. I forgave you a long time ago. Sure we had a hard time at first, but when I look back and think about how great things are now, well, I have to smile."

"I know. Me too. " Sally said then suddenly stopped.

Carl could see she was becoming emotional. "Sally, I forgive you. I did then and I do now."

"Really?'

"Really."

"Thank you Carl. You have no idea how much I needed to hear that."

Sally stood up. "I'm being silly. I didn't mean to bring up anything sad. Now make us some more drinks and we can visit awhile longer," she said as she left for the bathroom.

Kim looked at Carl and asked, "What was that about?"

"I don't know. I've never seen her like that."

"Do you think something's wrong?"

"How would I know? She say anything to you?"

"Nothing at all. I took the kids to her house the other day and everything was fine. We had a great time."

Carl made the next round of drinks. He looked across the den at Kim. "Do you think I should ask her if anything's wrong?"

"I don't know. She seems better. Let's see how the rest of the night goes."

"Okay. Sounds good to me."

When Sally returned she walked to the wall containing pictures and looked lost in thought. Kim and Carl became concerned again.

Carl walked up to Sally. "Is everything alright?"

Sally turned and smiled. "Everything is going to be fine, but you better sit down. I'm afraid I have some difficult news."

Difficult? Was it the business? Something with Peck? He had no idea what to expect but knew he was not going to like what he was about to hear.

Sally sat between Kim and Carl and held their hands. "I started to feel poorly about a month ago and thought it best to get checked out."

Carl felt like a hand reached into his chest and squeezed his heart.

"There's something wrong with my blood. There's a long name for it I can't pronounce. Anyway, my doctor sent me to specialists and they all agree..." she said her words drifting off.

"They all agree what?" asked Kim with concern. Carl could not speak.

"I don't have much longer."

"How long have you known this?" he asked.

"I've suspected for a few weeks. In fact I've already made all of the arrangements. Like I told you, I'm leaving the animal shelter to Ruth. God knows she's earned it. I've put money aside for Peck, he's been good to me over the years. Everything else is in a trust for you and the kids."

"But there's still hope, right?"

281

"I'm afraid not Honey. The doctor told me this morning. They have treatments that could help me last a little longer, but after talking to people in my situation I'm going to pass. It would just prolong the suffering."

Kim looked at Sally. "Why didn't you tell us before?"

"Oh, I didn't want to burden you. You're so busy and I was hoping I'd be okay. But after talking to my doctor today I couldn't keep it from you any longer."

It all made sense now. Sally's talking about old times and her need of his forgiveness. His mind filled with so many questions he could not focus on just one, and it took all of his strength not to sob. He finally got words out. "How long?'

"The doctor said a few months. Maybe longer."

"There has to be something we can do. Maybe get another doctor. You can't just give up."

"Honey, I'm not giving up. It's just my time."

Kim buried her face in her hands and Carl could no longer hold back his tears. He wanted to be strong for his Aunt Sally, but this was too much to bear.

"There has to be something we can do."

"Medically everything that can be done has been done. But I do have a request."

"Anything…" Carl said, his voice breaking uncontrollably.

Sally placed her hands on each side of his face, kissed him gently on his forehead and rested hers on his. With tears flowing down his face he looked up. "Anything…"

Sally pulled back just far enough to look into his eyes and said, "Carl, honey, I want you to build my casket."

CHAPTER 35
ALL GOOD THINGS

H e opened the large doors wide and sunlight flooded the wood-shop. In just under two weeks he turned shapeless boards of Santos Mahogany into a stunning work of art. The top was inlayed with different grains forming images of roses. Even though it was inert, it looked alive. Carl was never impressed with his work, it was what he did and he let the customers do the admiring. But this time he was proud.

Carl realized it had become a daily occurrence since he began this project as he wiped away a tear. Never before had he had to stop working because he could not see clearly through watery eyes. He did not sob; the tears just flowed without warning.

He walked around the casket; it was perfect. He decided to rub it down with oil one last time to coax out every bit of beauty the wood had to offer.

He spent the rest of the afternoon cleaning the woodshop. It did not need it, he wanted something to do and was not ready to take the last step. Not yet. He hoped he would find the strength the next morning.

After he locked up and walked back to the house he noticed the transformation from Carl the woodworker to Carl the husband and father was more subtle, almost unnoticeable. Before Sally gave him the bad news he was two different people but now they blended into one.

As he got closer to the house he saw Peck's truck pulling up the driveway.

"This is a surprise," Carl said.

"I tried calling but there was no answer at the house and your cell went to voicemail."

Carl reached in his pocket and pulled out his cell realizing he forgot to turn it on. "Kim is helping Sally and Ruth with the final details at the animal shelter and my cell wasn't on, sorry."

"I wanted to see if you needed any help."

"Not today, but tomorrow you can help me load it so I can take it to the funeral home."

"You know I've always been excited to see your projects. This time, not so much."

"I understand. Come in and I'll make you a drink."

They sat in the den. "Carl, I know I've asked you too many times why you don't want to teach…"

"Why do you want me to?" Carl interrupted.

"I think it'd be good for you and the students."

"Why?"

"It's not just woodworking; it's how it affects you. I've known you a long time and believe it's one of the things that got you through the hard times. I thought there might be other kids who could use something like that."

"If you said that to me a few weeks ago I would've thought you were crazy, but now I understand."

"So you'll do it?"

"I'll think about it."

Kim came home a half hour after Peck left.

"How'd it go?" Carl asked after giving her a kiss.

"Exhausting. There were so many details but we got it done. The shelter now belongs to Ruth."

"How is Ruth?"

"About the same as us."

"That bad, huh."

"I'm afraid I have some bad news."

Kim sent copies of Sally's medical records to every major hospital in the country to review in hopes they could find a treatment.

"No luck?"

"I heard from the last one today and they agree there isn't anything that can be done, but they did say she should have some time left."

"Well, I guess that's it."

"The house feels empty."

"The kids are hanging out with friends. Is Sally coming over?"

"No. It was a long day and she wanted to go home and rest. She'll be by tomorrow."

"I can show it to her then."

"You finished?"

"Just one final rubdown in the morning."

"Honey, I can't imagine what it must've been like to build that."

"It gets you thinking."

They shared a light dinner and settled in the den to watch TV. Neither felt like talking and had no idea what they were watching as they stared blankly at the screen.

Sally was glad to be home. It was a good day. She felt a little better and was able to accomplish what she wanted, but she was tired. The maid asked if she should make dinner.

"I'm not that hungry; maybe just a small salad."

As the maid went to the kitchen Sally walked around the house thinking about the changes. There were several walls filled with pictures of her and her family and friends. Most were of Carl, Kim, the kids and her. There were many with Peck and Ruth and older ones with Matilda. Sally remembered a time when the walls were filled with what she thought was art. The furniture had been replaced with Carl's creations. The house transformed from what looked like a French brothel, phony and stale, to a warm and inviting home.

The tables were filled with Carl's sculptures and the large bouquet of wooden roses was still her favorite.

She walked into the Kid's Zone and looked at the games and bean bags and wondered, "Did I spoil them enough?"

The maid served her salad on the patio. As she ate she watched the gentle waves in the pool and remembered the get-togethers she enjoyed over the years. She could not remember a single time the pool was used before Carl moved in. She looked at the empty dog run and realized she still missed that ugly dog, Mutt, even though it had been a long time since he died.

After she finished her salad she decided not follow doctor's orders and poured herself a healthy shot of brandy.

"What's it going to do, kill me?" she laughed.

As she sipped and looked around the kitchen she was reminded of her friend Matilda and her incredible cooking. She wondered why she was so fixated on the past. She knew she did not have a lot of time left but still had much to look forward to. She planed to visit Carl, Kim and the kids the next day and knew she would have a wonderful time. She always did. She thought about the upcoming weekend with Peck. She knew she was in love with him and questioned whether they made the right decision in not marrying.

Then it struck her. All of her affairs were in order. Signing over the animal shelter to Ruth was the last of many details and for the first time Sally found herself with nothing to plan or manage. At first she was unsettled, but the unease was soon replaced with memories. And that was okay; she had many to enjoy.

She drank her first brandy a little faster than she should but poured another before she went to her room. "This should really make that quack mad!" she laughed out loud.

She went into her office and looked through photo albums from the last twenty-plus years. Each picture had a story that was full of fun, laughter and love.

She was not sure if it was the brandy or that it had been a long day, but she was very tired. She decided to go to bed early.

As she changed for bed her mind was still streaming the good memories and she felt more contented than she could remember.

As she pulled the covers over her she thought about her life before the boy entered it. She thought about her youth and was glad she could now revisit those times and not feel sad, but happy. Then she remembered the marriage and what it turned her into. She cringed as she recalled that unhappy time. Then she smiled as she thought about what her life became after the boy and she decided to make it work between them. It was not easy at first, but it became very comfortable and important.

Her body was telling her it was time to sleep. She turned out the light and thought about how much she was looking forward to spending the next day with her family. Then for the last time in her life Sally closed her eyes and dozed off. Just before she did she whispered, "Thank God for Carl."

He got up early to oil the casket. It was ten o'clock in the morning when he stood back and said, "You're finished."

He always considered himself down-to-earth and did not read into things but he had to admit this project said exactly what he wanted. Its beauty spoke to life's complexities and its simple design to its fragility.

He was tired so he pulled a stool into the middle of the wood-shop and sat in front of the casket. He was not sure if it was the intensity he put into the work or the amount of energy he burned remembering so much from his past as he built it. It did not matter. Once Peck helped him load and drop it off at the mortuary he could take a break and focus on making Sally's last days as enjoyable as possible.

Carl was not sure how long he been sitting when he felt a presence in the shop. He turned and saw Kim. And right away he knew.

"Nooo..." he said in almost a whisper.

"Honey, I'm so sorry."

"When?"

"The maid found her this morning. She passed in her sleep."

"I thought I was ready for this, but now I'm not sure."

"I hope this helps, the maid said she looked peaceful and it didn't look like there was any suffering. She just slipped away and…" She stopped when she saw the casket. "Oh my God, Carl!"

He followed her gaze, "What do you think?"

She was speechless as she walked around it, letting the beauty of the work soak in. She lightly drew her hands across its finish and shook her head. "I can't find the words."

Kim had always been impressed with her husband's work, but this took her breath away.

"She didn't get to see it."

"She didn't have to. She knew she'd love it because you built it."

"Still…"

Kim looked at him and could see he was shaken. She held him close, he broke down and they stayed that way for a long time.

Peck and Carl were delivering Sally's casket to the funeral home later that afternoon.

"Carl, I've always been impressed with your work, but this is the best I've ever seen you do. Anyone do for that matter."

"I was motivated."

"She would have loved it."

"I know. How you doing?"

"To be honest I'm pretty tore up. I knew it was a matter of time but I was hoping for more of it."

"I know what you mean. Peck, for what it is worth, I know Sally loved you."

"I have no doubt and I hope she knew I felt the same."

"She did."

"Thank you for that…"

What should have taken a few minutes turned into over a half an hour when they delivered the casket. The employees were entranced when they saw it. The owner asked Carl, "Where did you get that?"

"I built it."

"You built this?"

"Yes. I'm a woodworker."

"Sir, I have to tell you. This is amazing! Do you have a card?"

"I'm in the book."

"But sir, I don't know your name."

"I'll give it to you later. Now can we get this unloaded? I have to start on the final arrangements," Carl said becoming agitated.

"Did you know the deceased?"

"Yea, I knew her."

After the casket was unloaded Carl and Peck were driving back to Carl's house.

"You were a little short with that guy," Peck said.

"I know. His timing sucked."

"Well I hope this doesn't, but have you thought about what we talked about yesterday?"

"You mean about the teaching?"

"Yes."

"A little. What you said made sense."

"I know there're some kids who could use your help and not just with woodworking."

"Well, like I said, I'll think about it. Right now I'm just trying to figure out how to help my kids through this. They really loved Sally and it's hard on them."

"It's hard on all of us."

Carl felt his tension melt as he understood his friend was also hurting. "Peck, have dinner with us tonight."

"You sure? I don't want to intrude."

"I'm sure. I want my friend to be around people who care for him."

Peck looked down. "Thank you, Carl."

If Sally's funeral and reception would have taken place thirty years earlier it would have been much different. Carl remembered the social circle phonies at the reception after his mom and dad's funeral. For them it had nothing to do with paying their respects or helping with the grieving process. It was simply dislikeable people trying to position themselves in society. Sally's was nothing like that.

The tears were real and heartfelt. The smiles were genuine as people shared memories of Sally. The sense of loss was deep.

The funeral was simple and attended by about thirty people. Everyone thought Carl should give the eulogy, but he refused. He knew there was no way he could share his memories of his aunt without breaking down. After a lot of coaxing and begging he got Peck to agree to take his place, and Peck was wonderful.

Carl was surprised as Peck shared his memories revealing things only a lover could know. He was happy knowing Sally's life was complete because of her relationship with Peck. He was saddened as he understood the relationship should have lasted longer and now his friend was alone.

The graveside ceremony was the hardest. As the rest of the guests where shown to the reception hall Carl, Kim and their kids were seated on one side of Sally's casket and Peck and Ruth on the other.

It was a beautiful day with a light breeze and with the full midday sun shining down onto the casket, it looked even more stunning. Carl saw the irony that his best work would soon be buried and hidden forever. It was as if Kim had heard his thoughts.

"I can't believe no one will see it again."

Carl thought a moment and smiled. "That's alright. I built it for her."

After the final words at the graveside service and the casket lowered they took turns saying their goodbyes. Carl could not remember a time he saw his kids cry so hard. Ruth hugged him, "It scares me how her life would've turned out if it weren't for you."

"It goes both ways."

Carl was the last to be alone with Sally. He thought of things he would say but as the time came the words were lost. He pulled a wooden rose from a box he brought. It was the same as the ones he had given her years ago with one exception. It had a ribbon tied around its stem with words that read, "Thank you Aunt Sally."

He placed it on the casket and whispered, "Rest well..."

He told the group he would catch up at the reception. His mom and dad's graves were a five minute hike, and when he got there he placed a lure he carved on his father's grave and a wooden daisy on his mother's. He filled his parents in, "A lot has happened since last I visited..."

Twenty minutes later he started toward the reception hall but still had one last stop. As he stood at the foot of Matilda's final resting place he reached into the box to retrieve the last item and placed it on her grave. It was a miniature bird house he made for her many years ago. He remembered the time Matilda, in about ten seconds, found the big old fashioned cell phone he threw in anger after he and Ruth had been searching through the thorny brush for hours. The memory made him smile. "I miss you, too."

When he walked into the reception hall he saw a large picture of Sally on an easel and people talking. He could feel the sadness but was glad there was an air of celebrating a life well lived.

He saw Kim and walked to her. Three times he was stopped by guests so they could tell him how impressed they were with the casket. A couple asked if he would consider building theirs when the time came.

"That was my first and last."

"Hey you!" he said to his wife's back.

"There you are! I was wondering what happened to you. Everything okay?"

"Fine, I had a couple of things to do."

The hour was filled with condolences and stories about Sally. Carl was surprised he felt better and was able to smile and talk without fearing his voice would crack.

As the reception was coming to a close he saw Kim standing next to the Champagne fountain waving him over. "What's up?"

She reached for two glasses, filled them half way with the flowing Champagne and topped them off with orange juice. She handed one to Carl.

"I thought we'd have one last toast to Sally, just you and me, and this was her favorite."

He looked at the glass then at Sally's picture.

"To Sally."

"Yes, to Sally," Kim said as she sipped from her glass.

Carl sipped and his stomach immediately turned into knots. He shook his head as he put the glass down, grabbed a beer and slugged a fast swallow to get the taste out of his mouth. He quickly felt better and was no longer worried he was going to be sick. He looked at Sally's picture, raised his beer and smiled.

"Sorry Sally, I really tried…"

CHAPTER 36
WHAT IF...

K im and Carl were sitting on their porch sipping coffee and enjoying a beautiful summer morning.

"I can't believe it's been a year since we lost Sally," Kim said.

"I know."

"I got more calls. A lot of people want you to build a casket for one of their relatives. Don't worry. I already turned them down."

"That was only for Sally."

"Might be worth a lot of money."

"We already have a lot of money..."

They sat awhile talking about the kids. They were doing well. The oldest would start college in the fall and the others would soon follow. Everyone in the house still missed Sally terribly, but it was getting easier.

"I better get going. I don't want to be late," Carl said as he stood and kissed his wife.

"Nervous?"

"A little."

"You'll do fine..."

Carl pulled out of the driveway. As he drove his mind started to wonder.

He wanted to prepare for the day but instead his thoughts drifted to why he was doing it in the first place. His thoughts became questions. And a lot of them started with "What If..."

What if he had slid the button on his alarm clock all the way? Would his parents still be here or was their fate sealed? He did not think about it often but still never explained to Kim his refusal to have an electric clock in their bedroom. He smiled thinking about having to take the old style wind-up one vacations. Neither could sleep without the ticking in the background.

What if his mother had had the time to get him in the computer class? Would he have found his way into woodworking? Would Sally and Peck have met?

What would his life be like today if he ended up at Boy's Town?

He wondered if his and Sally's relationship would have evolved if it were not for Ruth and Matilda.

Would he and Kim have found each other if her family did not move to his town?

He was confused with the "What ifs," then was reminded of how much he loved his life. His children were doing well and he was married to the love of his life.

He was thankful and understood things could have been different. He might not be enjoying the life he had today and would not change a thing with the exceptions of losing his mom and dad so young in life.

He thought a lot about Sally. She did so much for him. The money did not hurt, but it was much more than that. He wondered if Sally did not have the wealth that she had if their start would have been smoother.

Before Sally died, he would change while he worked with wood. But after his mind opened to new possibilities and saw different ways to handle bumps that came along. Carl still found it strange that his transformations at the beginning and end of his workday were much less profound since he finished Sally's casket. He knew he would never understand why but thought confronting his demons had something to do with it. When he was building the casket he could not help but think about the rough parts of his past. He was happy before, but he had to admit he was more comfortable with himself now. Maybe it was Sally's final gift.

He parked his truck and grabbed a tool box and a wooden sign he made. He walked through the front door to be greeted by the head of Boy's Town.

"Carl! It is great to see you."

"You too."

"Come on, let me show you around so you can see how we spent all of that money you donated."

The first stop was the new dorms. There was not a room that held more than four boys at a time and there were private showers. All of the furniture was new and the walls were covered with items that gave the rooms a feeling of a home instead of an institution.

They went to the dining hall and the food smelled great. The old tables were replaced with new ones that gave the place an inviting and homey feel.

"That cookbook made a huge difference and with all the money you gave us these boys are going to be eating well for a long time. No more processed crap here, only home-cooked meals from now on."

He walked to a table where a couple of boys were finishing their lunch and Carl recognized the smell right away. "That was one of my favorites."

"I don't blame you, this is really good!"

Carl looked at a spot above the entrance. "Do you have a ladder?"

Ten minutes later he looked at the sign he hung. "Matilda's Café."

"Let me show you some more," the head of Boy's Town said as he led Carl outside.

They walked through an area filled with dog runs.

"Looks like they're having fun."

"It's great. Before your help we didn't have the money to let the boy's have pets. Now with a lot of help from your friend, Ruth, we can!"

They continued to the back of the property where they came to a large, new building. As they walked inside Carl looked at the new woodworking tools. This woodshop was better equipped than his own and he knew Peck was going to be envious.

"Well, I'll leave you to prepare. The boys should be here soon."

One of the walls was filled with Carl's pieces. He brought them a few days before. The rest were filled with empty shelves. At the front of the room was a large desk, his, and the bouquet of wooden roses he made for Sally.

Thirty minutes later the room filled with fifteen young men.

Carl looked at each and saw a little bit of himself from a long time ago.

"Well, here it goes..." he nervously thought.

"I'm not one for formalities so there're not going to be any misters or sirs here. Just call me Carl."

He walked around the room and spoke with each of the young men. When he finished he went to the front of the woodshop. "Now I promise to try, but it might take me awhile to remember all of your names."

The shop was filled with laughter. Then one of the boys raised his hand. "Carl, we were told you were the one who donated the money to fix this place up. Is that true?"

"It is."

"This place is so much better, and the food! Why did you do it?"

"Good question. A long time ago I was in a situation many of you might be in right now. At least I assume so because you're here. I was alone and scared. I had no idea what my future held and it felt like no one was left who cared about me."

He stopped and could see they knew exactly what he was talking about.

"I had some lucky breaks and now I'm a very happy man. I guess what I want to do is give you guys some breaks and give you a shot at a good life."

"Don't get me wrong, we appreciate how you fixed up this place up and like my buddy said, the food is a lot better, but why the woodshop?"

"Another good question. A dear friend of mine once told me when he saw me work with wood he could tell it was about more than building something. I've had a while to think about it and he's right. It might sound funny to you now, but I hope I can help you learn that some of the principles we will be covering can be applied to many areas of your life. If you're focused on a project you can't be thinking about how bad things are. Just by you being here at Boy's Town you already know life's not always fair. Maybe this class can help you deal with that." He had their complete attention.

"Don't get me wrong, I want to teach you a skill I've developed over the years. In fact that's some of my work on the shelves over there."

"You made all of those?"

"Every last one," Carl said as he heard a couple of "Wow's."

Then he pointed to the empty shelves. "I want to fill those with things you build. And for those of you who like this and do well I'll provide an opportunity to expand. I'm hoping some of you will one day work with me in my business and I'm willing to commit to helping you become good enough to start a career in woodworking. Let's face it, not all of us can go to college and this beats the crap out of flipping burgers!"

The class laughed and Carl became comfortable. "I don't care if you've never touched a tool in your life. If you're willing to try, I'm willing to teach you and maybe we can throw in a few life lessons along the way."

He could see the boys thinking and again was reminded of his first day in Peck's class. Then one of the boys asked, "When do we start?"

"Right now. Our first project will be building a birdhouse." Carl handed out plans.

"A birdhouse!" one of the boys complained.

"I know, I know. But trust me. We all have to start someplace," Carl said with a smile.

A couple of hours after he gave basic instructions for the hand tools and how to use the plans Carl saw the boys were focused on building their birdhouses. They were not thinking why they were at Boy's Town and not worried about their future. He knew many had difficulties in front of them but he also had a degree of satisfaction in knowing he might be able to help some of them through those hard times.

The only sounds in the shop were from the tools, and he was satisfied as he sat on his stool and watched his students work. He reminded himself to thank Peck for not giving up on urging him to teach. Carl knew he was exactly where he should be and doing exactly what he should be doing, helping these boys.

He looked at the wooden roses, thought about his Aunt Sally, and smiled.

About the Author

Kent Walker is a national bestselling author who has been published by HarperCollins and Nelson and is a recipient of the Edgar Allen Poe Award. He has appeared on many television and radio talk shows, including *Larry King Live, The View, Fresh Air, Dateline, The Today Show, Good Morning America, To the Best of Our Knowledge* and many others.

He lives with his wife, the love of his life, in Southern California.

www.ingramcontent.com/pod-product-compliance
Lightning Source LLC
Chambersburg PA
CBHW020411260626
47156CB00007B/2339

* 9 7 8 1 9 4 9 0 0 3 6 6 6 *